A
FAILING
KINGDOM

Copyright © 2021 by William Rogers

Published by Thorncroft Publishing

Paperback ISBN - 978-1-9196343-0-2
eBook ISBN - 978-1-9196343-1-9

Printed in the United Kingdom

Cover design and layout by www.spiffingcovers.com

A
FAILING
KINGDOM

WILLIAM ROGERS

CHAPTER 1

Waiting for another thirty seconds was clearly not going to make much difference, Josh determined, as he huddled with others under the sharp angled canopy that covered the tables and chairs immediately in front of the coffee house. The un-forecast strength of the wind was driving the rain hard against the plastic, clattering onto its surface and then, like a curtain of water drawing itself around the boundary of the premises, it fell in waves onto the pavement.

"'S'cuse me, I going to make a dash for it," he said, easing his tall, athletic frame past a young lady standing immediately in front of him. He was already ten minutes late.

"One more street," he reminded himself, as he pressed on at increasing speed, avoiding the puddles which represented the greatest obstacles to maintaining any sense that he may be able to keep anything he was wearing damp, let alone dry.

Such was his pace, and so focused was he on making it to his lunchtime rendezvous, that this normally super-aware, ever-alert and, on rare occasions, slightly anxious former special forces officer, didn't notice the man who had been shadowing him, street by street, ever since he had left home.

Josh only slowed at the last moment to ensure no unnecessary collision with the old familiar etched glass door that would lead him into the lounge bar of the pub. *The Duke of Westminster* had been preserved, loved, and well maintained by successive owners.

Crucially, it still served a range of draught beers. Even the smell of the lunchtime food filled the air with the scent of typically English pub-grub. He hadn't been inside the pub for a few years, but as he stepped inside memories came flooding back. First dates, boozy nights out and, gladly less frequent, quiet reflections on lost friends.

As he stood in the doorway, he ruffled his hair a few times in a mirror to try and re-establish its more usual, bouncy, and fulsome look. He was now set. He smiled. He'd been relentlessly teased about such vain antics throughout his entire twelve-year military career. They hadn't called him "Mirrors" for nothing.

Josh scanned the room. The pub was surprisingly busy. He didn't recall it ever being as full, so early in the day. The rain, he thought. Then he smiled broadly, raising his right hand in front of his face to acknowledge the grinning figure ahead of him who was waving both arms in the air like an old semaphore operator.

He grabbed Micky Johnson and they held an extended tight embrace.

Josh took half a pace back and grinned. "Christ, you chubbed-up," he said. "What the fuck have you been doing?"

Micky was a couple of years older than Josh, a couple of inches shorter and a couple of stone heavier. The challenges of keeping weight off, which included his penchant for a glass or two of beer, too many days a week, had almost cost him his opportunity not just to enlist, but to gain a place in the special forces; an ambition he'd had since he was fourteen.

It was Josh who had supported him and backed him up on all too many occasions; back up that had eventually resulted in him finally achieving his dream. The two men had known each other since school and though their career paths had taken them in slightly different directions within the military, they both had a lasting bond and friendship that had survived the tests of time and circumstance.

"Piss off," came the response. And then, inevitably, "What you having?"

"Any decent ale will do. Or a new one if they've got one," responded Josh.

"Really good to see you," said Micky, slowly and deliberately patting each of Josh's shoulders with both his hands. "I'll get 'em in." He then turned towards the bar, heading off with his usual purpose and intent.

Josh found himself watching Micky's approach to the bar closely, immediately identifying differences in both physical appearance and gait, pondering the impact such a brief period of time had had on him since they'd last met.

This was a bulkier, less agile and very comfortable-looking man Josh now witnessed in front of him. His fair hair had greyed. And specs, too. He almost looked studious, something no-one would ever have considered an appropriate description for someone who had left school with no qualifications, ended up in a great deal of trouble in short order and whose life had been turned around because of his military career. Micky was a man never shy to use his fists as the first solution to almost any awkward and pressurized encounter; something that had been more than welcome on a mission, but something all too frequently deployed unnecessarily in civilian life.

Josh took a deep breath and berated himself for not making a greater effort to stay in touch. They'd occasionally communicated by email and text over the last year, but Josh was surprised to notice such a significant change in someone who had been perceived by all, including him, to be one of those fixtures that would always look, and be, the same.

Micky turned away from the bar and bumped into someone standing immediately behind him. The man engaged Micky in a brief conversation. It was only a few seconds and Josh was hoping that Micky's short temper wasn't going to come in to play, especially as some of the beer from one of the glasses had been spilt; something never readily forgiven by his friend. Thankfully, Micky headed back towards Josh and the other man moved towards the bar.

"I thought I was going to have to step in there," said Josh, reaching out for a drink.

"Fucking twat," said Micky, "I'd have been right fucked off if he'd done that to me years ago."

Micky raised his glass. "Cheers mate. Bloody lovely to see you."

Josh raised his own glass and both men downed about a half of the contents; always the first thing to happen to their first drink of any session.

The initial parts of the conversation covered the inevitable topics. Josh's impending fatherhood, married life generally, weight, looks, fitness, mates, deaths, the state of the military and old comrades, all wrapped up and bound by the usual ribbons of banter and laughter.

Josh was struck by Micky's frequent references to the country's political situation. He wasn't normally at all interested and would frequently discuss politicians from a position closely aligned to that of "a plague on both your houses."

Josh noticed that Micky was drinking more slowly than usual, and four rounds in, Micky was ready to disclose the reasons why. The conversation suddenly moved from casual and relaxed to serious and hesitant. Micky clearly had something on his mind and was drumming up the courage to share it.

"So," said Micky, "I wanted to talk to you about something."

Josh stayed silent to give Micky time to say what he needed to. He had always been a good listener, especially to the concerns of his men. Now it was time to be so again.

"So, we've both been out for a few years now and, er, I know it's been quite tough at times. Well, for me…"

Micky was surprisingly open about how he felt, though Josh had known him to be unhappy and certainly struggling with civilian life in almost all respects. Josh himself hadn't fully managed to make the transition to his own satisfaction. He was happily married to Becky, about to have his first child and had a reasonably good, although sporadic, job advising wealthy foreigners on their personal security and protection, but he had struggled to become de-institutionalised from military life.

"Well look… the thing is, as I said last year, I've done a few jobs abroad. All legit, mostly, but well… I've had an offer to do another." Micky lowered his voice. "It's a specialist civil job, Josh." The emphasis on the word "civil" told Josh everything he needed to know.

Micky paused and stared at his friend intensely. During their time in the forces, both men–for different reasons–had ended up in one of the most secret, elite special forces weapons teams in the British Army. The only military trained and recruited team to be managed and overseen directly by the security services.

Two years before Josh had left the military, he headed up the active field-based section of the "civil protection unit" - the CPU.

As a result of the emergence of a radical new platform of Chinese developed weapons–primarily to protect its leadership following serious civil unrest in major cities across China–all protection protocols for Heads of State and the most senior politicians in a small number of countries, had been changed.

Despite improvements to animal welfare, food hygiene and other measures introduced by the Chinese Government, standards remained poor, and a series of viral outbreaks and health management issues, some rumoured to be failed laboratory experiments, had seriously impacted millions of its citizens. With small pockets of the population also agitating for democratic reforms throughout the decade, inept and ineffective management of these matters internally had resulted in civil unrest and a failed coup by Chinese military leaders.

The response had been a ruthless three-month imposition of total censorship, enforced isolation and daily curfew, and the imprisonment and execution–without trial–of the leaders of any organization deemed to be undermining the state by military or other active means.

New personal protection systems had also been developed by China which had been made available to protect their government leaders. These systems were smart, mobile, intuitive weapons which created a virtual forcefield that could wrap itself around the shape of any person to whom it had been electronically linked, delivering comprehensive protection against any known traditional weapons system. The individual wearing it could run, sit, and move in any way and the device would adapt its shape accordingly.

The technology's details were acquired by various means by the Americans a year after the Chinese had developed the system. Once the USA had its hands on the technology, it was adapted a little and pressed into immediate use. Subsequently, it had been voluntarily shared with, and further developed for, the protection of leaders in the UK, Russia–an ally of the major NATO countries since 2029–and France.

CPU teams had been set up as expert operators of 'the sleeve.' Josh had been a trained operative and Micky a member of the support unit. Together with a team of twenty-eight others, they formed the first CPU team in the UK, managing personal security for the royal family, the Prime Minister and The Home Secretary. Ever since the Department of Defence and The Home Office had been brought together in 2027, creating a massive new mega-security and military department, Wolstenholme, the new Home Secretary, had become one of the most powerful people in the country and was second only in importance to the Prime Minister.

The CPU was deliberately constructed to limit those who had knowledge or access to the system to an absolute minimum. Once anyone had left the CPU, they were subject to the strictest limitations on their ability to refer to, discuss, or communicate with, anyone previously or presently involved with the team. There was also an automatic, without trial, minimum sentence in a military prison of twenty years for any breach of the protocols laid down.

"I think we should drink up here, don't you?" responded Josh.

Micky downed the rest of his pint and both men headed to the door.

Though it had stopped raining, the roads and pavements were still awash with water. Josh pointed ahead of him, moved off across the road and beckoned to Micky to follow him into a side street.

Josh looked around. "Are you fucking mad?" His voice was quiet but his tone firm and harsh.

"Hear me out," came the reply, as Micky struggled to regain control of the conversation. He knew that this was going to be an uphill struggle in any event but clearly, things hadn't started at all well.

"No, I fucking won't hear you out. This stops now. We know what we've agreed to, and this is not that. You leave the unit and you fucking leave. You take nothing with you. That's it. What the fuck is wrong with you?"

Micky lowered his head, and Josh felt bad for how he'd reacted. But as Micky looked back up, his lips were pursed, his eyes wide and staring. Josh straightened his frame, stood tall and upright, taking a small backward step as he did so. He had seen Micky look like that before.

"Micky, this conversation has to stop. Now."

"You need to hear me out for your own good." Micky knew he had one shot at convincing his friend, or the ramifications would be greater than Josh could possibly know.

"What do you mean, my own good...? Micky, I need to go. You need to stop this." Josh started to move off.

Micky grabbed his arm. "Josh, these people are serious, and they'll do anything to secure your involvement with this." The sentence sent a bolt of anxiety through Josh's body, the like of which he hadn't felt for some considerable time.

He knocked Micky's arm away from his own, grabbed his friend by the lapels and drove his entire body at pace against Micky's, thrusting him hard against the wall. Normally so quick to react, Micky did nothing.

"You're fucking lucky I don't report you for this!"

Both men stared at each other for what seemed like minutes, but was barely five seconds, before Josh relaxed his grip.

"You can't protect everyone who might get hurt." Micky was stepping into uncharted waters with his friend.

"What?"

"These people will do anything, Josh... Anything." A frown crept across Josh's face. "They know you're married," continued Micky.

That was the bombshell Josh hadn't expected.

"Don't you ever talk about her in that way. Ever! What the fuck are you doing Micky? Whatever you've got yourself into, you'd better get yourself out of it... I'm gone!"

With that, Josh turned and walked away from Micky at pace.

"Josh. I'm trying... Josh!" Micky called after the man he now suspected was a former friend.

As he watched Josh disappear around the corner, Micky became aware of the presence of the same short, balding man he'd bumped into in the pub. The man raised his eyebrows. Micky looked at him, shook his head a few times and looked down at the pavement.

The man took a phone from his pocket, dialled a pre-programmed number, and raised it to his ear. When the call connected, he said, without waiting, "It's a no," and then disconnected the call, turned and walked away.

Micky grimaced and lowered his head. "Shit," he whispered, to no one.

CHAPTER 2

Josh had managed to walk barely two hundred metres before he stopped and turned back towards where he'd left Micky. He was as shocked as he was angry. Why had he reacted so quickly and closed down the conversation instead of trying to understand what this was all about, and to persuade Micky to cease his involvement and report it to the CPU?

It was unlike him to have behaved in this way. Should he inform on his friend? Probably. Certainly. Should he go back and make a further attempt at reasoning with him to detach himself from this nonsense? Probably. No, too risky for himself, and Micky seemed to be in far too deep already. Josh pondered his options. It was Micky, after all. And why the threats?

He sighed. He would call it in as soon as he got back home and had some privacy.

As he approached Trafalgar Square, the noise of chanting, whistles and drumbeats hit him and he decided to avoid the demonstration by cutting through to Embankment, past Old Scotland Yard and head across the river to the Southbank and home.

Since the renewal of emergency regulations and powers, the almost weekly–and occasionally violent–demonstrations across the country had become the norm, and they seemed to be getting bigger.

The recent decision by the Government to seek authority to rule by decree, had not been approved by Parliament, though it had prompted the latest spate of protests.

Much of this public activism was tolerated by the authorities as it reflected "the norms of democracy and free speech," as the Prime Minister could be heard frequently arguing. Most people across the UK believed that the restrictions in place were too restrictive and their application undemocratic but the fear of a second wave of the latest viral pandemic was greater.

It had been seven years since anyone had had the opportunity to express their views at the ballot box, and as a result, the fragile political atmosphere was continually being tested.

Indecision, incompetence, and confusing messaging had led to a pervading anxiety that had infected all areas of society, which had taken a savage toll on the reputation of the previous Government and the last general election had seen an extreme right-wing party take power, led by a charismatic, young leader; Tony Eddington.

As he ran up the stairs from Embankment to make his way across the river to the Southbank by way of the footbridge, Josh became anxious about Becky. Was she at home yet? Was Micky serious about involving her? Surely not. He removed his mobile from his pocket and, pace quickening as he progressed, called her again.

It rang and rang. "Pick up... answer the bloody phone," he quietly urged.

"Hi, it's Becky. Please leave a message and I'll get back to you as soon as I can."

That wasn't what he'd wanted to hear. He broke into a gentle jog. He wasn't even sure why he was becoming increasingly concerned but once he'd allowed the thought to enter his mind, all his protective instincts had taken over. Josh checked his watch. She should have been at home by now. Even if she wasn't, why wasn't she answering the phone?

He quickened his pace again. Just a few more streets to go and then he was there. He slowed a little to allow himself the balance and control to call once more.

"Hi, it's Becky. Please leave a message and I'll get back to you as soon as I can." The beep seemed to take ages.

"Hey, it's me, you there? Can you call me back, please?"

Josh began to run. The dull brick façade of the block of flats where they lived rose ahead of him. He crashed through the main door and bounded up the stairs, three at a time. The added security of their fourth floor flat now punishing his lungs. As he got to the last few steps, he stopped sharply.

As he peered around the stairwell and along the hallway towards his flat, he battled with two competing thoughts. How much of a fool he would feel if he were to open the door only to find Becky unpacking the shopping and listening to her favourite playlist. The alternative, though, that someone had intervened to change their chilled, relaxed, and loving existence, was currently winning.

Nothing. No people, nothing suspicious. Perhaps the first possibility was going to be the case after all. He was just being paranoid. Of course he was.

Nonetheless, he gingerly climbed the final three steps and walked slowly, but deliberately, towards the front door of his flat. He listened intently for a few seconds. Silence. Once again, he scanned the landing before leaning further forward and placed his right ear to within an inch of the door. Silence.

Josh removed the small bundle of keys from his pocket, selected the front door key and inserted it into the keyhole, slowly unlocking the door and then easing it open. More silence. Becky had clearly not arrived home.

Pushing the door wide open, he stepped in and closed it firmly shut behind him. He eased himself out of his wet coat and headed along the passageway towards the bathroom to hang it above the bath to dry.

Josh returned to the kitchen, filled the kettle, and started making himself a cup of tea. He grabbed two mugs, one for him and one for Becky, for when she walked through the door a little later. It wouldn't be that long now.

He paused, thinking about his meeting with Micky. He should make that phone call.

Realising he'd left his phone in his coat pocket, he returned to the bathroom to recover it and, having done so, walked towards the lounge area, pushing the door open as he scrolled through the names and numbers on the screen.

Every cell in his body screamed at him. He stood bolt upright and scanned the room. The silence was only punctuated by the noise from the kettle as it switched itself off.

A cold shiver ran the length of his body. He knew that he was not, for the moment, in control of anything.

CHAPTER 3

Becky sat on the sofa, mascara smudged around her bright green eyes. She was slumped forward, her hands resting on her pregnant stomach, staring at Josh intently.

Three of the four men who stood around Becky were holding guns, one pointing at her and the other two directly at Josh. The men were clearly professionals – the silencers signalled that any resistance could lead to instant, noiseless retribution. No alarm would be raised. No one would be saved.

Josh felt a surge of cold anger run through his body as he fought back the urge to launch at them all to protect his wife and child, but his training dampened that prospect, at least until he had more information.

He had one option. Wait, watch, listen and learn. The next moves he–or they–made would determine whether Becky and their child, let alone himself, had any chance of survival.

He thought his way back to the pub, to what Micky had said. Why hadn't he called this in earlier on his way home? Too late, and now he was on his own.

His one consolation was that whoever these men were, if they were going to kill him, they would have done it already. The fact that they'd involved Becky in this situation cemented the idea that they weren't here to kill him. Becky was leverage.

"Hello, Josh." The older of the four men spoke, fiddling with the gold signet ring on the little finger of his right hand. Josh stared at him, without response.

The man brushed fluff from his immaculately tailored suit before continuing.

"You're a smart man, Josh. You've looked at my charming colleagues here and already thought, can I take them? But, of course, you can't."

Josh stepped towards Becky, determined to make her safe but the much younger man who was pointing his gun towards her cocked his weapon, causing her to flinch and cower back into her seat. Josh stepped forward again, raising his right arm, hand outstretched, "No, no!"

"Ah, ah, ah!" exclaimed the man, with a machine-gun staccato, breaking the tension. The situation calmed instantly. He instructed the younger man to reverse his threatening action and he obliged, un-cocking his pistol and casually resuming his previous position. Josh, along with the other two men who had also taken a step forward, all returned to their previous positions.

"Young Ryan is such an excitable character. You can never be certain how he'll react."

"I understand," came Josh's response.

"So pleased we understand each other, Josh. It makes for a much more pleasant and productive relationship." His smug, superior manner irritated Josh intensely.

As for "young Ryan," if that was his name, the first chance he got, Josh was going to send him straight to hell. Josh took a few seconds to assess him. Very early twenties, short brown hair, striking tattoo of an eagle's head on the left side of his neck, which continued behind his ear and disappeared below his shirt collar. He had an air of invincibility that made him extremely dangerous.

"Now," the grey-haired man continued, "let's get to know each other a little better, shall we? I think that'd be nice, don't you?" The man smiled at Josh. These faux pleasantries were grating beyond belief. Josh continued to focus on maximum self-control. He knew that, for the moment, it had to be maintained.

"Do you trust me, Josh?"

Josh nodded. He had no other option.

"Good. It's so important to have trust in troubled times, don't you think?" The man smiled. Josh didn't smile back.

As he took in more of the man, he spotted that he wore black and gold cufflinks bearing the initials CM.

"I was so pleased to see that you're expecting your first child. Given that you'll be doing a few bits and bobs for us over the coming days, it's important that your lovely wife is well cared for and looked after."

Josh pondered where exactly this was all going.

CM continued. "So, I thought it would be lovely if she spent a little time being pampered. Nice little country house, well fed, nice glass or two of wine in the evening. You know the sort of thing."

"Please..." Becky's entreaties interrupted the moment. It pained Josh but he knew he had no choice but to comply and he needed to encourage his wife to accept her present situation.

"Becky, trust me, it's for the best right now. You'll be okay. I love you and I need you to go with them."

Becky shook her head. She began to sob.

"Becky... Becky... look at me,"

Her pain was too great for him to bear and he slowly moved across to her. CM raised his hand, instructing his team to hold position and not to intervene. Josh sat alongside Becky and embraced her tightly. The tears flowed and her sobbing increased.

After a few seconds, Josh put his hands on her shoulders and eased her away from him.

"I need you to do this. You'll be alright. Trust me. I will sort this out."

Becky, her face contorted, tears still trickling down her cheeks, slowly nodded. "I love you," she whispered. "I love you too. It'll be okay, really. Trust me..."

They both stood, Becky clinging to Josh briefly as one of the other two men, whose previous focus had been on Josh, took her

William Rogers

by the arm and led her out of the room. A few seconds later, Josh heard the front door open and close.

Josh looked around the room once again. Young Ryan, CM, still seated, and one more man, impressively built - his bearing suggested ex-military and that he was capable of looking after himself. Perhaps thirty years old, stubbly beard and short, straight black hair, with a parting on the left. He had maintained the same position throughout the incident and only moved when Josh had taken a step towards his wife a few minutes earlier.

"Please do sit down Josh," said CM. "Oh, and gentlemen, let's lower our guns, shall we? We are all friends here now, aren't we?" Both men took a few paces back and lowered their weapons.

Josh sat in the same spot where he had just sat next to Becky and waited for CM to tell him what he wanted. The team were proficient, well organized, and more likely than not, part way through something which was almost certain to be well planned and competently executed. And Micky? Where does he fit in to all this?

"Let me start by re-assuring you that your lovely wife and your unborn child will both be fine. Clearly there are certain conditions to that, but I'm sure I don't need to go into that?" CM raised his eyebrows, seeking assurance that the message had been received. Josh nodded affirmatively though he suspected that CM's assurances were worthless and that they were all likely to be found dead in a ditch somewhere as soon as he'd done what they needed him to do.

In the short term, he knew he needed to commit to helping, to keep Becky safe for as long as possible, but he also understood that at some point he not only needed to foil the plan, whatever it was, but needed to find out where Becky was being held and get her out safely. His heart was thumping at the prospect.

Both men were playing a deadly game of control and manipulation and they each knew that the other was doing exactly that. Josh hoped that something might crop up to change the

20

dynamic at some point. Military life had taught him that no plan, however good, remains intact after engagement commences.

CM raised an eyebrow to Ryan who was now standing by the window. He peered down into the courtyard behind the building and looked back towards CM and nodded.

Rising to his feet for the first time since their encounter, CM stood up, reached for his coat that had been resting over a chair to his right, slipped it over his shoulders and raised his hand towards the doorway.

"I think it's time to go. Do please get your overcoat. Can't have you catching a cold in this weather, can we?" CM smiled that sickly smile once again.

As Josh came back from retrieving his coat, Ryan took up position in front of him and the other man stood behind him, carrying a hold-all. CM was already at the open front door. The guns had been safely pocketed out of sight but were still readied for deployment were the situation to require it.

"Stairs... not lift," said the taller, more imposing figure.

All four men set off down the steps in a line, one behind the other, and, shortly afterwards, made their way along the outside of the building and on to the pavement.

A blue SUV was parked twenty-five metres away from the building, its engine running. As they made their way towards the vehicle, Ryan jogged ahead and opened the rear passenger side door, beckoning Josh to enter. As he ducked his head inside he was nudged towards the central seat, as Ryan and the other armed member of the team sat either side of him. CM climbed into the front passenger seat, the doors were closed, and the car pulled away.

CHAPTER 4

Micky was worried. He knew that the call he'd seen his newly acquired colleague make after Josh had left would set plans in motion that would heap considerable unwanted pressure and worry onto his old mate. And onto Becky.

It had taken him just over forty minutes to get home to his studio flat in Ealing. No sooner had he removed his coat and headed to the kitchen for a glass of water than there was a knock at the door. He peered through the viewer. It was the man from earlier. He had clearly followed Micky home and was now, presumably, going to reveal his next set of instructions.

He opened the door and stepped to the side to allow the man entry. "What now?" he asked, closing the door firmly as he did so. As the man moved away from the doorway and down the corridor towards the lounge, Micky closed the door and called after him. "What do you want me to do?" There was no reply.

Micky followed the man down the hallway and into the lounge. "What's the position with Josh?"

As Micky entered the lounge, he observed the man standing in front of the small fireplace, his back towards him. He pressed for an answer. "Well?"

The man slowly turned to face Micky. He fired the gun he was holding twice in quick succession. Once in the chest and another to the head as soon as Micky's body hit the floor.

The man stared at his victim through dark, almost black eyes, and slowly unscrewed the silencer before placing both items in his coat pockets. His face bore no emotion as he raised a mobile to his ear. "Done," he said, disconnecting immediately, removing the battery and SIM card from the phone ready to dispose of.

He stepped over Micky's body, walked calmly towards the door, and exited the property, pulling the door tightly shut behind him. Once outside, he pushed against the door a few times to ensure that it was locked, and then, left. He knew Micky was single, and that his body would not be discovered for at least a few days, by which time, it would be too late to matter.

CHAPTER 5

The SUV transporting Josh and the four other men had travelled east through London and then, north onto the M25. Josh couldn't figure out what was happening. Micky's conversation at *The Duke of Westminster* had been less than illuminating. He could understand why they'd taken Becky – as leverage. But leverage for what?

The only other voice he'd heard was at the other end of the briefest of phone calls moments earlier. He'd caught the single word "Done" before the call was terminated. He was certain at this stage that it could not relate to Becky as that was the one thing that would result in them totally losing influence over him; they would know that. Which meant that it could be Micky. Or may be not. Though anxious about the situation his old mate might be in, Josh knew that there was little he could do.

* * *

As the car continued its journey northwards, junctions passed, and no clue emerged as to where the destination might be. Josh was attempting to remain calm, clear thinking and level-headed. He tried to maintain complete focus on every little detail, every little remark, comment, and instruction, in order to bring all those things together and start building a picture.

The car came off of the motorway towards Cambridge and headed through the city and out towards the suburbs. As Josh began to wonder whether they were to leave Cambridge completely, the car slowed and turned into the entrance to what appeared to be an airport. He had no idea that there was a functioning airport close to Cambridge, other than Stanstead, and certainly not one which seemed to be in the city itself.

As the barrier was raised to permit the vehicle to gain access, Josh saw hangars filled exclusively with private planes.

The SUV pulled up outside the main airport building and all those inside the car exited the vehicle.

"This way," said CM, indicating that they should all follow him along the front of the building. As he got to the end, he turned and made his way across a little patch of open tarmac.

The runway had now come into view. It was much longer than Josh had anticipated and looked like it might even be able to accommodate a small passenger jet. Spotting a small twin-propeller powered plane about fifty yards ahead, it was now clear that wherever they might be headed, it was much further away than he had initially thought .

The pilot was already in place, carrying out a variety of checks ahead of take-off. All five men climbed aboard: CM first, Ryan second, then Josh, followed by the other member of CM's team. The last on board was the driver of the SUV. He was utterly non-descript, Josh noted; the sort of person you'd forget moments after meeting him.

The pilot powered up the aircraft and a few moments later began taxiing into position. It was a comfortable twelve-seater plane, had beige leather seats and was surprisingly spacious for such a small aircraft. Other than the pilot, there was no-one else on board. Ryan's quip about the "wonky seat" having been fixed confirmed that this was not the first time the men had seen the inside of the aircraft. A small bottle of water was suspended in the elastic mesh attached to the side of each seat.

Josh had been sat on his own in the second row, with both Ryan, and his more impressive colleague, sat in the row behind. The SUV driver was sat in front of CM, who was on the other side of the isle.

The power of the engines ramped up and the plane shook a little before the brakes were released and it made its journey down the runway, building speed. Seconds later, it began to climb sharply, banking right. Josh saw Cambridge shrinking below them and with the sun well to the west, three hours or so before setting, he had assessed that they were now heading north. But to where and for what purpose?

CHAPTER 6

Prime Minister Eddington rose to his feet to make a much-anticipated statement to the House of Commons. It was widely assumed to announce a relaxation of some of the measures which had curtailed the movement of much of the population over the last two and a half years.

Prime Minister Eddington paused and surveyed a packed House of Commons. What noise there had been quickly evaporated. Every time Eddington made a major statement in Parliament, the hush that descended always seemed to add to his stature and enhance the anticipation of those waiting to hear what he had to say.

He leaned forward, theatrically grasping either side of the Despatch Box and standing bolt upright. He cut an authoritative, powerful figure and presented himself as the master of all he surveyed. Though he had a growing number of critics, most of his corps of lieutenants–all packed into the rows behind him–still loved him. They knew that the vast bulk of their party membership would follow him anywhere.

His salt and pepper hair was now more salt than pepper but far less so than many might have anticipated, given the turbulent times his leadership had endured. His bearing demanded attention. Six feet and stocky frame, he was always immaculately dressed. His collection of cufflinks was the envy of anyone interested in such things.

"Mr. Speaker."

He cleared his throat.

"As the House will know, the last few years-"

"Not few!" bellowed the sartorially colourful Member for Dorset Central. Roger Spencer was given to frequent heckling of the Prime Minister and had gained a reputation for independent thinking, as well as a unique ability to irritate Eddington. Ever since Spencer had crossed the floor of the House to join the opposition, his barbs carried even more weight. That he had then systematically voted against every measure of social and population control that Eddington's Government had introduced, ensured his status as a thorn in the PM's side. Dorset Central had never had such a famous advocate in Parliament. Outside the House, he was rarely seen without his Fedora hat and certainly never without one of his flamboyant bow ties.

Eddington briefly looked towards his most vocal critic, sat, as he always was, on the benches barely ten metres opposite. The Prime Minister delivered an icy, contemptuous stare before returning to his script.

"As the House will know, the last few years have been extremely difficult for the people of our country. Unprecedented times have demanded that the Government take unprecedented action. Such measures were vital, right and delivered by a government that had the courage to do what was necessary."

The usual loud chorus of "hear hears" erupted from behind him. His Party, he thought, was both in good heart and good voice.

"A Government that had the courage to do what was necessary and, which will always do what is necessary, whatever the circumstances, to secure the safety of our people, the security of our borders and the stability of our country."

"As the House will have anticipated, we wish to see many of these unprecedented measures relaxed as soon as is practicable. Something every Member would, I hope, support: not only an easing of the control measures and orders that presently give additional power to our Police forces across the country, but also the lifting of orders that will then permit the restoration of full democratic accountability, and the holding of elections, here in the United Kingdom."

It seemed the whole of the House of Commons had suddenly found a singular voice to echo such sentiments, as a wave of supportive, enveloping noise greeted the Prime Minister.

Was this the moment that the population of Britain would start to see elements of normality return? The noise died away in anticipation.

Eddington lifted his head, slowly and deliberately looking at every part of the chamber in turn.

"I had, today, anticipated seeking the permission of this House to agree to the cancellation of a number of orders relating to all such matters. However, whilst I do raise the prospect that such an intention will soon be given practical effect, and I would re-assure all Honourable Members in this regard, I must report to the House that after careful consideration of all the detailed advice I have been given by the various departments of state–as well as the different elements of our security services–such orders will now not be available for some time."

Irritated voices now joined the clamour from the benches opposite Eddington, the cacophony making it too difficult to discern in terms of its support, or opposition, to what had just been said.

"Order! Order!" bellowed the Speaker, the Prime Minister resuming his seat. "Order!"

It was clear that there was little order to be had.

The Speaker rose to his feet. "Order! I am on my feet... I am on my feet. Please will some Honourable Members resume their seats."

Slowly, the House resumed a state of calm, and the Speaker resumed his seat. "The Prime Minister," he boomed.

"Thank you, Mr. Speaker."

Then, nothing. Silence. Eddington looked around. The few

seconds seemed like a lifetime. Looking down at his notes, it was as if he were debating with himself whether to present the next part of his speech at all. Members of Parliament seemed to sense the dilemma, many leaning forwards as if to engage even more directly in the moment. .

Again, with both hands clasped each side of the Despatch Box, Eddington drew himself upwards, taking a deep breath.

"Mr. Speaker, I know that on this side of the House, and against all the protestations and whining from Members opposite, we have striven at all times and in all ways–unlike those opposite–to make the right decisions for the people of this country..."

The provocative tone was having the desired effect and generated the response he wanted. Eddington looked across to his left and towards one of his most fiercely loyal of advisors and supporters, Edward Strong.

Holding down the two posts of Party Chairman and Chief Whip, he represented a new breed of Prime Ministerial enforcer. Strong's remit spread across both voluntary and Parliamentary Party.

"Strongy," as Eddington called him, was a barrel of a man. In his early 50's, he was a former Army Colonel, tough as old boots and–since entering politics at Eddington's side–had taken on the role which represented a combination of enforcer, fixer and party manager. He had taken to shaving his head shortly after gaining his seat, joking that it made him look more menacing. Those who had faced his wrath all took the view that he was menacing enough as it was.

The Prime Minister had always relied upon him at critical moments for his sense of where the Parliamentary Party stood on a variety of different matters. Today was no different. Though he was sure he would carry them with him if he took the next step, if Strongy nodded, he'd proceed. If not, he'd consider quickly changing tack.

The nod came.

"Making the decisions to finally tackle those small pockets of troublemakers and anarchists who still inhabit a small number of cities and towns across the UK, will accelerate a return to normality. Something I am sure the whole House will welcome. We have tolerated such individuals and groups for too long. If our country is to get back to its normal ways of working, we must sort this out once and for all." Much support, and noisy endorsement from the benches behind him, confirmed that Strong's instincts were right.

"As a result, I am exercising the powers afforded to me under the Control Orders and Suspension of Elections Act 2029 to end jury trials for those charged with offences relating to the provisions of this Act and extend the time people may be held without charge to one hundred and twen--"

No-one heard the last few words. The explosion of noise which greeted that most authoritarian of measures produced truly extraordinary scenes. No amount of effort by the Speaker to calm things down was going to be equal to the task. Fingers pointing across the House were accompanied by insults hurled between MPs from every bench in the chamber. Foul language and wholly unparliamentary threats spewed from Members, on their feet ranting at their opposite numbers.

Crucially for the Prime Minister and his Party Chairman, the response was exactly as planned, and required. Eddington's own party roundly supported their leader in what they perceived to be his determination to sort out the groups of anarchists they saw as wrecking the chances of a return to normality. The opposition, outnumbered and furious about what they perceived as a further erosion of liberties and democratic norms, introduced by a petty dictator, exploded in a torrent of rage and uncontrolled anger.

Eventually, after five minutes of trying, the Speaker gave up on his efforts to bring matters to order and advised the House, most of whom could barely hear him, that he was suspending the sitting. Eddington made his way out of the chamber to cheers, jeers, and insults, exiting behind the Speaker's chair. Strong followed him immediately.

"Bloody good job, Prime Minister," he said, patting Eddington on the shoulder. "You couldn't have hoped for better than that. Perfectly pitched."

"Let's hope so," Eddington replied. "Number 10. You can ride with me."

Both men headed at a brisk pace down the long corridor and made their way into the courtyard, to the waiting cavalcade of cars that would ferry the Prime Minister back to Downing Street.

Their tactic to split the House had worked absolutely. Not a single question was raised, no scrutiny applied and, even better, the suspension of proceedings had given them valuable additional time. It would not be until next week that MPs would be able to re-convene.

MPs would have returned to their constituencies on Friday, all no doubt ready to share their thoughts with local and social media channels.

For Eddington, it had been critical to cement his position amongst his Parliamentary Party and get opposition members to demand change. Both objectives had been comprehensively achieved. The two men now had the four days that they had craved to accelerate their already well-advanced plans.

Just before climbing into his vehicle, Eddington turned to Strong and fleetingly raised his finger to his lips. His instruction was understood. No chat in the car, at all. Both men knew that too much was now at stake to risk the consequences of idle chatter.

As the convoy moved away, one of the younger, more outspoken Members of Parliament from the main opposition party, lunged at the Prime Minister's car and hammered on the window. "You're a fucking disgrace! You're a --" Police wrestled him to the ground in a matter of seconds.

CHAPTER 7

Except for a few brief moments of turbulence about twenty minutes in, it had been a smooth flight. Josh had spent the time trying to establish their ongoing direction of travel. They had taken off towards the north, but it would only have taken a small shift by a degree or two to significantly change where they might be. The clouds made any assessment of the ground below impossible.

They had been airborne for about an hour and a half. Josh felt the wave of butterflies that he always got when an aircraft he was flying in started its descent. There it was again. The second time in about a minute. Wherever they were, this plane wasn't too far off its destination.

The cloud broke below them, and Josh saw small, open fields punctuated by more rugged countryside and numerous rocky outcrops as the plane continued its descent. Just as Josh started to become concerned about where they planned to land in such problematic terrain, with barely a thousand feet of air below them, the aircraft banked sharply to the left. As they flew over a hilly outcrop which had obscured the view beyond it, he saw a small landing strip, at the end of which sat a vast manor house.

Josh looked across the landscape stretched out below him, dusk beginning to settle on the hills and fields below.

The aircraft levelled itself as it lined up for landing. As it approached the runway, the pilot made a few adjustments. It was clear that this wasn't a particularly easy approach, and he was clearly trying to ensure that he landed the plane as close to the start of the landing strip as he could. Josh could not remember ever landing on grass before. Yes, helicopters, of course, but never in a fixed wing aircraft.

This wasn't a strip built with the intention of delivering the smoothest of landings. The plane rocked and tipped as it roared along the strip.

Within seconds of landing, the plane slowed sharply, and the passengers lurched forwards in their seats. Then, almost as quickly as it had begun, calm was restored and the plane briefly taxied the remaining twenty-five metres to the far end of the runway, before it finally stopped. The pilot switched off all power and commenced a few necessary checks. The propellers slowed and finally ground to a halt.

Josh estimated a dozen men in their twenties and thirties standing around watching the plane park up. As was becoming all too familiar, thought Josh, they looked like they had military training. Two walked towards the plane and opened the doors either side.

Ryan nudged Josh in the side, indicating that he should follow his colleague out of the plane. Josh obliged. Having all disembarked, CM turned to Josh. "This way. Ryan, Paul, you two with me."

All four men made their way towards the building. Though part of the property was castellated, it didn't look original. The central part of the building was three storeys, the two wings protruding left and right each had two stories and looked more modern.

Across to the right were several outbuildings and, to the left, behind the main property, were some relatively new buildings, all utilitarian in design and construct. The entire complex was a hotch-potch of different construction styles and, as a result Josh thought, uses.

Walking up the three steps which fronted the main door to the property, CM reached for the handle and walked into the large, open, cathedral ceiling hallway. All three men followed. To Josh's surprise, the interior was basic. A few paintings, no ornaments and little furniture to speak of, save for a lonely looking chair by one of the windows to his right.

The one concession to luxury was an ornate wooden staircase which clung to the walls of the hallway as it circled the entire room. The steps were painted white, and ornamental floral styled metal railings ran up the sides topped off with a smooth dark mahogany handrail.

"Take him to his room," instructed CM. Both Ryan and Paul made their way towards the staircase, guns once again in hand, and pointed Josh in the same direction.

"Scotland?" enquired Josh as they started climbing the stairs. No reply.

"Left at the top, here," said Paul. It was the first time he had spoken a decent sentence, and Josh detected a slight Yorkshire accent. "Second door along on the right."

Josh entered a small, single bedroom. Stripped bare of all but the essentials, it contained a bed and one folding metal chair. A door just to the right of the bed was ajar, revealing an even smaller room that housed a toilet and sink. The smaller room had a tiny window, barely twelve inches square. The larger window in the bedroom itself was closed and had both horizontal and vertical metal bars, which looked newly fixed, in place. A single light bulb hung in the centre of the room.

It was hardly a home from home, but Josh recognized that it did at least confirm more time being allotted to his stay; something he would seek to take full advantage of.

"We'll be outside." With that, Paul pulled the door shut, locking it immediately. As the key turned in the lock outside, Josh was immediately drawn to the same spot on the inside of the door. No door handle and no lock. Just a flat, metal plate. As he scanned the whole of the door, which he noted was firmly set into its frame, it was clear that this wasn't an exit option.

He reached out with his left hand and flicked on the light

switch. The single bulb gave off just enough light to bring a warm glow to the room.

Barely taking three paces, he walked across to the window and peered out. His room overlooked the rear of the property. There were no extensions or other buildings in sight, but–although he was unable to make it out clearly in such poor light–some fifty metres from the building there appeared to be a large open area which had different sections marked out with white lines.

He returned to the light switch and flicked it off to improve his view of the exterior, but Josh was still unable to make any sense of what he could see. He switched the light back on and then sat on the bed, taking in his new surroundings, as well as his predicament.

Every so often, he would hear the voices of assorted men passing his door or going up and down the staircase. It was mostly the sort of chatter you would expect from young men. Football, sex, women; banter, even the occasional whinge about the food. What was also clear was that as they acknowledged their colleagues on each occasion, both Ryan and Paul were "just outside."

Josh laid on his bed and returned again and again to the same range of questions about why he was here, how Micky was involved, and where Becky was and whether she was safe.

There wasn't a thing he could do but wait and gain as much information as he could about his surroundings, the plan, and his part in it, and equally as important, assess the various people he'd encountered so far, as well as those he'd yet to meet.

At some point, all these things would become clear. Until then, he knew that he needed to do exactly what he had trained so many others to do; deploy all the techniques at his disposal to get back to Becky and the baby. Whatever they wanted him for, it was clearly something that only he could do. Which meant that he held at least some of the cards.

The key turned in the lock and Josh swung his legs over the side of the bed and sat bolt upright. Ryan entered–with Paul lingering a few steps behind him–and lobbed a small, cardboard box towards

Josh and backed away, pulling the door shut and locking it once again. Josh opened the box to reveal four large cheese sandwiches, a banana, and a bottle of water. He hadn't eaten for hours and whilst this wasn't his ideal supper, it was something.

He checked his watch again. It was getting late.

* * *

Josh rested the spent water bottle alongside the banana skin in the now empty box, closed the lid and placed it on the floor by the side of his bed. He lay back once again and waited.

Barely ten minutes after finishing his food, the door was unlocked and pushed open. Ryan entered and gestured, gun in hand, for Josh to leave the room.

Paul was waiting down the hallway and turned and walked towards the staircase as Josh came out of the room. Ryan stuck close behind. There were two more men at the bottom of the staircase, awaiting their arrival. Ahead of him, just before Paul got to the last step, one of the men turned abruptly and headed in the direction of one of the doors to the right of the staircase and they all followed.

On entering the room, Josh was surprised by its scale, especially compared with his own tiny shoebox of a bedroom. At least forty feet from one end to the other, and twenty wide, four large windows stretched from the floor to the ceiling. The carpet was luxurious in comparison to everything else he had seen, slightly worn in places suggesting a decent age. It had a medieval design incorporating shields and knights on horseback. The furniture was also much more the style he would have expected to see in a house of this size. Chippendale style chairs and rich deep red leather sofas and chairs presented a sense of class and quality. A few paintings adorned the walls: horses, military and landscape and the entire room had an unexpected warmth to it. Two large chandeliers hung from the ceiling. They were not particularly grand, the cascades of long crystal droplets looking too plain for such a room. The electric bulb fittings, which had long ago replaced the original candles, lit the room.

All four men entered with Josh and took up various positions around him. Sitting at a dining table in front of him were CM and an older man, their empty plates, and glasses, still in front of them. It felt incongruous that these men had sat down to a rich meal, given the circumstances.

The older man stood up. He was elegantly dressed, his shoes immaculately shined and he had long, flowing, but neatly brushed, grey hair. His eyebrows were bold and a darker shade indicating how his hair may have looked some years ago. Josh was certain he'd recognised the man but couldn't put a name to the face.

"Have you had something to eat, Josh?" the older man enquired, his deep, clipped, slightly gravelly Scottish tones emitting an unexpected warmth.

"I have, yes." Josh had determined to keep his responses brief, seeking to draw as much information and comment from his captors as possible.

Using a knuckle to scratch his nose, the older man took a couple of steps forward and looked Josh up and down a few times.

"I think it's probably time to explain to you what you're going to do for us." The man smiled. Josh remained silent.

With a wide, sweeping gesture of his right hand, he intimated that Josh should sit on one of the chairs close to the table.

The man followed him and sat immediately opposite, relaxing into one of the comfy looking red leather chairs. Josh looked back across towards CM. He hadn't moved. CM was obviously not the man in charge, Josh thought.

"You're a former member of the CPU."

Josh remained silent.

"A senior member. An officer."

Josh continued to pay attention in silence.

"Your skills will be used to facilitate…" The man was making an effort to provide enough information to explain what would be required of Josh, whilst keeping some things back from him, "… to facilitate some necessary changes for the benefit of our country. This is a patriotic endeavour. That is why you are here, Josh. For your country–and that is why you'll do what needs to be done."

Josh remained silent.

"Now, you'll want to know about Becky. I am sure you are concerned about her. You need not be. She is well cared for and safe for the moment. And she'll remain safe and be returned to you once you've completed your task."

The man paused.

Josh knew that such a promise rang hollow. Given that this was so obviously a clandestine operation, and clearly illegal, the prospects of either he or Becky emerging from this alive were near zero. Though he could feel his heart pounding and his desire to react was intense, he knew that staying calm and in control was the only course of action that might see both he and Becky through this ordeal.

"Where is she?" Josh enquired.

"Quite safe," CM spoke from across the room.

"'Quite safe' is not something that remotely re-assures me, coming from the man who's responsible for dragging my wife into a mess she has nothing to do with. I want to hear it from you," responded Josh, turning back to the older man.

CM remained silent. The man stood up and walked slowly towards the large fireplace before turning back to face Josh.

"Come, come. You know we're not going to disclose that my dear fellow." He smiled, as though it were all some sort of party game being played out for the amusement of all involved.

"I suspect you're anticipating your… involvement. Yes?"

Josh remained stony faced. No response, no flicker of interest.

"But first let me show you something that will underline our intent and determination. You will do as you are told, Josh. To not do so would be particularly unfortunate. For Becky… and the child."

Josh struggled to keep calm. In spite of the fact that his mind was raging with hatred and his body anxiously coiled, ready to serve upon them a vengeance that he could not wait to inflict, he knew that the only way out of this was to remain focused, controlled and alert.

Josh noticed a coat of arms etched into the large stones which propped up the mantle on both sides of the giant hearth. Below each was one word chiselled from the rock: *Ardoon*.

Josh now immediately identified the man he'd earlier recognised but hadn't been able to place. Lord Ardoon.

Although Josh knew relatively little about him, he was aware that Lord Ardoon had been one of the founders of The People's Justice League and was one of its key financial backers. He was a colourful, outspoken figure, both revered and hated in equal measure. There was no middle of the road view when it came to Lord Ardoon. He was known to be a close friend of the Prime Minister and was very well connected politically.

"I want you to watch this, Josh," the instruction cracked the air and brought Josh back into the room. The sickly, faux smile that had crept across the man's face evaporated, replaced with a cold, ruthless and steely look.

With that, he beckoned to CM to attend to the screen. CM reached for the remote device resting on the table beside him and turned on the 'foldaway.' Completely wireless, capable of delivering visuals from any connected source, and of rendering 3D images, "foldaways" had been launched into the market three years earlier and were able to fold up into one eighth the size of the opened-out screen. As a result of an innovative fixing system, they could be attached to any surface, even under water, without any physical attachments being required.

Josh watched attentively as CM flicked through a small number of options before alighting on one marked "Tramp," and the screen lit up. In the centre of the screen sat an unkempt figure, his arms and feet tied to the chair, completely isolated in a small cell. The lonely figure was, presumably, the "tramp." He looked sleepy, possibly sedated or, if he were a "tramp," quite possibly suffering from alcohol abuse, or worse.

Josh looked at his captors. Only CM was watching the screen. All other pairs of eyes were looking intently at Josh. He returned his gaze towards the foldaway.

A second man then appeared in the picture. Though he kept his back to the camera, he was clearly holding a syringe, which he raised and squeezed gently; a spurt of clear liquid shooting upwards a few inches.

He then held the tramp's arm and injected the entire contents into his veins before backing away and disappearing from view. A stopwatch appeared in the bottom right-hand corner of the screen. Tenths of seconds rolled into seconds, into minutes. The man seemed completely oblivious to his predicament.

By the sixth second, the man became distinctly anxious, moving his entire body, trying to wrestle himself up and away from the seat. By the tenth, he was starting to shout. By the fifteenth second, he was screaming in agony.

Josh looked down. He had seen all too many unpleasant things in his life, but this was different. This was cruel, vicious, deliberately inflicted pain, clearly doing immense damage to this helpless victim.

Twenty seconds: the man began to foam at the mouth.

Twenty-six seconds: blood began to pour from his nose and eyes.

Josh looked away again but could still hear the anguished screams of an inconsolable man whose body was being systematically destroyed by the vicious cocktail injected into him.

Josh glanced towards his host with contempt, and noticed he wasn't looking at the screen. He stared directly at Josh.

Silence. Josh looked back at the screen. The man was slumped in the chair, his life extinguished. The clock had stopped at just thirty-six seconds. Thirty-six seconds to inflict pain, suffering and death in an unimaginably dreadful manner.

CHAPTER 8

Edward Strong had left 10 Downing Street twenty minutes earlier and had made his way the short distance to meet Wolstenholme at his home for a long-arranged supper.

His host was a well-educated, wealthy man and Strong didn't care much for his unerring self-confidence, which he felt, often bordered on the arrogant. Nor did he care much for the sense of "entitlement to rule" which was so often exhibited by those of his type. As for the oft-deployed sarcasm that masqueraded as humour, Strong despised it.

Strong knew he wasn't in the same league, either intellectually or financially, but he did have Eddington's rock-solid support; something he was sure that Wolstenholme didn't have. For the moment, he had a job to do, and he was doing it.

As he approached the grand London townhouse, the two armed police officers standing guard outside acknowledged him, both stepping back to allow him to approach the heavy dark blue door.

Trotting up the tiled steps of the double-fronted three-storey building, Strong looked back down the street. A large, black SUV was parked close by–the additional close arm protection provided to senior Government politicians. Strong had always been impressed by the level of security it had bestowed upon Wolstenholme. As Party Chairman, he had always been put out that he wasn't considered worthy of such support and protection.

He lifted the large, heavy door knocker and banged it as loudly as he could five times. Both police officers smiled. They knew, like him, that such a flourish was certain to have annoyed the man he was about to encounter. Strong smiled back at the officers and winked at them both.

The door opened and he was invited to enter the large, grand hallway, by a member of staff.

"It's got a touch colder Mr. Strong," said the lady who had welcomed him into the house.

"It has," replied Strong, rubbing his hands together as if it were winter.

"This way please." He was directed into the usual room to the left of the front door. It was a beautiful room, rich in colour and blessed with some fine antique furniture. A small collection of Newlyn School paintings hung on the wall. The Home Secretary was a keen collector of paintings, primarily those depicting real life in times past, rather than the more abstract, modern styles. He was particularly disparaging of such art. That said, the Home Secretary was disparaging of pretty much anything, other than his own views, tastes, and opinions.

"Mr. Wolstenholme will be with you shortly. Do please sit down." Strong obliged, sinking into an elegant sofa, cushions enhancing his slow progress.

"Usual drink, Mr. Strong?"

"That'd be great, thank you," he replied.

"I'll be right back," she said, turning away and leaving the room.

His usual was a vodka, with a splash of soda, but he'd always felt that it was more appropriate to request a gin and tonic when visiting Wolstenholme at home.

Strong looked around the room. He may not have cared too much for Oliver Wolstenholme, but he had to admire his style. He never failed to be impressed by his visits to this most impressive of townhouses.

"In the sitting room, sir." Overhearing voices outside the room, Strong rose to his feet, anticipating Wolstenholme's arrival any second. He still didn't know why he always felt the need to defer, but he did.

"Edward, lovely to see you. Thanks so much for coming over." Hand outstretched, Wolstenholme walked straight up to his guest and shook his hand warmly. "Drink on the way?"

"Good to see you too Oliver… and yes, I'm sure it'll be here in a tick."

"Sit down, sit down," gestured the host to his guest.

Both men sat, Strong taking his place on the sofa once again and Wolstenholme settling into one of the large chairs which appeared, somehow, to complement, and even enhance, his status.

The lady re-appeared with two glasses on an elegant tray. Strong removed his gin and tonic, and Wolstenholme retrieved a small cut glass tumbler within which was a neat whisky. No doubt it was an awfully expensive single malt, mused Strong.

"So, how's the party Edward? All good? Everybody happy?"

Strong balked at the pleasantries.

"Certainly appears to be," he replied. "We've had a torrent of emails supporting the PM's statement this afternoon and, as far as I can tell, the Parliamentary Party is firmly behind him all the way. We have not had the slightest criticism from anyone."

"I'm sure," came the half smiling reply. Loyal and committed in words, but not at all so in reality. Wolstenholme always managed to loyally express whatever statement needed to be uttered, even though Strong knew he didn't mean it. It was quite possible to interpret most of Wolstenholme's answers in whatever way you wished. It was a technique honed to perfection by one of the most ambitious, manipulative, and cunning men in Parliament.

Strong acknowledged the smile with a half-hearted one of his own. Like every meeting he had with this most Machiavellian of politicians, he would need to wash every word spoken before it emerged from his mouth.

Wolstenholme was well turned out, with a sartorial elegance unmatched by most, his light brown hair was swept back as if to accentuate the curious blond streak reaching back across his scalp from his forehead. His face was angular and the little cleft in his chin meant he was favourably compared to Kirk Douglas. During the now infamous prison riots which took place barely a month or two after his appointment, he was depicted as Spartacus in one cartoon; a re-affirmation of precisely the image that he had so painstakingly cultivated over the early years of his political career. Inevitably, the original of the cartoon had found its way onto the walls of Wolstenholme's house.

Ever since he had entered Parliament, Wolstenholme was all about projecting an image of toughness, competence and authority and, to date, he'd managed to do so.

The conversation moved entirely predictably from the party to policy, policy to their political opponents and then, as usual, on to individuals and where they might stand on certain challenging issues of the day. They were like two men boxing shadows. Many well aimed punches but none ever landing with effect.

The housekeeper re-appeared at the door. Both men stopped their conversation and looked up.

"Dinner is ready sir, if that's convenient?"

"Thank you, Mary," said Wolstenholme, at once rising to his feet and urging his guest to do the same.

Strong followed Mary out of the room, but instead of heading in the normal direction of the dining room, she continued past the staircase and down the narrow hallway to its side. This was unexpected. *An adventure in itself*, thought Strong.

They had passed several closed wooden doors, all with gleaming brass handles, before Mary turned sharp left and disappeared into a room, the last one along the hallway. Strong followed her into what was a much smaller room than he had expected, considerably less grand than any other he'd seen to date. He took a few paces into the room to make access easier for his host.

Other than the impressive antique bookcase flattering what was a distinctly modest room, there was a small dining table, beautifully laid with all the necessary cutlery for a four-course meal, two wine glasses in each setting. Strong was particularly drawn to the beautiful, long, central flower arrangement adorning the table. He was certain he could even smell the scent from it. There was a small fireplace, a wooden mantle-piece, and a large-framed mirror hanging above it. The frame had a fussy design of flowers and leaves.

"Thanks Mary. Do please serve when you're ready," said Wolstenholme, gesturing at the same time for Strong to take a seat. As he eased one of the chairs backwards, his host interjected.

"No, no," he purred, in that faux warmth he'd cultivated for years, "nothing worse than facing the door. Take that one. It'll be far more pleasant."

It was a strange request. Not only was Strong not in the least bit bothered where he sat, but he had suddenly felt a tad claustrophobic, particularly now that he was to face the room rather than the open door.

An open door was also unusual. Normally, Wolstenholme was the first to close doors and usher in hushed tones to any private or politically clandestine meeting. Strong was even more conscious of his language now, as well as his opinions.

The first course came and went, as did the main. More innocuous chat about this Member and that Member, including the appalling state of the main opposition party's leadership. The Hon Member for Dorset Central, who represented a particular irritation to Wolstenholme, came in for a serious amount of grief. "If he carries on like this," said Strong, "don't you worry. He'll go too far, and I'll nail the bastard." That view was warmly endorsed by his host.

Then, just as the empty bowls of what had contained fresh fruit salad and clotted cream had been cleared, Wolstenholme rose from his seat and walked around the table towards the door.

"Mary, give us twenty minutes or so to let that all settle before you bring in the coffee and petit fours, will you please?"

With that he slowly closed the door and returned to his seat. Strong broke the silence.

"Well, that was a dramatic flourish. Must be something important."

Wolstenholme eased his chair backwards a couple of feet and crossed his right leg over his left easing himself into a more relaxed and comfortable position.

The two men looked at each other, each considering at what point and in what style their next intervention should come.

Strong tried again. "So, Oliver, what's on your mind?"

Wolstenholme stared directly at Strong and barely blinked, which unnerved him. It was almost menacing.

"We've never really got on well, have we Edward?"

Where on earth was this going, Strong pondered.

"We've had our differences on occasion, of course, but I've always regarded you highly." Wolstenholme continued. "I've always valued your advice. You have your ear to the ground. You... well, you're particularly well informed. I value your insight."

Wolstenholme paused, testing how well the opener had gone down.

"Thank you, Oliver, I appreciate that."

"Well, you don't, of course," continued Wolstenholme, "but I wanted you to know that and hear me say it."

The conversation was taking a bizarre course. Compliments and a dose of honesty, all in the same sentence.

"Here's my take," Wolstenholme continued. "We are different, you and I. You probably feel that you must tolerate my presence but you don't really trust me, and you find me irritating, perhaps even arrogant. However, whatever you may think, I regard you highly and think that you are the best possible Party Chairman we could have right now."

This was all becoming distinctly uncomfortable for Strong. "Not at all, really," he interjected.

Wolstenholme raised his right hand, intent upon continuing

his point. "Maybe I am difficult to get on with, I don't know. I may even deserve some of the criticism I know others are inclined to make. Whatever our personal views, I am totally onside with you in policy and political terms. But more than that, I'd like you to know that you'll have my full support in the event that anything threatens your position within the party."

"Threatens my position?" questioned Strong.

"As I say, whatever may get thrown up, you can rely on my absolute support."

Strong was taken aback, but suspicious of the motive and reasoning behind Wolstenholme's remarks. Nothing this man ever said, or did, was without some ulterior motive. The political chess player extraordinaire, he had just moved a whole load of pieces around the board, all at once.

"Oliver, I appreciate you being as frank with me as you have, but I have to tell you that I don't believe that anything is in the offing, for you or me, other than maintenance of the status quo. The PM has no plans, as far as I know, to do anything other than keep us both in place." Bare faced lies sometimes need to be told, he thought.

"Supposing certain marks were… overstepped?" enquired Wolstenholme.

"Certain marks?"

"Yes… challenging times, I know. But if things were being done or advocated that were not in the interests of the country, Edward. The PM has my full support of course. But supposing he were to veer off course in some way. What then? There are all sorts of rumours whirling around at the moment."

"I haven't heard them. And…" Strong checked himself.

"And?" pressed his host.

"And if anything, were to be considered to have overstepped any mark, by anyone, I'd come down on it like a ton of hot bricks. It ain't going to happen. The PM is totally committed to maintaining the status quo and he'll do whatever it takes to do so. And, of course, if he didn't act in the national interest, I'd obviously be supportive of any action you felt was necessary to deal with that situation."

Wolstenholme paused before answering. His smile had a hint of resignation about it.

"You're really saying you'd support any action necessary to deal with the PM if he didn't act in the national interest?"

Strong re-iterated his position. "That's what I said. Yes"

"And next week? Monday or Tuesday? Nothing likely to be announced that will take policy in a different direction?"

Strong held his ground. "What do you mean?"

Wolstenholme paused briefly. "I understand. Your loyalty is entirely appropriate, and I apologise for bringing all this up in this way. I hope I can rely on your discretion, Edward."

Wolstenholme unfolded his legs and moved closer to the table, resting his weight upon it. "We have much more in common than might appear to be the case."

For the first time since they had served in Cabinet together, Strong felt a hint of positivity towards Wolstenholme.

"It gets late. I think I'd better go. Thank you for a lovely meal."

"Of course," replied Wolstenholme, "always a pleasure."

With that, both men stood and made their way out of the room and down the hallway towards the grand entrance hall.

As they reached the main door, Strong turned, "Thank you Oliver, it's been lovely, as usual. Do please thank the chef, and Mary, for me."

Wolstenholme reached out his right hand and gripped Strong's hand tightly, shaking it a touch too long.

"Thank you for coming Edward. And remember what I said."

Strong smiled. "Thanks again."

The door closed behind him with a thud. Both police officers wished Strong a good night and he made his way down the street towards his flat in Victoria. A pleasant evening, albeit getting late, he decided to walk home.

* * *

Strong's mind was working overtime as he replayed the events of the evening. He simply couldn't reconcile the direction the conversation had taken with the history the two men shared. His pace quickened, his powerful strides reflecting the thinking which was now taxing and testing his brain. What was it that Oliver knew, or, thought he knew? Did he actually know anything at all, or was this just an attempt to cast doubt in his mind? But what was the point?

Strong knew that he had the support of the PM. Yes, of course he did. He was sure. Wasn't he? But then who knows? No, there was no doubt. As Strong walked on, with every step he took the seed of doubt planted by Wolstenholme seemed to germinate ever faster.

Wolstenholme had done his work, and well.

Strong opened the door to his flat, entered and closed the door behind him. He was unlikely to get to sleep too quickly tonight.

After Strong's departure, Wolstenholme had returned to the small dining room in which he had shared the meal with his guest. The table had been all but cleared away, just two glasses and the flower arrangement remaining in place.

Wolstenholme looked around the room and then, standing upright, he gazed at himself in the mirror and adjusted his tie. A smile slowly cracked across his face. As Mary re-entered the room, his eyes latched on to her movements, watching her retrieve the two glasses and leave.

He leaned forward a little, slightly stooped, and raised his right hand towards the mirror, tapping it with his index finger. Tap, tap, tap. Tap. He stepped back, turned, and walked out of the room.

Walking back down the narrow hallway, he went into the room next door and immediately closed the door behind him.

The two men sitting at the table, one much older than the other, stood up. It was an even smaller room than that which had hosted dinner. It contained a table, two fold-up metal chairs with shallow cushions tied in place to provide a little comfort, a laptop connected to an electric socket in the wall by the door, and a large glass window. But this wasn't a window with a view to the outside world. It was a window through which all the activities and conversations taking place in the small dining room next door could be watched and recorded.

"We have everything we need; I trust?" enquired Wolstenholme. Both men nodded. "It's clear there's no shifting him. He had every opportunity to say something. He's obviously anchored to the PM's position. It'll be interesting to see how long it takes before we get something back. We have to hope that it's sooner rather than later," said Wolstenholme.

"We'll leave you to it and catch up tomorrow morning once we hear something," confirmed the older of the two men.

"We'd better," Wolstenholme almost insisted.

Gathering up their equipment, the two men followed Wolstenholme out of the room. "Tomorrow," he said, shaking hands with both men as they headed off into the night.

The older of the two, David Wilson, was smart and ambitious but had upset some around him because of his sometimes more outspoken authoritarian political views. He was never averse to using the powers vested in him and his department, to take whatever action had been necessary–across many fronts–over the last three to four years. He was certainly a trusted ally of Wolstenholme.

His colleague and subordinate, Dave Welling, who looked about ten years younger, was taller than Wilson. His fair hair had flecks of ginger running through it, enhanced in certain light, and he could just about claim to have a head of hair. Always more casually dressed, he had been assigned to his mentor and immediate superior two years ago and had frequently been relied upon to "get his hands dirty" as required.

After the men had left, Wolstenholme climbed into his bed,

reached across towards the bedside lamp, and switched it off. He lay there in the darkness, still, calm, and relaxed. His evening had been well spent and the next forty-eight hours would indicate whether the carefully laid plans now in place, could produce the desired result.

Never had Wolstenholme risked so much, prepared so comprehensively, and put his own position, potentially, even his life, on the line.

* * *

As Strong lay in his bed, desperately trying to focus on the sleep he knew he needed to catch up on, his mind continued to play the tricks Wolstenholme had so skilfully placed within it.

What made no sense at all was that if Wolstenholme was even close to identifying a problem, why now? What on earth would the PM have to gain by dumping his key supporter, given what was about to transpire.

CHAPTER 9

Having let the final image linger for all too long, CM shrunk the grim picture from the screen. No-one spoke.

"It's important that you understand us, Josh." Ardoon seemed more distasteful by the second. "It would be an absolute tragedy if this unpleasant experience should befall your lovely wife."

The threat was all too clear.

"I understand."

"Good. It's important that we know you are aware of the consequences of any failure on your part to carry out your instructions to the letter."

He emphasised the last three words, making the instruction even more chillingly clear.

"Who was the man?" Josh enquired.

"No-one. Just a tramp."

The contempt Josh had for his leading captor grew by the minute. No-one is just anything, he thought.

"Now, we should all make our way to our rooms. It's late and we all need our beauty sleep." The man concluded before Josh could ask more questions.

Josh looked around the room and caught Paul's eye behind him. Josh's eyes were drawn to a quick movement of the fingers on Paul's right hand. As quick as it was possible to be, he had crossed and uncrossed his index and middle fingers before returning the gun and hand to a more appropriate position.

Josh continued to look around him, anxious not to draw suspicion to either himself or Paul. If he had seen what he believed he was meant to see, he wasn't quite as alone as he thought. The quick crossing and uncrossing of two fingers was a sign that the CPU, and some other personal protection units used, to covertly signal support, assistance, or even the cue to respond to a threat.

Whilst the signal was known to Josh, Paul was not, and he was urgently considering whether Paul could have worked with the CPU after his departure, or, if he'd worked with other units of close arm protection alongside the CPU, if he had at all. The answers to these questions would need to be established, and fast, if Josh were to trust this potential new ally.

Josh determined to await further developments rather than pro-actively engage with Paul. There was still far too much uncertainty surrounding everything to make an ill-judged hasty move, based upon a couple of finger movements.

Ryan opened the door and beckoned Josh through, watching his every step closely, gun in hand. Paul followed Josh out across the hallway and up the stairs. As he climbed the staircase and made his way down the first-floor passageway towards his room, he felt his hand being roughly grabbed and a small piece of paper being thrust into it.

Josh quickly put his hand in his pocket to deposit the piece of paper, and left it there, so as not to arouse Ryan's suspicion.

Josh was concerned that this could well be a trap, but he didn't have much else to go on right now.

As he reached his bedroom door, Paul put his hand between Josh's shoulder blades and shoved him into the room making Josh stumble towards the bed.

"Sleep well," Ryan sniggered, as he closed and locked the bedroom door.

Paul and Ryan made their way down the staircase and across the hallway towards their own shared room. "What do you think of him? He doesn't seem like much to me," smirked Ryan. "Well, it doesn't mean he's not a bloody handful if he wants to be," Paul responded.

"No, I mean, exactly," affirmed Ryan, "but he's, just, well, not what I expected."

Paul shook his head. "Don't underestimate him."

* * *

Josh immediately retrieved the piece of paper from his trouser pocket and unravelled it.

With no curtains at the window, the pitch blackness outside yielded a few stars in the sky, sparkling in the distance; something rarely seen from the windows of his home back in London.

He moved to the bathroom and flushed the piece of paper Paul had given him down the toilet. As he watched it disappear, Josh again pondered whether help really was about to materialise or whether yet more games were being played.

On it had been written four words.

Co-operate. Wait. Be Ready.

CHAPTER 10

Strong hadn't slept well.

The question that troubled him the most, was whether to raise certain aspects of his conversation with Wolstenholme with the Prime Minster at all, or brush it away until he knew more.

Could this be an elaborate test of his discretion? Wolstenholme may well be assessing Strong's reliability and loyalty. He had given his word that he'd respect the confidences just shared. What if he didn't? Should he anyway? Despite everything going on, as things stood that morning, Wolstenholme was the only likely successor to the PM and Strong realized that if things went seriously wrong, he'd certainly need to ensure that he was at least recognized as being politically indispensable to Wolstenholme.

As he started preparing his breakfast porridge, things started to settle. As he lifted a spoon from the cutlery drawer, he was certain of the actions he would take that day.

* * *

The Prime Minister's alarm sounded, as usual, at 06:00am, and he unwrapped himself from the duvet and walked across the small bedroom towards the bathroom to wash, shave and prepare himself for the day ahead.

The small flat was perfect for Eddington's use. With his wife barely there and his younger neighbour, The Chancellor, needing larger accommodation, this suited his needs perfectly.

Eddington personally liked his neighbour, not only as an individual, but politically. The Chancellor was personable, had a profound sense of humour, and was naturally full of the kind of bonhomie that he himself wished he could better deploy. Apart from that–and to Eddington, even more important–was the fact that his neighbour had always, both publicly and privately, made it clear that he didn't wish to be, and never would be, Prime Minister.

Chancellor Bonato, had acquired a reputation as a hard worker, highly effective Government spokesman and loyal lieutenant to the Prime Minister. Having come from a business background initially, Bonato had decided to go into politics following a whole series of debacles made by the Government in the mid to late 2020's. Indeed, it was Eddington who had persuaded him to stand for a party he was not entirely sure about himself at the time.

Michael Bonato, now thirty-eight, had arrived in the UK as a baby after his parents had emigrated from Italy. Blessed with classically strong, handsome, Italian features, he was very much the "pin-up" of the party. His husband, a Yorkshireman by birth, had also previously been an accomplished Parliamentarian. They were a formidable pairing.

The Chancellor and Prime Minister were to meet later that morning and Eddington was looking forward to it.

After a breakfast of scrambled eggs and toast, accompanied by two cups of tea, the Prime Minister made his way down the flights of stairs, past the multiple pictures of former Prime Ministers adorning the walls. As he descended towards the ground floor and "the guts" of the operation, as he referred to it, he looked up at the clock on the wall and checked his watch. It was a habit he'd had ever since taking up office and, as his wife spent most of her time in his constituency in outer London, his first phone call of the day was almost always to her.

Despite his desire to check in with Strong, he made the obligatory call to Helen, making it as brief as possible. He needed to ascertain how Strong's supper with Wolstenholme the previous evening had gone. He was acutely aware what a slippery character his Home Secretary was and knew that he needed to keep his Party Chairman firmly onside over the coming days.

"Morning, Prime Minister."

"Good morning, Edward. okay?"

Eddington sensed Strong's hesitation.

"I think so," came the less than committed response.

"Oh, you under the weather?"

"No, no, not at all. Fighting fit."

Another pause confirmed Eddington's sense of something amiss in Strong's attitude.

"So, what did the little shit have to say for himself?"

Edward Strong pondered the degree of openness he should deploy when giving his answer.

"He was extremely supportive. Couldn't have been more supportive in fact. Best conversation I've had with him for years. Surprised really."

The Prime Minister creased his forehead.

"Supportive as in… me… you… party? What?"

"Generally supportive. Even told me he was on-side, particularly with me. Nothing too specific, but he went out of his way to make that point."

"What do you think he meant?" The Prime Minister was immediately suspicious and spoke in clipped tones.

"I was going to ask you the same question."

The Prime Minister paused before gathering his thoughts.

"No idea, Strongy. We know how bloody slippery he is. I suspect he was fishing. Trying to draw you on what's actually going on. Seems like he was testing you… mind you, can't blame him if he's suspicious. I suppose he'd be right to be, eh? Let's face it, he'll hate being so unceremoniously dumped when all this is over."

"Suppose so," came the reply. "Is everything still on as planned?"

"Yes," replied the Prime Minister, firmly. This was a course of action to which he was totally committed. "I'm seeing Michael later this morning to try and lock him in, and then, this afternoon I'll prepare for all the other changes."

"Do you need me to do anything at this stage or is it all set to go as planned?" Strong enquired.

"I'm not anticipating any changes, though who knows."

* * *

Wolstenholme could not have been less of an early riser than Edward Strong if he tried, but today was different. He'd headed to the offices in Whitehall and, by 07:45, had already completed his first meeting by conference call and was due to make a private but important call immediately after.

Prior to both, he'd checked in with Wilson to get an update on plans to selectively use some of the information and remarks from Strong that had been obtained and recorded during the previous evening. All was progressing well.

It was a minute before eight and Wolstenholme flicked through the contact list on a second, personal mobile phone and spotted the name he was after. Tapping on it to make the call, bang on time he lifted the mobile to his left ear and waited for it to be answered.

"It's me. Did everything go as expected?"

He listened intently as the answers he was seeking were relayed in quite some detail.

"Understood." He was pleased by the response but continued to seek some further reassurance. "And you think we'll be ready to deal with all of this once I've managed to get what we need sorted this end?"

All appeared to be going satisfactorily. He terminated the call.

Wolstenholme knew he had to dig deeper to get clarity on the Prime Minister's plans. That he had been completely excluded from what he now knew were a series of private meetings over the last two months, had made him determined to intervene.

This was going to be a terribly busy day.

CHAPTER 11

Josh had woken early. His first thoughts were of Becky. He feared for her. He had no idea where she was and was completely helpless to do anything about it, even if he did. He knew that the only way to have any prospect of rescuing her was to play the game that had now commenced and see where it took him. But whatever else might happen, he knew he would not rest until they were reunited.

As he peered into the darkness through the bedroom window a shaft of light on the horizon caught his eye. The hills and the silhouettes of isolated trees and rocky outcrops were picked out and brought to life as the sun rose slowly, crafting an array of colourful transformations in minutes. The multitude of dark shadowy limbs from trees reached out across the landscape, slowly recoiling back to their places of origin as the sun edged further above the horizon.

The silence of the moment, along with the vastness of the open spaces before him, enhanced Josh's sense of isolation and added to the weight of responsibility he felt to rescue his wife and unborn child.

The house began to stir as the dusky dawn turned to a fulsome morning light and Josh took advantage of every second his solitude provided him with to carefully examine the area to the rear of the building.

In front of him, some fifty or so metres away , was an area of grass with a narrow path cutting across it, covered with carefully drawn white lines which he felt were clearly intended to mark out a location. But for what?

The sound of a key in the lock interrupted the peace. Josh moved away from the window. The door swung open and a man unknown to Josh appeared, holding a plate in one hand and a mug in the other. "Breakfast." Both plate and mug were placed on the floor to the side of Josh's bed. The young man stood back up, and left the room as quickly as he had entered.

Josh demolished the breakfast as he watched proceedings outside. He observed three men move across the grass, on each occasion adding more definition and substance to what appeared, initially, to be a spider's web of white lines.

As he watched, just like a Magic Eye picture that was held too close to his eyes and suddenly came to life as it was slowly withdrawn, Josh gradually became aware of what could be a street, junction, slip road and what, potentially, might be various buildings and obstacles. It reminded him of a poorer version of some of the training areas he had experienced during his military service.

A key turned in the lock, Ryan and Paul appearing.

Neither men spoke but Paul tilted his head towards the door, beckoning to Josh to make his way out. Ryan took the forward position as the trio made their way back along the hallway, down the stairs and towards the same room Josh had been taken to the previous evening.

As he entered the room, Josh was joining a group of another twenty-five people, all sitting in rows. There was no sign of Ardoon, only CM, who was sat on a dining chair, motionless but watchful of all the movements in front of him.

Josh was once again instructed to sit in the same chair he'd occupied the previous evening. Once he believed Josh to be settled, CM commenced, what turned out to be, the start of a briefing.

There were no initial pleasantries and there was no slow build-up to the reveal. Once CM had brought the foldaway to life with various pictures and images supporting his remarks, he commenced his explanation, the trickle of data soon turning into a tsunami of information and, bit by bit, the picture began to emerge. The group of two dozen men, and the one woman, were all ex-military personnel. This was an interesting mix, thought Josh.

They were all advised that Josh had been "recruited"–a bizarre word to use given the circumstances, thought Josh–to provide the necessary technical and operational knowledge, particularly in respect to his CPU service. As Josh had already suspected - the area mapped out in the grounds of the property was an exact scale representation of a location yet to be confirmed, but one which he would be required to become thoroughly acquainted with . Once in situ at the actual location, he would be called upon to conduct his part in the operation.

On top of the training that the team had already undergone, there would be two further days of intense training ahead of an assault on a convoy of vehicles. The details of the target, and the reasons for the mission were left out of the briefing.

Whatever it was, someone had spent a good deal of time and money planning it all. It would have been impossible to have kept all this as secret as it clearly had been kept, without some high-powered people being involved. Josh had assumed that the skills he was required to bring related specifically to the protection "sleeve" which, itself, caused him great angst as he knew that there were only a few people allocated such sophisticated personal protection.

Given the potential target list, it was no wonder that his wife and unborn child were being held as leverage. The choices he knew he would face, were already causing him to agonise, and the pit of his stomach slowly ground away, producing waves of anxiety and even, at times, physical discomfort.

Whilst the actual objective remained unclear at this stage, the expectation wasn't.

As CM continued, his arms became more animated, conductor-like, as he worked his way through each component part of the plan. His voice became louder as the pace quickened. He was clearly relishing the moment, and his role in it. The phases of the mission, the number of cars to be attacked and in which order, the weaponry to be deployed and the "critical" timings required of each group; all led to the final slide.

Taking small steps towards the team as he reached his conclusion, without any indication, CM suddenly paused. Silence. He looked around the room at each member of the team, every one of whom was sitting deathly still. No noise, no response and not an eye-lid blinking.

Now softly spoken, CM confirmed, "We are going to take out some of those at the heart of Government who stand in the way. Our targets will ensure that strong Government can be restored. That, lady and gentlemen, is our task. When the training is completed, and we are ready, you'll be told exactly who. But I will tell you this. It doesn't get much bigger."

Josh now, at least, knew where he stood and what was personally expected of him. It didn't get any more serious than this. During the silence that followed, he felt the tension in the room. Some sat back in their seats, others looked at colleagues. Moments later, having completed the briefing, CM left the room, and the assembled men and women made their exit, some quietly starting to discuss what they had all been assembled to deliver. None seemed unnerved. Ryan, ever the enthusiast, led Josh down a passageway and out of a door to the rear of the building, immediately under the window of his bedroom.

Ryan stopped and turned. "Right, you're with him," he said, pointing at Paul and gesturing for another man to follow him towards the training ground set out before them.

As Ryan and his colleague walked on, Josh was held back by Paul with a backward flick of his left hand. Josh slowed and Paul looked down to his watch. He tapped it and put his hand to his mouth as if feeding himself something. He looked at Josh, who nodded that he had understood. Paul's next move, or communication, would be at lunch time.

Josh was still not entirely certain as to Paul's reliability and trustworthiness, but it was all he had to grab hold of and, given the circumstances, he'd settle for that. Either his potential new comrade was playing a clever game of manipulation and control on behalf of his captors, or he was risking a heck of a lot to establish a contact that could only put him in more danger. Time would tell.

As all four men reached the spot at which training would commence, Josh surveyed the scene ahead of him. He counted eighteen men, included himself, all of whom had taken up positions at various points on the training ground. The entire area was roughly three-hundred-and-fifty square metres, larger than it had looked from the vantage point of his bedroom window.

The man accompanying Ryan opened the plastic box he had been carrying and retrieved from it a rectangular wooden box about one foot long and eight inches deep. He handed the box to Josh. The size and weight of the item was consistent with the operational unit that controlled the protective sleeve technology.

"Now," said Paul, "this is what's going to happen."

Training was underway.

CHAPTER 12

Eddington was struggling to keep his schedule on track. He had asked his private secretary to reschedule his meeting with the Chancellor. It was important to have a popular figure like Bonato lined up and solidly in support, and he dared not risk another day.

One of the two telephones on his desk rang. He could do without the interruption and hoped that whoever it was, and whatever it was about, he could despatch the matter swiftly. He answered. "Tell him I'm bus-" His reply was interrupted. "Fine, put him through." It was the third time Wolstenholme had called and the Prime Ministers "gatekeeper" was reluctant to put him off yet again. Eddington composed himself for what he anticipated may be a difficult conversation.

"Oliver, sorry I've been a touch elusive. Trying to keep on top of things."

"No problem at all. I just wanted to check in with you about Monday."

"Monday?" The Prime Minister wasn't sure where Wolstenholme was coming from. Did he know something he shouldn't? What had Strong said at their dinner?

"I'm assuming there's nothing we need to be preparing for other than your planned statement to the House?"

"No, nothing else. We can co-ordinate further on Monday." Eddington tried to shut down the conversation quickly. He had things to do and was worried about where this conversation was going.

"It would be useful to have a copy of your planned statement to look at sometime today, so that I can make sure I'm on message. I may be able to feed in a few positive additional elements about the need for continued vigilance, adherence to orders in place, security measures. That kind of thing."

Eddington paused before answering. He knew that he could not send any such draft.

"It'll be in decent shape over the weekend and I'll get a copy over to you Sunday night."

"Thank you, Prime Minister. I'll look forward to seeing it. Have a good day."

"And you Oliver, and you."

"Oh, Prime Minister." Wolstenholme quickly intervened before either man could disconnect the call.

"Yes?"

"Sorry, just whilst I'm on," he paused dramatically, "it's about Edward."

After his conversation with Strong earlier that morning Eddington was keen to discover what Wolstenholme had to say.

"You probably don't know, but I had supper with him last evening and he was somewhat concerned about his position. Nothing too specific but it was most unlike him. I thought I'd let you know; for what it's worth."

"What did he say?" asked Eddington, increasingly suspicious of Wolstenholme's machinations.

"As I say, nothing specific but he seemed anxious and, to be honest, for the first time I've known him, less than rock solid and effusive in his support for you. Kept referencing the future and how uncertain he was about choices you were making. Anyway, I told him I didn't know anything that was going on that would be a problem for he, or I, and he'd be fine. I was certain."

The Prime Minister listened attentively, picking his way through a mirror image of what he'd heard only a few hours earlier from Strong.

"I see. How bizarre," responded Eddington, cagily.

"There isn't anything, Prime Minister, is there?"

"Ha! No, of course not. He's fine. I'll take an opportunity at some point to re-assure him. I won't refer to this conversation obviously but thanks, Oliver, appreciated."

"Presumably, we both are." Wolstenholme's question was presented as a statement. Eddington realised that he had to be incredibly careful how he answered it.

"Christ Oliver, I've got shit loads to do without upsetting both relationships. Thanks for the call. Bye for now."

As soon as he'd disconnected the call, Wolstenholme looked at Wilson, who was still sitting opposite him. "He's definitely going to fuck me over." The normally calm, determined, and steely Wolstenholme was showing signs of the stress and strain he had so far kept under control. "He's not going to show us his statement. And we both know what that means."

"We'd better move quickly in that case," came Wilson's reply. "Do we go?"

Wolstenholme stared ahead, deep in thought. Allowing the Prime Minister to do what he feared was being planned, would be an afront to everything he had been working towards.

"When the Prime Minister lies to you in the barest faced way, you know you're no longer part of the circle," Wolstenholme asserted.

"Do we go?" repeated Wilson, in clipped but clear tones.

Wolstenholme was jolted from his deep and intense gaze. Looking towards Wilson, he nodded, "Prepare… only prepare." As Wilson headed to the door, Wolstenholme stopped him.

"David." Wilson turned, "Check on Michael Bonato's diary. We need to know what he's been doing for the last few weeks and what he's got planned this weekend. He may end up being a player in all this. Check on Strong and Taylor's diaries too. Details. We'll meet later."

Nodding his acknowledgement of the instruction, Wilson left Wolstenholme's office and headed straight back to his own. Things would now move at pace.

CHAPTER 13

The morning of intense training and briefing that Josh had endured had been called to a halt by Fitz, the middle-aged man who had taken charge as soon as the team was in place. Paired up for the task ahead, Josh and Paul had been working together since rehearsals had got underway, with Ryan standing watchful guard.

All morning Fitz had coordinated the training, his knowledge of the plan was so detailed that every second was accounted for. Each time he stopped barking orders – something he seemed born to do–they all broke out to zero in and analyse every single variable. He was a hard task master and was obviously from a military background.

As they broke for lunch, it looked like Ryan would have to wait for his as the man delivering them turned and walked away.

"Go and get yours mate," said Paul. Nodding towards Josh, Paul suggested to Ryan "I don't think he's going anywhere, and even if he had plans to, I'll handle it." Paul smiled at Ryan as if to dismiss and prospect of such a situation developing.

Pausing for only the briefest of moments, Ryan turned and walked off towards the building. On two previous occasions in the last week, he'd missed out on lunch and was determined not to do so again.

As Ryan moved off, Josh waited for him to be out of earshot before whispering his first direct remarks to Paul since receiving the paper message which had been thrust into his hand the previous evening.

Lowering his head and peering down at his lunch to obscure as much of his lip movements as he could, Josh opened the conversation.

"Who are you?"

"MI5," Paul responded. The country's domestic counter-intelligence and security agency was an organization familiar to Josh, as he'd been reporting directly to senior officers of it during his time within the CPU.

Josh took another bite from his sausage roll. Paul reached into the box and withdrew another sandwich. Sitting alongside each other on a small, flattish container, both men, but particularly Josh, were the subject of much scrutiny from others dotted around the training arena. Although the closest pairing was a good thirty to forty metres away, communications had to be carefully managed and completely disguised.

As Josh wiped away some of the pastry crumbs from his mouth, he whispered his second question.

"Is it just you?"

Paul took a bite from the sandwich, "Plus you."

"What is going on? What's all this about?" enquired Josh.

"It's Monday I think," responded Paul. "This is all about Monday coming."

"And what is it?"

"After the earlier briefing, we still don't know who the specific targets are yet. That's been kept quiet, but we all know they're bloody important. That's why you're here."

"An assassination? Then what? What's the point?"

"No idea," came Paul's reply. "He's coming back," he whispered.

Ryan had emerged from the building, eating a sandwich from one hand, and holding a small cardboard box containing the rest of his lunch in the other.

The conversation ended and Paul stood up, intentionally distancing himself from Josh by a few steps.

"Got it then?" smiled Paul to his young colleague.

"Not only that, but there's also some actual food in there too!"

A shout from some forty metres away interrupted the conversation. "Not starving now then?" Clearly everyone had a view on Ryan's food issues.

Ryan's extended his middle finger, waving his arm from the elbow backwards and forwards with purpose. Giving the finger to so many of his colleagues was something he'd obviously had to do many times before.

* * *

Josh finished his Diet Coke and folded the lid of the box shut. He then placed it on the container beside him. Paul quickly followed suit.

"Me again, I suppose," remarked Ryan. Paul smiled at him and nodded. Tutting to himself as he picked up both empty containers, Ryan made his way back to the main house, finishing off his own Diet Coke en-route.

"Who's in charge here?" whispered Josh, rubbing his nose with his elbow to obscure this latest set of communications.

Paul stroked his stubble and turned his back away from his erstwhile colleagues scattered across the training field, his answers completely obscured from their gaze.

"Lord Ardoon. It's his show here. Trying to find out who's pulling his strings."

"But this makes no sense," responded Josh. "Why is he doing something like this and what's the point of it all. He's already got the influence he wants; hasn't he?"

Paul was unable to give any response that enabled either man to make sense of the situation.

"We've got to wait." About that much, Paul was certain.

"Where is Becky?" Josh waited for the reply, but none came. As Ryan made his way back to take up his usual position, Paul shouted towards him. "Oi, where's the bloody pack?"

Ryan looked heavenward, turned, and made his way back to the house. Whatever it was that Ryan had forgotten, Josh was grateful for a few more minutes alone with Paul.

"She's not here but I think you can get her here. Push hard later. You'll get the chance and when you do, take it. Without you, they're totally fucked, but they will kill her. So, we need her here if we're going to save her... as well as stop all this bollocks."

The message from Paul was unequivocal. The softly spoken whisper had landed on Josh like a thunderclap.

"Right, let's go again," shouted Fitz as he emerged from the building. Ryan also re-emerged immediately behind him, this time holding the pack.

Everyone took up their position once again, waited for Fitz to give the go ahead, and, for the fifth time that day, the practice session was underway.

Both Ardoon and CM had, at that moment, taken up position at one of the windows on the second floor at the rear of the main building.

The plan required the entire exercise to be completed in under four minutes. CM observed his watch and noted a time of four minutes and twenty-five seconds.

Ardoon was happy. "We'll get it nailed tomorrow, possibly even later today," he said, confident in his opinion. "The real issue is what sort of delay we get if our expert decides he's not going to co-operate."

CM nodded in agreement. "He seems compliant so far."

His Lordship was less convinced than his subordinate.

"Don't assume anything. He's smart. Almost certainly playing us as much as he can. That's what these people are trained to do. If the boot ever ends up on the other foot, he'll kick us to death."

Turning to CM, Ardoon stared directly at him, "That's what you're there for. To make sure that does not happen. That said, we do have at least one trick up our sleeve, eh?"

CM smiled knowingly.

"Let me know how the final session goes. I need to make a call." With that last request issued, Ardoon turned and walked away from CM, out of the door and out of sight.

Now alone, CM once again looked out across the mock location stretched out before him, all the players reviewing their roles in small groups before coming together for a team review. And there, of course, was Josh. CM didn't trust him, nor like him. Josh represented all the things that CM had striven to become but failed. Thirty seconds passed before CM blinked his way back to reality and away from the all-enveloping hatred he held for this one man. He would enjoy taking the opportunity to shorten his life.

CHAPTER 14

Lord Ardoon settled into the large, fine, comfy leather chair in his small private study on the ground floor of his home. The sun shone through the large window, bathing the entire room in waves of light. It was a beautiful day.

"Good afternoon," he spoke into the receiver of the phone on his desk. Those deep but delicate Scottish tones enriched the greeting. Ardoon might be an outspoken and colourful character, but he could also be given to the use of few words on occasion. He was definitely a mood conversationalist.

After pausing to allow for the response, he waded straight in with the only question that mattered.

"Where are we for Monday?"

The short briefing kept his attention focused and intense. As he began to realise that everything was moving inexorably towards receiving the go-ahead, he made his way to the window and gazed across the countryside spread out before him. These were momentous times.

"We'll be ready if it's a go. All is on time here. And Monday's statement? Is that all prepared?"

The short answer brought a nod of approval from Ardoon. "Good. It's at least started… you'll get your bit done, no doubt. It's now up to us to make sure it's delivered," he acknowledged. "So, Sunday night, no alternative, we decide on the go ahead."

He disconnected the call and looked out upon the beautiful

landscape before him once more. As he drank in the vista of the place of his birth, he marvelled at the range of colours, the contours, windswept trees, rolling hills in the distance and rocky outcrops that all came together to produce this most outstanding of Scottish landscapes.

He knew that every minute spent perfecting the rehearsals taking place just a few hundred metres from him, would ultimately determine the course of history for the country: quite possibly forever. *Upon such risks were countries built*, he quietly asserted to himself.

Ardoon retraced his steps and walked back into the room where CM waited.

"Christopher."

CM was still looking out of the window and turned to face Ardoon.

"Monday. It's looking like it'll be on."

CM coaxed half a smile.

"I'll start turning up the heat on the boys then." With that commitment given, he started to make his way out of the room.

"Christopher," CM was stopped in his tracks and turned to face Ardoon.

"We have waited years to get to this point. Strong government, holding the levers of power, discipline, and control. No more weak democratic interference in our plans and ambitions. This is not just a mission; it is a dream to seize power and rest that power in our hands. Do not leave a single stone unturned."

With that, CM nodded, turned and left the room.

Ardoon walked over to the window and watched Christopher Mason emerge from the building. Walking at pace, he made his way across to Fitz, took him aside for a private conversation and then returned to the house.

No sooner had CM delivered his message than Fitz began barking orders to the team of men scattered before him.

CHAPTER 15

It was now half past twelve and Eddington was getting a little irritated at Bonato's lateness. However, for all his irritation, he knew that he had to take the time to bring his neighbour onside and ensure his support was locked down. Either that, or he would need enough time to make alternative plans to sort out a different solution. Whilst he'd thought about that, of course, he knew that there would be significant political risks involved without the Chancellor firmly on board and he'd rather try and tie it all up with Bonato in support; however difficult that might prove to be.

As he considered all of this, there was a knock on the door and his private secretary walked in, quickly followed by Bonato.

"The Chancellor, Prime Minister,"

"Thank you. Michael," he said, smiling, "do come in. Good to see you."

"I'm so sorry about that. I had to take a call and I just couldn't end it."

"Oh, don't worry about that. Totally understand. Even Prime Ministers can't take precedence over everything." Smiling broadly, Eddington was at his most charming and gracious.

"Sit down, do, Michael."

As he took his seat, Bonato noticed the buffet lunch arranged on the low-level table between he and Eddington.

"The egg and tomato ones are on your side of the tray," Eddington offered.

"Crikey, I am being well looked after," said Bonato as Eddington leaned over and passed his guest a plate.

"Orange juice?"

"Thank you. No notes needed today, Prime Minister?"

"Notes?" Eddington filled his own plate, having poured the two men a glass of orange juice each.

"Well, not often you get served in this way by the PM. Just wondered whether it was a more formal meeting, or personal, if you like."

Eddington detected a slight nervousness in his colleague. Unsurprising, given the circumstances.

"Oh, no, no. Just a chat. There are a few things I wanted to run by you, and I just thought it'd be best to do it like this. Nothing more than that really."

Eddington had carefully planned the structure of the conversation well in advance. He began with a summary of the present state of the country. Eddington was a master of description and could link policies together in a way no other member of the cabinet could, and Bonato was impressed by his boss's grasp of all areas of policy and his ability to summarise complex positions with ease.

Eddington leant over and topped up Bonato's glass once again.

"Michael, can I just stop at this point and ask if this is what you would broadly accept as being your own position. Well, maybe not position but, perhaps, assessment?"

It wasn't a question that Bonato was surprised to hear. The Prime Minister would often use this gradual and segmented strategy to gain backing for his position. It was both effective and politically smart. If the answer were a yes, he'd press on having tied you to his policy wagon. If there were areas of concern, he would unpick them, debate them, and then seek to resolve the issue either by force of argument or, alternatively, with an occasional compromise. Either way, he would have made considerable progress with his agenda, and your support for it.

Bonato looked away and then back towards Eddington, clearly in thought. Eddington remained silent. He would be prepared to sit in silence for minutes, if necessary, always affording time for the subject of his attention to think and produce a considered response.

"You've summed up the situation well. I don't really have any fundamental differences with that. I might argue about timing or degree in some areas, but I am totally aligned with the general position."

Eddington was quietly delighted with the response. It could not have been better, given what he was about to disclose.

"So, to the tricky part; people."

Bonato's gentle smile was unexpected. Though an immensely personable man, he was normally quite serious when it came to the big issues of the day. He was also the most people friendly and focused personality in Government, frequently banging on about culture, values, and approach to people, much to some others' irritation. People issues were always given a completely serious look.

Eddington paused, an expression of slight surprise across his face. It was a look which encouraged a response from his lunch guest.

"Oh, sorry... nothing about what you've said. I was just thinking back to an earlier conversation I'd had. The predictions might be about to come true."

Eddington was intrigued. "What do you mean? I don't follow."

"Oliver was saying he thought there might be a problem for some of us–specifically Edward. It was why I was late. I couldn't get him off the phone."

"Oliver rang you about this?" Eddington felt pangs of doubt creeping into his mind. He started questioning the wisdom of discussing this whole business with Bonato. It was a lengthy conversation if all they were talking about was a potential re-shuffle. What else had been said? What was Oliver's game?

Eddington had always suspected that Wolstenholme not only had his suspicions that there was something going on he'd not been consulted about, or would be, but was also likely to work behind the scenes to stop it if he knew.

Bonato ploughed on. "He was on to me for quite a while. He was particularly focused on Edward. Don't know why, as I don't think he's ever liked the bloke."

Eddington found his focus drifting. Why was Wolstenholme so focused on Strong? Why did he call Bonato? It was a long conversation. They must have talked about other matters. What was Edward doing to be the subject of such attention? Worse still, had Edward Strong spilled the beans and warned Wolstenholme? Was that why Wolstenholme was throwing up this smokescreen around Strong?

Looking once again at his guest, Eddington found himself in two minds as to whether to continue or to divert until he had checked a few more matters.

His mind was made up. Caution in these times.

"Michael, I'm keen to know your personal views on every member of the cabinet. I have some thinking to do about the structure of the Government and I'd value an objective and considered view."

This wasn't the next step originally planned. Nor was it what Bonato had expected.

"I have my views Prime Minister, but I think it's a matter for you entirely. Your cabinet is a choice for you."

"But you must have a view, Michael."

Bonato took a deep breath. He felt instinctively uncomfortable about sharing his views about everyone.

"I've made my views privately known to you about some of the cabinet, and if I've had a disagreement with them, I've let you know privately as well as reflecting those thoughts at cabinet itself. I really think it's not for me to say."

That was exactly what Eddington had assumed the honourable

Bonato would say and was relieved that he didn't need to press any further.

"I'm sorry I haven't really given you what you're looking for. I just think it's best that I don't," Bonato concluded.

Eddington leant across and shook Bonato's hand. "Thank you, Michael. I understand and appreciate where you're coming from. Happy to leave it at that."

That was The Chancellors cue to leave. He shook Eddington's hand, stood up from his seat and started to walk across the room to the door.

"Thank you for lunch and I do appreciate the chat. I am onside with your assessment and if it's helpful to meet again to discuss this in more detail, I'm happy to do that, anytime."

"Thank you, Michael. Appreciate that."

As he closed the door behind him, Bonato was re-assured, though struck by the abrupt termination of their conversation.

Once Bonato had left, Eddington lifted his mobile phone from his desk and quickly scanned the names for the one he needed.

Placing the phone to his ear, he waited for it to be answered.

"Adam, I need to see you, and smartish. Come in the back way."

The call was disconnected, and Eddington made his way back to his desk and took up position in his seat behind it.

He lifted the receiver, "Jamie, can you bring in some coffee in about five minutes please, and two cups and saucers. I'll be joined by the Foreign Secretary shortly. Just show him straight through when he arrives."

Replacing the receiver, he sat back in the chair, staring out into the space in front of him. His caution with Bonato had set many conversations back by at least a day or so, but it was all still manageable.

Leaning forward, he placed both elbows on the desk and rested his head into his hands.

CHAPTER 16

Frustrations had been growing amongst certain sections of the team, that the pace of each of the last three rehearsals was still not quick enough to deliver the timings necessary. One group of three seemed to be on a perpetual mission to thwart the efforts of their colleagues. After yet another inadequate performance, Fitz had changed some of the personnel around in an effort to correct and improve things.

"We'll be here all fucking night if necessary!" barked Fitz. "Go again!"

For the fifth time that afternoon, they ran the drill. Eight basic elements amidst all the complexities of each.

First, a signal came from the right. Second, a tractor moved into place to block an exit to the rear. Third, an assault on the last of the three vehicles in the convoy. Fourth, the lead car blocked, 200 metres further on, before being surrounded and strafed with handheld automatic weapons fire. Fifth, Paul, Ryan and Josh were to wait for the main vehicle to appear between two gate posts after reversing away from the attack launched on the lead car at point four. Sixth, Josh was to hack and disable the device controlling the sleeve, which would, by now, have been activated, at point three. Seventh, as the main target vehicle sped across the field, having entered between the two gate posts, it is hit with two RPG's, to destroy both the car, and whoever was inside. Eight, complete the escape.

This time, everything went like clockwork. Three minutes, fifty seconds. With a day of further practice sessions to come, all seemed set and Fitz was clearly pleased with the improvement.

In spite of that, Fitz knew, as did all those taking part, that nothing could be taken for granted and that there was always the probability, as military personnel well knew, that no mission, however well planned and executed, would survive contact with the enemy intact.

"We'll call it a day on that last one," shouted Fitz. "That's what needs to be repeated all day tomorrow... and live rounds tomorrow... don't forget that, or you'll get yourself killed."

As the men made their way back to the main house, half a dozen of them were called back and instructed to reproduce their part of the engagement some distance away to the left. Josh had been amazed that the ground had stood up so well to the onslaught it had faced.

"Add the hedges in those critical areas." That additional request from Fitz confirmed what Josh had already presumed. This was to be an assault on a convoy of three vehicles, taking place on a road in a relatively isolated location, and someone was going to be assassinated, along with those intended to protect them.

Josh had performed his role without complaint and, for the most part, flawlessly. He had determined to take Paul at his word and await further instructions and had made himself indispensable to the plan.

Paul and Ryan accompanied Josh back to the main house and through the hallway, but instead of heading back up the stairs to his room, he was told to keep going and head off to the right. A few doors later, he was directed into a small shower room.

"There's some shower gel and a towel in there and some clean clothes we nicked from your wardrobe at home. The rest you'll have to use again. You've got ten minutes." Ryan seemed to begrudge Josh this most basic act of cleanliness, but whatever he felt about it, Josh was delighted to get himself freshened up. A day of travel, and a sweaty day's work meant a wash was in order.

Once he'd finished, he banged on the door. Paul and Ryan were waiting and accompanied him up the stairs and back to his bedroom where he was locked in and left alone. He threw his old clothes onto the bed and walked straight over to the window, looking out and across to the training ground as three men erected mock hedges at various key points.

As he watched this new model killing zone take shape before him, he became aware of the setting sun. A few hours of daylight left, at best, he thought and sat down to remove his shoes.

Paul entered the room followed by the ever-present Ryan.

"You can leave them on. You're wanted downstairs," instructed Paul, and they ushered him out of the room, Ryan leading the way. Paul took hold of Josh's arm, stalling his exit from the room just as he reached the open doorway.

"It's time. Hold your nerve." With that he then pushed Josh out of the door causing him to stumble. Though well down the hallway, Ryan had turned in time to watch Josh lose his balance as he was pushed from the bedroom and gave a brief smirk of pleasure.

* * *

Awaiting Josh's arrival in a room downstairs was CM, who had settled into what looked like a distinctly comfortable and relaxed mode in one of the four armchairs dotted about the room.

"Sit down," CM said to Josh. A guard took a small, wooden chair and placed it in front of Josh.

"Sit down," came the repeated instruction.

Josh eased himself around the chair and sat down. He was facing CM, who recapped the day, adding a few bits of detail which had not been obvious during the actual training period itself; the shortened distance between the first phase and use of the tractor and the first assault groups brought forward attack time, once the tractor had been deployed. He'd also noticed, as had others, that

Josh had done exactly what was asked of him and had done it as well as they had all thought he would.

"You'll have picked up that we are only a matter of a few days from the actual operation being carried out," said CM.

Josh nodded but remained silent.

"The purpose of this discussion is to re-affirm a few points."

Josh took his moment and promptly interrupted. "We can rehearse all you like. You can "re-affirm" all you like, but until I see Becky, there'll be nothing from me on the day. And you can kiss your fucking plan goodbye." It was a substantial risk to take but the moment seemed right and if Paul was who he said he was, this was Josh's moment to seize it.

CM paused for a moment and began again.

"The purpose of this discussion is to re-affirm a few points. First, without your full co-operation, your wife and child will be killed. Then you."

CM waited for a response.

"You've had my response," replied Josh. He held his ground, and his nerve. He hoped Paul was right.

"And is that your final response?" CM enquired.

Josh looked at him and remained defiantly silent.

"Very well. The responsibility for what follows rests with you."

CM pulled his mobile from his pocket, looked up a contact detail and tapped his finger on the screen.

"Do you have the syringe?" Waiting a few seconds for the response, CM continued. "Good. Administer it. Right now."

This wasn't the response Josh expected, and yet he sensed this was his only chance to leverage his position. His heart was pounding. He continued staring at CM, barely blinking. If it were a show of personal strength and resolve CM wanted, he'd got one.

CM tapped on the screen again and held his phone, speaker on, in the air towards Josh. Allowing the sound at the other end to puncture the silence of the room, added further extraordinary emotional torment and pain to Josh's already anxious state.

The shouts and the screams all banged further nails of anguish into Josh's soul.

Josh looked directly at CM. He didn't flinch. He didn't waver. He didn't move a muscle. "Nothing from me," re-iterated Josh, in whispered tones, "Nothing."

As the noise the other end rose to an uncomfortable and distressing crescendo, Josh neared breaking point. He continued to stare at CM, willing a response.

CM looked once again at his mobile, tapped the screen which silenced the noise and placed it to his ear.

"Stop." He then hung up.

Josh maintained vice-like control over himself. He had won out.

CM sat back into his seat and allowed the moment to settle.

"Very well… but let me be clear. No more fucking games and no more fucking hero shit. If we get either, there'll be no more fucking wife."

"Nothing, unless I see her in person," re-iterated Josh.

CM stood up and took two steps towards Josh and bent over, looking him straight in the eyes.

"You'll see her tomorrow. She'll see you, tomorrow. But if you fuck anything up, it'll be the last time you see each other alive."

With that, CM walked past him and left the room.

"Let's go." Paul intimated to Josh that he should follow him and return to his room. Ryan, Paul, and Josh all retraced their now usual footsteps and, a minute or so later, Josh was stepping into his room. As he turned to look at Paul for what he hoped would be at least a modicum of reassurance, Paul was already closing the door. However, just before he was out of sight altogether, Josh received a wink. Mission accomplished.

Josh walked over to his bed and lay down. He had been so close to caving, but Paul had been right and whilst suspicions about his newfound ally still lingered, for now he'd take this small but important win.

* * *

In response to hearing the footsteps yet again making their way along the passageway towards his room, Josh checked his watch. It was nearly 7:00pm. As Ryan came in, carrying yet another plate of cold food, Josh lay still, looking straight up at the ceiling, barely acknowledging him.

"Here, you'll get a drink later."

Ryan bent down and placed the plate on the floor by the bed, stepped back, turned, and headed out of the door, pulling it tightly shut behind him. The key, inevitably, turned once again in the lock.

Ryan had appeared on his own, thought Josh. No Paul. He presumed they thought that until Becky showed he wasn't going to do anything risky. They were right.

He lifted his legs off the bed, swivelled around and placed both feet firmly on the floor, leaning across to pick up the cling-film covered plate. Unfurling the awkwardly applied covering, he looked at his supper. More sandwiches; tuna and cucumber by the looks of things, a couple of medium-sized tomatoes, a chunky piece of cheddar cheese, a bag of salt and vinegar crisps, and an apple. It could have been worse.

Having devoured all but the crisps. Just as he started to open them, yet more footsteps could be heard.

This time it was Paul, and he was on his own. "Finish those, and then I'll take your plate. Here's your drink." Paul then nudged the door and let it ease its way towards an almost fully closed position.

"We've got about a minute, max, so just listen." he said, before continuing. "I was planted here about a couple of months ago, but I've not been able to get in touch with HQ now for three weeks so we're running blind here. It's certainly one, or multiple VIP targets as per the briefing. The use of the sleeve also tells us that much. No idea who or exactly when but with the number of people involved, it's going to be a hell of a fire fight. I've kept gathering what I can but if I'm honest, I've still no fucking clue exactly what's going to happen. It looks all set for Monday, though I'm not a hundred percent certain. We've got to stay close and be ready to act. We're both only going to get out of this fucking mess if we stick close together. Becky has no chance unless we do."

Paul glanced back towards the bedroom door. "I'm going to need to get back now." He concluded the conversation and turned to go.

"What do you mean you've no clue?" Josh whispered "What's the plan? What's going to be done? What about Becky?" Josh had too many questions and Paul made to leave.

"Becky's on her way. I overheard she'll be here tomorrow, she's ok. I'm pretty sure we're to move out on Monday. All I can say is when it all starts to go down, however things pan out, stay close. We'll have to re-act to the situation as best we can. I've got to go."

With that Paul left the room, locking the door behind him.

Josh stood in silence. Time was running out. Neither he nor Paul was close to understanding the detail of what was going on. But at least he felt that he now had a better chance of saving Becky, albeit a remote one.

But who was the target? Was there more than one? If Paul was going to make a move, what did he need Josh to do? So many questions, and nowhere near enough answers. All Josh knew he could do was respond and back Paul up when the time came. It was his only hope.

As darkness slowly enveloped and then obscured every view from his window, Josh decided to get his head down and try and sleep. He knew that he'd be no good to anyone if he was completely exhausted, and though difficult, he'd need to overcome his anxieties and maximise the hours of shut eye. How quickly his years of training had returned to influence his thinking.

He slipped off a few of his clothes and, partially dressed, pulled back the covers of his bed and climbed in, folding the sheet and blanket back across his body. Closing his eyes, he hoped that sleep would come to him more easily than he was concerned might be the case.

* * *

Lord Ardoon had finished his evening meal and was enjoying both his own company and a small glass of Port, his favourite after dinner tipple. Sat in his leather chair, he felt relaxed and calm. It had been a satisfying day and his confidence in the successful implementation of the plans had increased substantially during the last few days of training.

The door to his study opened and CM entered. Ardoon looked up, irritated at the intrusion.

"I've just had a call from the boss," confirmed CM. "It's looking like mobiles on Sunday."

"I see. And we're certain about this? That's potentially bloody risky."

"They seem to think it's the only way to make sure we can get this done with the cover that we'll all need at the end of it. They seem to be pinning a lot on that. Assuming Paul does what we think he will. It always has been the plan, bear in mind."

"Do we think Paul's spoken with Josh yet?" asked Ardoon.

"Possibly, once or twice and, almost certainly, this evening."

"Almost certainly?" retorted Ardoon. "We'll need to know with a bloody site more certainty than that, Christopher."

"Well. Yes, we do."

"You don't think that this whole mobile phone thing is all too risky?" Ardoon was clearly not as certain about this part of the plan as others.

"They're convinced it's the only way to finesse the whole thing. As long as it's managed to the second by the rest of us, it's almost certain to work… and work well."

"That's the second time in a minute you've used that bloody phrase," replied Ardoon.

CM looked at Ardoon, a frown appearing across his face whilst slightly cocking his head to the side like a puppy waiting for approval from his owner.

"Almost certain. Almost… we can't do bloody almost!" raged Ardoon.

There was a brief period of silence before CM decided it might be better to wrap up both the conversation and the meeting.

"Anyway… we'll get the final instructions about the mobiles tomorrow."

Ardoon nodded in acknowledgement and looked away as CM made his way out of the room.

The silence which accompanied CM's departure gave Ardoon, a former military man himself, the opportunity to take in the moment and privately wrestle with the concerns he had about this element of the plan.

He rose from his seat and crossed towards the door to leave. As he switched out the light, he pulled the door shut behind him and headed to his bed, port in hand.

CHAPTER 17

Wolstenholme's 8:00pm meeting with Wilson had been as productive as he hoped. He had been anxious to confirm exactly who would be supporting Eddington next week and, despite all his efforts thus far, he'd been unable to get absolute confirmation beyond Strong.

It was confirmed that Edward Strong was meeting the Prime Minister on Sunday as expected, as was Adam Taylor. According to their diaries, both men were to join Eddington at the Prime Ministers official country residence at Chequers, a beautiful 16th century manor house set in the Buckinghamshire countryside, where Eddington would spend most weekends ahead of important events and discussions with colleagues.

They were scheduled to arrive mid-morning and the entire day had been pencilled out. Interestingly, Bonato was not attending. Either he knew nothing about it, was unable to attend for whatever reason, or was not invited. Wilson also advised that the Prime Ministers Parliamentary Private Secretary, Marie Standing, would also be present.

Marie Standing had acquired a reputation as a formidable politician and one of the best speech writers in the business. The two men continued their discussion for another hour, reviewing, over and over, the information they had before coming to the same conclusion that they had each privately reached. Though the Home Secretary was still unprepared to commit, he acknowledged that they had to prepare and be ready for all the eventualities.

"If Eddington weren't such a dithery bastard, we'd know exactly what we needed to do... in the absence of anything else. We'll need to make the final call on Sunday," said Wolstenholme. His colleague nodded in agreement.

"Let's reconvene tomorrow. I'll let you know the time. Keep digging. We need as much info as we can get. Monday will be here before we know it and we must find out what Eddington is proposing before we decide to act."

Wilson acknowledged his instructions, as Wolstenholme rose to his feet, quickly followed by Wilson who would now take his leave. Both men still had much to do before they could head to bed and each recognised that time was against them.

With Wilson having departed, Wolstenholme took a few moments to quietly assess the last two hours of conversation, analysis, and outcome. For the first time, his nerves were getting the better of him. He made his way to his bedroom and determined to get as much sleep as he could.

CHAPTER 18

With at least five hours of sleep behind him, in the privacy and peace of his home, Wolstenholme had risen early to start to write the statement that he would need to have available from Monday coming, acutely aware how important it was, as well as how confidential it needed to be kept. He would continue to draft it himself and, only shortly before it was to be delivered, would he share the contents with his closest aides and supporters. Wolstenholme had long since learned that in politics, there is many a slip twixt cup and lip.

When drafting important speeches–though none previously crafted were as momentous as this one–he'd always written them by hand first. It was a habit he'd got into as a younger activist and one that had served him well over the years. It helped him to think at his own pace and he could structure the content, and style, as he went.

The noisy arrival of Mary outside in the hallway brought Wolstenholme out of his work and he rose from his chair, crossed the room and reached towards the light switch. As he turned off the light, the room appeared dull, dark and bleak with only tiny shafts of light illuminating the smallest fractions of space. Crossing to the windows, one after the other, he rolled back the deep, soft, and heavy curtains, each sweeping along the edges of a beautiful Indian silk carpet. The light streamed into the room re-establishing all its class and vibrancy.

The short, sharp, double tap just a few minutes later, confirmed Mary's arrival as she appeared around the half opened, thick set, mahogany door.

"Breakfast? A cup of coffee?" she enquired. "Oh... no, I see you've sorted yourself this morning."

"Thank you, Mary, but I'm okay... apart from a fresh cup of coffee. That'd be lovely."

"I'll just clear all that for you and then I'll rustle one up," she said.

Mary made her way across to the desk and retrieved the bowl, plate and cup and saucer before making her way back across the room and out of the door. "I won't be long," she said, pulling the door shut behind her. Wolstenholme had been so lucky to find Mary. She was simply superb. He'd made certain she was well looked after, not least as his wife had made him aware of how lucky he was and had insisted that Mary should be properly valued.

* * *

The empty mug of coffee, and half-eaten slice of toast on the crumb covered plate on the table to the side of Eddington, confirmed that he too had been up early and was already well into his day.

The loneliness of the role was sometimes overwhelming, but Eddington knew that he, and he alone, was going to have to make all the critical decisions over the coming few days. He had been re-assured by the support of his three key lieutenants but remained anxious that he had not yet felt able to bring Bonato on board. Perhaps he should have another go.

As he made his way from the comfort of his private apartment, down through the levels of his Downing Street headquarters towards his office, he heard the familiar voice of his PPS engaging in conversation with one of the office team.

As the staircase curved around in front of him, the unmistakable, formidable figure of Marie Standing came into view.

"Morning Marie," he called.

"Good morning Prime Minister," came the ever respectful and polite response as she looked up towards her approaching boss.

As she entered his office, Eddington had taken up position by the desk, perching on its side, legs straight out in front of him.

Eddington beckoned to her to close the door.

"So, you wouldn't be here unannounced if it wasn't important Marie. What's up?"

Standing took a few steps forward and, as usual and without hesitation, came straight to the point.

"Tony, I don't think we should do this unless we have Michael on board. We have to isolate Oliver completely."

Eddington raised his eyebrows. Whilst he agreed with the sentiment, and had pondered how best to achieve exactly that, it wasn't clear yet whether it was at all possible.

"We know this will all boil down to a few things," she continued. "Speed, surprise and, most important of all, being able to bounce the Parliamentary Party into support, with little, if any, notice. Oliver will be hostile from the second we open up, and without Michael there's a real danger we could lose vital support. I think you have to speak to him again."

Eddington untangled his feet and stood upright from his more relaxed, perch-like position, slowly walking across the room to help him think. The walking around assisted him in mapping out the route he should take in his mind.

With no reply to her urgings, Standing continued to press her point.

"Oliver will be no push over. He's got control of too many areas and still has a half-decent following on the backbenches, despite what you've been doing over the last few months to lock people in."

Still no reply. She was relentless and she always took the opportunity to fill silence.

"We've got seventy-two hours Tony, seventy-two hours. You can't just leave this bit to chance. You've got to speak to Michael."

Eddington knew that she was right. Whilst he didn't need to hear the relentless logic of that position rammed down his throat, he also acknowledged that her motive and intent was bang on point. He'd always admired her capacity for total public loyalty, and private berating. And, as far as he knew, never a leak, never any tittle tattle and never, ever, a worry about what alternative position she might be espousing to others. Though Eddington trusted her completely and valued her being anchored in the role she performed so brilliantly, he could never understand why she had always refused promotion on the two occasions he had discussed it with her.

"Yes. okay," Eddington interjected for the first time. "I get that, but we also know he's spoken to Oliver and it's not clear what happened. That's why I didn't follow up when I spoke to him last. I've updated everyone on that. What if he's already agreed to side with Oliver?"

"You have to speak to him Tony," Marie said, after a few seconds, "We need to know whether he's onside or not… you can't not follow up on this… he's too well liked to leave on the side lines. We know he's not Wolstenholme's biggest fan but if you don't tie him down, that little shit will."

Eddington looked at his PPS, not a hint of his likely decision in his expression.

"Tony…"

"I'm trying to think." His curt response persuaded Standing to remain silent. She had landed her point and now knew that she needed to wait.

After what seemed like an age, Eddington agreed to speak with Bonato that day and make the best effort he could to establish where he stood.

"Satisfied?"

"Of course. It's completely the right course of action, Tony. If I can help, let me know."

Eddington nodded, "will do."

* * *

Next door, Michael Bonato had already said goodbye to the children before they headed off to school, hugged and kissed his husband goodbye, as he had done every morning before and since their marriage, and had arrived, bright and early, in his office at Number 11.

The Chancellor was already on his third cup of coffee and although he'd been trying to cut back on his total caffeine intake recently, this particular battle was one he was evidently losing.

One of the two phones on his desk rang. His Private Secretary had just been asked to arrange a meeting with Eddington that afternoon.

"When did this request come through?"

"Just now, Chancellor."

Bonato looked at his watch. This would be the third such meeting requested by Eddington in as many days which, if the other two were anything to go by, would seem to have been convened for no apparent reason. In spite of this, he gave his assent and replaced the receiver.

Briefly rubbing his eyes, he began to wonder whether he'd missed something. Two face-to-face conversations in as many days, both requested at short notice and nothing of any substance either raised, reported, or resolved.

CHAPTER 19

Looking out from his bedroom window as the sun crept into view, Josh, once again, was up early to greet it.

Whilst it didn't stop him worrying, Josh had been confident throughout that Becky would remain unhurt and relatively well cared for. For her captors not to have done that would have sharply reduced the leverage they had over him, and as far as he could tell, their plan was far more dependent on him than they might care to admit.

The silence of the early morning was cracked by the splutter and intense revving sound as the aircraft which had stood quiet and stationary to the side of the property, roared its presence at the morning sun. He listened as the plane's engines seemed to sing tunes and test volume levels before a more consistent sound indicated take off. The plane soared above the building as it banked hard, heading south. Those few seconds watching it go had given Josh the kind of emotional boost he'd lacked for almost two days. He anticipated that it was the flight to bring his wife closer to him and he'd hang on to that thought for the rest of the day, right or not.

* * *

The sun was just about high enough in the sky to begin warming the ground and those stood upon it. All, including Josh, had now assembled for the first run through of the day, and were listening intently to Fitz as he outlined all the various components, as well as offering some of his unique home-spun advice.

Josh glanced back towards the house, spotting Ardoon and CM standing at different windows, observing the scene from the first floor.

All of those surrounding him, just as he'd thought previously, could have been lifted straight out of a recruitment poster and plonked into any regiment and then into any theatre of war, ready to do their stuff.

The briefing continued. Arrival, timings, order, weapons, expectations, exit, over and over. Questions peppered the monologue and, if there was just the slightest of variation from the plan, or any element of it, the entire process went back to the beginning of that particular component part.

It was close to an hour before Fitz pronounced that everyone should disperse to their positions for the first run through of the day.

Accompanied by both Paul and Ryan, Josh took up his position roughly mid-way along the mocked-up road, this time squatting behind the make-shift substitute hedge that was now in place. Ryan handed Josh the dummy sleeve control in readiness.

"When do I get the actual piece of kit?" asked Josh.

Neither man replied.

"Well, don't blame me if it gets fucked up because you haven't given me enough time to re-acquaint myself with everything."

Ryan and Paul looked at each other. It was exactly the point Paul had made to CM the previous day. This was a complex piece of equipment, and one which Josh hadn't used for a few years.

Fitz sounded his whistle. That was the ten second warning.

Rather than just the one vehicle involved in the rehearsal as had been the case the previous day, this time there were three. The mock hedges made observation more difficult. Although everyone knew where their comrades were supposed to be, this was the first time that it wasn't possible to actually see any of them. Communication was clearly going to be critical.

The quiet was interrupted by the engines of all three vehicles bursting into life. Two large, black Range Rovers and one silver Jaguar saloon took up position at the beginning of the grass road which stretched out ahead of them.

As they proceeded along the pre-determined course, at various intervals, each part of the plan was triggered. The use of blanks in all weapons created a crescendo of noise as events unfolded. What this would sound like amidst all the inevitable chaos and response they would provoke, could only be imagined.

Inexorably, the plan unfolded and the middle vehicle in the convoy inevitably ended up precisely where the plan said it would, driving through an open gateway and into a field in an attempt to escape via the only route apparently available to it.

The car appeared through the gap, having slowed sharply to make its way through the opening. Paul readied the imaginary RPG, as Josh fiddled with the wooden box, trying to recall the actions he needed to take and imitating them as best he could.

Ryan, standing to one side, without an obvious role, simply watched his colleagues perform their tasks, arms folded, looking generally disinterested. Josh knew what Ryan's job would be, come the day, but for now, he'd simply take the necessary time to consider how he and Paul would deal with that, when the moment came. There could be no loose ends allowed and Ryan was obviously going to deal with a certain loose end called "Josh." Whatever he might be expecting, thought Josh, with Paul onside, they'd at least have the element of surprise.

The Silver Jaguar came to a sharp stop about thirty metres away, the driver attempting to imitate the consequences of being hit by the RPG. Paul had reflected on the proximity of the vehicle to them at the point of explosion. Thirty metres wasn't a huge distance to be from an exploding vehicle if everything went up with a hell of a bang. Irrespective, they were told to stick to the timing and the distances in the plan, as no risks could be taken in terms of delay between de-activation of the sleeve and the attack on the vehicle itself.

Josh knew that stretching out the distance to over fifty metres wasn't an option, as the sleeve would have been re-activated around that distance.

Much as Josh was still, in his own mind, determined to try and thwart whatever he was to be confronted with, he recognised that this was a plan that was comprehensive, well thought through and obviously crafted by someone who knew everything there was to know about the chosen location, the target, the different equipment being used, likely responses of those to be attacked, and, more concerning from his point of view, had access to some of the most secret equipment in the country.

There were few people who would know about this. Facilitating both its acquisition and use would require involvement at the highest levels of Government, the military, or the intelligence services; possibly all three.

Fitz blew his whistle three times, a signal for everyone to return to the briefing area. Josh, Paul, and Ryan all made their way along the make-shift hedge until they'd reached the open area at which the lead vehicle had, theoretically, been blown apart. They crossed in front of the car and walked the remaining fifty metres or so to the briefing spot.

As Josh surveyed the area around him, he observed the convergence of all involved, like ants returning to their nest, towards the ever-present Fitz, who was once again standing on a metal container ready to hold court.

"Time was fine, everyone was on point and that was the smoothest run so far."

Everyone looked around, like a class of school children, each smiling, and all pleased with their collective effort.

"We're going to have one more run through before lunch and if that goes well, we'll hit the live ammo this afternoon. There'll be a more detailed briefing before that for obvious fucking reasons. We don't want any of you getting topped before we get there, do we?"

Fitz was clearly delighted with what had been achieved and, amongst the team, there was a new sense of optimism about the whole mission. As Josh allowed his eyes to wander, almost everyone present had a smile on their face.

"Right," continued Fitz, "Fuck off back to your places and wait for the whistle."

The team dispersed in many different directions, each heading to their respective starting position on the lay-out carefully crafted around them.

A few minutes later, everyone was once again back in position and awaiting the sound of the whistle giving them ten seconds to prepare. Shortly after everyone was crouched, and with surprising haste, the shrill sound of Fitz's whistle heightened everyone's level of awareness as the seconds ticked away for the final run through before lunch and the live ammunition that would then be used during the afternoon.

Blanks continued to be fired, as the mayhem which greeted all three vehicles in the convoy drove them to follow the deadly path which had been laid out for them.

A matter of minutes later, and right on cue, the Silver Jaguar once again manoeuvred itself through the open-gated gap in the hedge. Paul was prepared and a matter of a second or two after Josh had confirmed that he'd disabled the sleeve, feigned the release of an RPG towards the back of the vehicle. Just seconds after that, a second was launched. Kill complete.

Ryan had stood some ten feet away from both men on this occasion, slightly further than previously, measuring up the most appropriate place to stand in order to safely carry out what would certainly be his instructions that day.

Everything seemed to go like clockwork and the time taken to complete the run through seemed even shorter than before.

As they were all called back for the de-brief, it was clear that confidence was high, and a sense of achievement had been established. This was a team really coming together and confident in each other.

Fitz took his time to look at the assembled group, it seemed, locking eyes with each and every one of them.

A broad smile crept across his face. "Lunch… back at 1330 hours," he exclaimed, raising his arms, and clenching his fists above his head. It was a gesture of strength and confidence and one not lost on every member of his team. Chatter, banter, and bonhomie followed as small groups split off from the assembled team and made their way to the main building for lunch.

Josh, Paul, and Ryan made up their own little grouping, Ryan taking up the lead as they headed for the main building along with the others.

For the first time since his arrival, Josh was surprised to be allowed to join the rest of those involved for a meal. Following Ryan into a large, impressive room on the ground floor that had been temporarily turned into a dining hall, he was led towards a small table near the entrance.

There was a long table in the centre of the room, easily capable of seating sixteen people and a small number of individual tables to make up the numbers of covers required.

At one end of the room was a trestle table which had been set with three large metal trays of hot food and a number of large bowls and baskets containing salads or bread. Taking their places at one of the smaller tables, all three men quickly devoured their food and sat in silence, a sharp contrast to the loud and often lewd banter which was surrounding them.

"I need to take a piss," Josh informed his table companions.

"You wanna take him?" asked Paul, looking across to Ryan.

"You do it, I'm gonna get another plate of chilli."

"Come on." Paul motioned to Josh and both men made their way out of the room.

They waited in silence for the toilet to become free as another man washed and dried his hands, nodding to Paul as he left.

They pushed inside the cubicle, Paul bringing Josh up to speed on what he'd learned since they last spoke.

"There's been a lot of chatter about moving on Sunday, but I don't know if that means we ship out then, or the operation date's been moved."

"What about Ryan, he's not been involved in any of the run-throughs," asked Josh, already knowing the answer.

"Ryan's only job is to make sure you do as you're told, and then clean up afterwards. Well, clean you up afterwards."

"So… you got a plan?" enquired Josh. "We have to do something. We have to find an out."

"Until we know more, I'm not sure what we can do."

Paul started to get concerned about the time they were taking. "Josh, we need to get back."

"I actually do need a piss," came the response.

"Well get on with it then."

Josh obliged and, as he exited the cubicle, another man pushed open the door and stood aside waiting for Josh to make way. The man went into the cubicle and closed the door behind him. Josh washed his hands and, together with Paul, left the bathroom and returned to their table in the large dining area.

Ryan was already halfway through his second helping of chilli and barely looked up as the two men approached the table and sat down.

"You want anything else?" Paul asked Josh.

"No thanks."

"Right!" Fitz had both silenced the room and gained everyone's attention. "That's your lot. Now, everyone needs to switch on. We're doing a live ammo run-through next."

CHAPTER 20

Wolstenholme entered the chamber of the House of Commons and was greeted with the usual loyal murmurs of "hear, hear" and an occasional cheer. Taking up his seat next to the Leader of the House, Sir James Phillips, he opened his file to afford himself the briefest of moments to scan his statement.

"Order! Order! A Statement… the Home Secretary," bellowed Speaker Morris, doing his level best to bring the House to order and move business along.

Eddington, watching from his office, raised the volume on his screen, sat back in his seat and waited to hear how well his most significant critic would fare, hoping that the tricky issue would do Wolstenholme a good deal of damage.

Unfortunately for Eddington, Wolstenholme's speech was superb and from a shaky start, with little if any vocal support, he rose to the challenge and used the opportunity to roundly condemn opposition spokesmen, and MPs, as they: "Reveal their true colours and do all they can to encourage smears, lies and outrageous calumnies against the forces of law and order in our country."

Having neatly turned what was a difficult task into an all-out attack on the Opposition, Wolstenholme had ended up rousing the Government benches to noisy endorsement.

Eddington had seen enough. He closed down his screen and returned to the task of drafting of his own statement for Monday.

This was the fourth attempt in as many days to try and get something substantive down on paper, but to no avail.

Not only were there still too many elements to draw together, but he also had to get the balance right between apology and vision–a difficult task at the best of times.

The knock at the door interrupted the tension and gave him a much-needed break. As it opened, a welcome tray of coffee, sandwiches, and his usual daily banana, was carried over to his desk and deposited in front of him.

"Thank you. That's just what the doctor ordered," he said.

As he made his way out of the room, Eddington's secretary paused and turned.

"Oh, Prime Minister, apologies. Gosh, I nearly forgot. The Chancellor has just called and profusely apologised because he can't get to your meeting. One of his children has had an accident at school and has been taken into hospital. He's made his way over there. He was sure you'd understand."

"Oh, no. Which one? How bad is it?" asked Eddington.

"Ah, sorry. I don't know… I can make some enquiries if you'd like me to?"

"Yes, please. Do let me know how things are as soon as you hear. We can re-schedule for another time."

No sooner had the door closed than Eddington clenched his fists and banged them into his forehead several times. "Shit, shit, shit!" He spat out the "t" with force. This wasn't at all what he needed.

Pausing for a few moments to gather his thoughts, Eddington lifted his mobile phone from the desk, swiped through the contacts and tapped on Marie Standing's number.

"Marie… one of Bonato's kids has been taken into hospital after having a bloody accident and he's cancelled this afternoon's meeting. He's headed over there now. Of all the bloody timing!"

Clearly, equally unimpressed at this unhelpful turn of events, Marie started suggesting various alternatives to Eddington, none of which were palatable.

"I'm going to have to wait to speak to him until the weekend, maybe Sunday. For now, we'll just have to assume we'll have to manage without his support and hope that on Monday he swings behind us."

Eddington thanked Standing once again for her support and reminded her that much still needed to be done.

"Sunday is going to be a full-on day," he said. "Oh, by the way, did you see Oliver's performance? You've got to hand it to that bastard. He can pull it off when he's up against it. Bloody impressive."

With that, he finished the call and placed his phone back on the desk. The die was cast.

* * *

As Wolstenholme left the chamber in triumph, he was congratulated by many backbench MP's, several wanting to chat about the subject, as well as his speech. Conscious that he needed to respond to every one of them with time and courtesy, particularly at this moment, he was happy to take far more time than usual to do so.

As he concluded the last of a dozen or so conversations, he turned to make his way down the corridor towards his Commons office. He stopped and paused for a moment, conscious that he was being watch by Eddington's Parliamentary Private Secretary, Marie Standing.

"Good afternoon Marie," he said.

"Good afternoon Oliver… excellent speech. I know the PM was impressed."

The conversation between them was interrupted by the comings and goings of other MPs in the corridor but both persevered.

"Very strong and robust defence. I presume we're confident there's nothing to be concerned about?" Standing was as direct as usual.

More interruptions. "Well done, Oliver… excellent speech."

Wolstenholme smiled and nodded in appreciation.

"Nothing we should be concerned about?" repeated Standing.

"Marie, rather than having this discussion here, I'm just headed to my Commons office... Would you join me?"

Standing looked at her watch before answering.

"I've got to be elsewhere at two-thirty, so I can join you for a few minutes if you'd like."

With that, Wolstenholme set off towards his office, and Standing followed behind, the brisk pace being set by Wolstenholme almost causing her to break into a gentle jog.

Once at his office, Wolstenholme opened the door and stood to one side to allow Standing to enter ahead of him. The two members of his team in the outer of his two-office suite, both looked up, smiled, and returned to their respective tasks.

"Would you like a cup of something, Marie?" enquired Wolstenholme.

One of the staff members prepared to rise from his seat to deliver on the answer but soon retook it.

"No... no thank you."

"Come on in," said Wolstenholme, indicating to Standing to enter his inner office ahead of him.

She walked slowly forward and stood to the left of the large round meeting table which seemed to occupy so much of the available space. She looked out of the third storey window ahead of her, before turning to face her boss's most vehement internal critic.

By this point, Wolstenholme had closed the door, after instructing his team that unless it was urgent, there were to be no interruptions for the next ten minutes or so.

He took the few steps forward that closed the distance between them, reached out both his hands and, holding both her shoulders, pulled her gently towards him, enveloping her entirely in his arms.

They kissed each other passionately, their embrace getting more animated as they did so. Breathing heavily, neither saying a word to each other, all their attention was focussed on the unexpected, rare moment of intimacy that they were enjoying together.

Wolstenholme slowly moved his hands around Standing's body, caressing and exploring every curve and angle as he pressed his body against hers with greater pressure and passion.

Their tryst was over almost as quickly as it had begun, as the phone on Wolstenholme's desk sprung into life, bringing a halt to the intimacy they had enjoyed.

Standing made an immediate effort to tidy her appearance, first focussing on her clothes and then, checking her make-up. Her lipstick certainly needed re-doing.

By this time, Wolstenholme had answered the telephone and asked that the Leader of the House–who wanted to speak with him urgently–be informed that he'd be called back within a few minutes. It was certainly urgent enough for him to have been interrupted, but not quite yet.

Marie took a handkerchief from her handbag and wet it with her tongue. She then wiped away all trace of lipstick from Oliver Wolstenholme's face, fiddled with his hair until she was satisfied it looked as it should, and then, stroked the side of his face with her right hand.

"Looks like he's going to go ahead... exactly as we suspected, Oliver."

Wolstenholme remained silent, breathing slightly more heavily.

"We're all at Chequers on Sunday... well, you know that... but he's now said that it's definite. He's going to go ahead... So, Chequers is now about how, not if. Speeches and tactics for Monday. He's just told me that Bonato is not included, his kid has been taken to hospital and Tony's not seeing him. Oliver, you can now take your chance. Do what needs to be done."

Standing moved closer to the man she had been having an on-off affair with for two years. She grabbed hold tightly of both of his arms, just above the elbow, and gently shook them as she quietly, and in whispered tones, encouraged him to make the moves she knew he now needed to make.

"It's now…" he interjected.

"…or never. We can change our country." came the immediate reply.

"You'd better go. And keep me posted. Everything… every little detail, Marie… and I will, seriously, now think about it."

Standing kissed the fingers of her right hand and pressed them against Wolstenholme's lips. He briefly held her hand in place before letting it, and her, go.

CHAPTER 21

The team briefing had gone as well as could be expected. About halfway through, both Ardoon and CM had joined, sitting at the back of the room like a couple of school inspectors.

Repeatedly, Fitz had reminded everyone of their weapons training and, time and again, he emphasised the need for care and attention whilst taking part in the live ammunition exercise.

Each person involved, with the exception of Josh, would be issued with both a semi-automatic weapon, as well as a pistol, which was to be used for back up in more populated areas were it necessary to defend themselves during their escape from the scene. At this stage, whilst grenades would be used during the mission, for these rehearsals, each of the three RPG teams would use smoke grenades to imitate impact. All three of the cars had been fitted with steel mesh sheeting strong enough to protect the drivers during these exercises.

"And, once more," Fitz repeated, "you're firing your automatic weapons into the air, or ground, and if the latter, always at a safe distance from you and your designated target, not at the target. This is for timing, and feel, and not so you can wipe out half of the rest of us in the process. If anyone shoots anyone else, I'll fucking shoot them."

All was clear.

"One final point, I'm also going to be firing live ammo at various stages and towards various positions, as the plan gets executed. If you're in the right place at the right time, you'll be fine. If not, you're likely to get shot. There will be return fire. These people aren't just going to sit back and let us kill them. You need to understand how that might be when we're in the thick of the shit-fight. If everyone does what they're supposed to, we'll all be okay."

The sense of anticipation and nervousness was all pervading. Things had suddenly got real. Everyone knew that live ammunition exercises were always fraught with their own unanticipated dangers. Anything could go wrong, and, sometimes, it did.

"Next door are your weapons with your names attached to them. Retrieve yours, no-one else's, and make your way back to your position within the mock target area. Take up your positions and wait for my signal. Questions?" Fitz enquired.

Scanning the room slowly for any indication of uncertainty, or someone seeking further clarity, Fitz took his time to fix everyone present, one by one, row by row, in his gaze.

"Good, let's go."

The team dispersed, all making their way to the adjoining room, where there was a veritable arsenal of weaponry. As they were expecting, each set of two guns had a label attached, each containing the first name, then followed by an initial, of each member of the team.

As each person retrieved their allocated weapons from the table, once outside, there was much checking and pointing of both semi-automatic and pistol.

Paul and Ryan grabbed the final two semi-automatics from the table, each having tucked their pistols into the holsters they were now wearing for just that use. Paul also picked up two smoke grenades.

"Where's the RPG?" enquired Josh.

"None of your fucking business," came Ryan's retort.

"It'll be there for us," replied Paul immediately.

Josh nodded. Obviously, these pieces of weaponry were well protected and cared for. He looked once again at the empty table, which confirmed what he had heard just minutes earlier. There was certainly no weapon for him.

As all three men made their way out of the main house and towards their allocated positions, Josh became increasingly aware of the noise of what sounded like an aircraft. Gazing up into the sky, at first he couldn't see anything, but as he looked back over his right shoulder, he saw the same plane used to transport him to Scotland dropping through the intermittent, wispy cloud cover, lining itself up for landing.

By the time Josh, Paul and Ryan had arrived at their respective positions and readied themselves for the next run through, the aircraft had touched down.

Allowing his mind to wander back towards the main house and, what he hoped, would be the arrival of Becky, he was jolted from his mental meanderings by a nudge in the ribs, clearly enjoyably delivered by Ryan. "Be ready!" he advised, with a distinctly impolite reprimand.

Josh refocussed, just in time to hear the blast of a whistle. Seconds later, the now instantly recognised noise of an approaching convoy was suddenly interrupted by an explosion of noise, and, what sounded like complete chaos.

The sound of a loud explosion ripped through the immediate atmosphere, some smoke drifting into the air. The third vehicle in the convoy had been hit. If all were going to plan, the front and middle cars in the convoy would now speed up, with their occupants, and those in the third car, potentially starting to return fire. The second explosion came a little later and yet more smoke signalled completion of the first phase.

Engine noise seemed to increase markedly as both surviving vehicles accelerated their way out of trouble, and, as they did so, more gun fire could be heard as the assault team at the rear of the convoy moved in to finish off those occupying the crippled third vehicle.

The two remaining cars drove at speed past the open gateway to which one would have to shortly return, the newly erected hedges hiding the three men who'd have the task of delivering the decisive and final blows.

Barely twenty-five seconds later and the sound of the third and fourth smoke grenades hitting their target, roughly five seconds apart, starkly declared to Josh that he and Paul were up next.

The loud, foot down revving, screeching engine noise of the reversing central vehicle towards the open gateway provided ample warning of the imminent arrival of the final target.

As the car drove through the gap, at a much faster pace than in any of the previous run-throughs, it slid sideways and rammed into the makeshift hedge, knocking it up into the air by six to eight inches and forcing it out of position by some three feet.

Regaining traction, it sped forwards, wheels spinning and churning earth and pebbles into the air. Josh had imagined doing his stuff and signalled to Paul that he could commence firing. The first smoke grenade was released from the weapon and slammed into the rear of the vehicle with a deafening noise. Smoke instantly filled the air around the car , and, seconds later, Paul launched the second grenade which brought with it more noise and clouds more smoke.

Two men, initially observing throughout the earlier runs, had now joined Paul, Josh, and Ryan and, immediately after the second smoke grenade had been unleashed, closed in on the vehicle, firing their semi-automatic weapons into the air as they approached it. It was clear what their responsibilities were to be on the day itself. Josh now realised that there would be him and Paul against three more people if things remained as they were.

The driver of the vehicle emerged unscathed but obviously concerned about the physical state of the car, immediately wandering around its entire body, checking that all was okay. He looked both pleased and re-assured having completed his inspection.

Fitz sounded the whistle summoning everyone back to the

central outside briefing point and everyone obliged making their way across what was now starting to look like a less than pristine battleground.

Once everyone had assembled, Fitz confirmed that the entire run through had taken just under three minutes and twenty seconds. Smiles all round.

It was clear from the following disclosures, that each man had been allocated to a particular small unit for the purposes of "exit and escape," as Fitz had called it, and within three minutes of the assault being concluded, everyone involved would be in a vehicle and on their way, dispersing in multiple directions.

They had all been instructed to get as far away as possible within ten minutes of the action to ensure that they escaped any roadblocks as well as the initial response from the Police, and, potentially, security services, some of whom it had been assumed would be on-site approximately fifteen minutes later.

"We have one further run through this afternoon," said Fitz. "This time, we'll actually have the sleeve unit in play."

Josh had wondered exactly when he would be able to re-acquaint himself with the machine, upon which everyone's hopes of a successful mission, were resting.

"Right, fuck off for an hour and be back here at 16:00 hours… Josh, you're with me."

With that, Fitz jumped down from atop his metal container and headed back towards the house. Josh followed, joined by both Ryan and Paul, as usual. Additionally, this time, another man was also enlisted to accompany Josh. Clearly, things were stepping up a gear and no-one was taking any chances.

Following Fitz in the direction of the same meeting room in which he'd met both Ardoon and CM the previous evening, Josh became full of anticipation that he may see Becky once again. The door was opened and as he looked into the room, he spotted Becky sitting on a chair by the fireplace.

She immediately jumped up from her seat, ran across to Josh

and threw her arms around him, bursting into tears. Josh enfolded her in his arms and held her as tightly as he could, closing his eyes in huge relief as he did so.

Ardoon allowed the reunion to continue uninterrupted for well over a minute before he spoke.

"Becky… please sit down… Becky." His second mention of her name was more forcefully delivered than the first.

Josh eased her away from his body and placed his right hand behind her head, stroking her hair slowly and tenderly. They looked at each other intensely, she with tears streaming down her cheeks and him, eyes also awash with emotional angst.

Josh nodded at Becky as if to encourage her to take the seat offered. Slowly she moved away from him and returned to her seat.

"Sit down please, Josh," said Ardoon, pointing towards a chair opposite Becky.

"I'd wondered whether to show Becky a short film about a tramp, but I assume that won't be necessary?" he said. That was the last thing Josh wanted Becky to see. "No, of course not," immediately offering his response.

"Good. I'm so sorry to break up your re-union so soon but I'm afraid time is pressing. There'll be plenty of time to catch up over the weekend, I'm sure." Ardoon could be nauseatingly annoying, thought Josh.

"Ryan," His Lordship continued, "please take Becky to her room and I'm sure she could do with a nice cup of tea." The sentence was so extraordinarily normal as to sound completely absurd, given the circumstances.

Josh looked at Becky, half smiled and nodded. "You'll be fine." His whispered tones were calm and re-assuring. Becky rose from her seat, and accompanied by Ryan, left the room.

"Your equipment has arrived, and it's just being checked over. You'll be acquainted with it shortly. Once you're satisfied it's all in order, there'll be a final run through this afternoon. You'll operate it as if… well… as if it were being operated."

Josh nodded once again, confirming that he'd understood everything said to him.

"Paul, perhaps you'll take Josh back to your position," said Ardoon, "the sleeve control unit won't be long."

Both Josh and Paul made their way out of the room, and then out of the main house, heading towards their usual designated positions.

Both men, albeit with considerable caution and care, began their next whispered conversation once they'd left the building and there was sufficient distance between them and the other members of the team who were also, by now, starting to assemble.

The exercise itself, and primarily their desire to consider how best to foil it, the possible targets, Becky and her rescue, their collective all-important exit, and how long they had, were all matters briefly and furtively considered.

Both men arrived at their positions as instructed and sat down in the open gateway. Paul became pre-occupied as they sat opposite each other, Josh following up on a few points, particularly with regard to precisely where Becky might be being held.

"Paul. What's up? You're not with me mate." His one known ally looked across towards him, frowning as he did so.

"This is not right. Something's not right."

Josh pressed for an explanation. "What? What's not right. What do you mean?"

"We're alone. We shouldn't be left alone together like this. Once we got to live ammo stage, I had specific instructions that when we were outside the main house there were to be always two people with you… never ever were you to be left with just one of us…"

"Do you think they know?"

"Know what?"

"That you're undercover?"

Paul considered the consequences of such a situation. "Shit. We'd better hope not, but we'd better be fucking careful."

With that, he looked back towards the house. Ryan had emerged and was on his way towards them, carrying the sleeve operating system.

"How the hell they got hold of one of these is a fucking mystery," was Paul's final contribution to their latest conversation.

As Ryan approached, he handed the device to Josh. "Here. Get it ready."

Josh knew that it would take about three to four minutes to prepare it for full operation and began to initiate the various elements required.

"Done?" enquired Ryan.

"Not yet," came Josh's reply.

"Done?" came the same enquiry about half a minute later.

Josh stopped and looked up at Ryan. "Not fucking yet! I'll tell you when." Ryan had only to open his mouth to irritate Josh; and it showed.

A row of six small green lights in the top right hand corner of the device all lit up in sequence, one after the other. The device was primarily black in colour, had four main rectangular numeric digital screens, one under the other on its left-hand side, and a small keyboard taking up about a third of the unit. A chrome-coloured knob was alongside each of the screens to their right, and a red and green light alongside each of those in turn.

"Now I'm ready," Josh confirmed.

Ryan stepped out into the gap, waved his arms high above his head and stepped back behind the mock hedge.

It wasn't the first time that Josh had wondered why, during the exercises, there were no radios or communications devices of any description. It was a strange and unexpected gap in an otherwise thoroughly professional operation.

A minute or so later, Fitz blew his now familiar whistle and, once again, yet another run through was underway. Less than three minutes later, the tyres of the middle car threw up debris and earth as it manoeuvred its way through the open gateway in between Ryan, to one side, and Paul and Josh to the other. They were all crouched up against the hedge, awaiting the emergence of the vehicle through the gateway.

It sped past them, accelerating away. As far as Josh could tell, he should, by now, have identified the code, inserted it into the device and terminated the signal. Though it had taken a little longer than he'd remembered it might, that additional four to five seconds didn't prevent the vehicle remaining in range, and then, for Paul to unleash the two smoke grenades within seconds of each other. Both hit their target and it was job done.

"You'll need to be quicker than that!" exclaimed Ryan.

"Then fucking do it yourself next time," came Josh's swift and blunt retort.

"Ryan," interjected Paul, "leave it."

Ryan looked distinctly unimpressed and started to walk over towards the vehicle that was now a good fifty metres away. The driver had extracted himself from it, once again unscathed.

With an evening ahead of him, Josh determined that he would use the time he would now have to think through his options. He would try to engage with Paul, to get some kind of plan together and, if at all possible, see Becky again and find out where she was being kept. For most of the team involved, the latest exercise had represented a conclusion to the business end of the day. For Josh, it was the start of a second period of reflection, scheming and preparation.

As Paul, Josh and Ryan made their way back towards the de-briefing area together, few words were exchanged. Neither Paul or Josh tried to communicate with each other, and Ryan, always a few steps ahead of the other two men, didn't look back once.

Fitz was pleased, and, if he was happy, so was the whole team. Paul appeared to be paying attention like everyone else, but his mind was elsewhere. Increasingly concerned about his cover being blown, and all the ramifications of that particular scenario, he was starting to think far more urgently about what he, and Josh, were going to have to do to foil the plan itself, get Becky out and then manage their exit, and eventual escape. None of this was going to be easy, if achievable, at all.

CHAPTER 22

The afternoon had flown by and Eddington was becoming increasingly frustrated that he had been unable to finesse his discussions quickly enough in preparation for both Sunday's session at Chequers, as well as the more important Monday initiatives.

The two scheduled long-standing meetings at Downing Street that afternoon had overrun terribly. The first, with the United States Ambassador, who was hosting the visit to the UK of the country's Trade Secretary, had taken forty minutes longer than anticipated. The second, with the Prime Minister of Portugal–one of the UK's oldest allies, and a nation which had been far more supportive and diplomatically positive about the UK throughout the last ten or so turbulent years–had overrun by a further thirty minutes. Eddington knew that it was time he needed and was unlikely to be recovered.

Standing outside the world famous big black door, Eddington waved goodbye to Prime Minister Santos, and turned and walked back into Number 10.

Once inside, Eddington headed straight for his office, brushing aside a series of interventions by various aides to grab even more of his time. He was determined to focus the next two to three hours on concluding some of the necessary preparations ahead of Monday.

The first call he made was to Marie Standing. No reply. The next was to Adam Taylor. No reply. The third call was to Edward Strong. No reply. He left short messages for each of them to call him back. Tapping his fingers on the desk in front of him in frustration that no-one was available when he wanted them to be, he suddenly sprung into life and reached for the third drawer down of his desk. He retrieved the notes and scribblings which had already started to form the basis of his statement to the House of Commons on Monday afternoon.

At that moment, a familiar knock on the door heralded the interruption of the Cabinet Secretary, an interruption it was always difficult to ignore.

"Prime Minister, I need twenty minutes to run through a few things, then I can leave you alone."

Though it was an unwanted interruption, it was at least to be mercifully brief. True to form, and reputation, the Cabinet Secretary had concluded everything in less than the twenty minutes estimated and promptly left the Prime Minister to himself.

No sooner had he been left alone, than, almost immediately, and in quick succession, all three of his unanswered calls resulted in call-backs, each of which were positive, responsive, and confirmatory of his requests surrounding Sunday and Monday.

The last call, that of Marie Standing, was necessarily cut short by the announcement of the arrival of the Police Minister, Sarah Bradley, and her lead civil servant. The aide was asked to show them both in and Marie's call quickly despatched. Another unwelcome meeting but one which he could not put off.

Outside, as Downing Street slowly emptied of its complement of staff, all heading off to enjoy what was likely to be a very sunny weekend, through its rear entrance, strolled David Wilson. Minutes later, he was sitting in front of the Prime Minister, joining Eddington for his meeting with Bradley and her colleague.

The report into police corruption would not make particularly great reading, but in the view of everyone present, the damage would be limited. The actions proposed were decisive, and those identified as being responsible would be held to account, an accountability policy Eddington had championed as part of his public sector reforms. For decades, the public sector had failed the "accountability test," as Eddington had described it, but that had changed markedly since his Premiership.

"Sarah, thank you for coming over. Good job," said Eddington, rising to his feet after only twenty minutes and giving a very clear indication that their meeting was now over. Bradley and her colleague made their way out of the office, the Prime Minister, and Wilson, now left alone.

Eddington indicated to Wilson to take a seat in the less formal and more comfortable section of his office.

"Coffee top-up David?"

"No, I'm fine thank you, Prime Minister."

Both men settled back into their chairs. The change of physical position might have been, of itself, relaxing and more casual, but the conversation was certainly not expected to be.

"Monday, David; where are we?"

"Everything looks set. We've obviously had to be ever more careful as the numbers of people involved have risen but it's been kept to a bare minimum and, thus far, no leaks and no hint of a problem anywhere." Wilson certainly seemed in confident mood.

"And the operation in Scotland. Do we have an update on that?"

"We're not expecting to get full details until our man makes contact, and we are expecting that to be on Sunday when everybody is issued with their communications devices. We understand that'll be mobiles... well, almost certainly."

"And we're still confident of our man being there? Alive, I mean."

"Oh yes, we'd know if he wasn't," came the re-assuring reply.

"As you know, I have my meeting with Taylor and Strong on Sunday. Oh, and Marie of course. So, we'll have everything sorted as regards timings, statements etc. by late afternoon, I should think."

Wilson looked away to his right momentarily, obviously thinking about something that was perplexing him. "I'm going to think about doing something to accelerate the armed police response… something like a pre-alert or warning of some kind. I'm not sure yet but I think we might need to hasten response and shorten reaction times… anyway, I'll have a think."

"I thought we were happy with all that. It's a bit late now."

"Not sure it's ever too late, Prime Minister," responded Wilson. "What matters is that we cover off all the bases and make sure we get everyone involved. I appreciate that this will have been unbelievably difficult, not least the intense secrecy. But, if this is to be successful, we must maintain this level of confidentiality until it's all finished with. We just have to trust each other and trust the plan."

Eddington looked away himself, gently nodding in acknowledgement.

Looking back towards Wilson, Eddington concluded the conversation and rose to his feet.

"Thank you, David," he said holding out his hand. Both men shook hands and agreed that they would speak on Saturday evening after what would be a hugely busy day for the Prime Minister in his constituency. Fortnightly visits made for intense, packed constituency activity every other Saturday.

Left alone, Eddington once again sat down in the armchair he'd only just vacated and leaned forward. Rubbing his eyes and face, he then peered out into the space in front of him. Three days, he thought. So much at stake and still so much that could go wrong.

After a few moments, he stood up, retrieved some papers from his desk and left the room. He made his way back through the building and up to his flat. He may have been hoping for some solace in the silence that awaited him but realised that wherever he might be over the next seventy-two hours, he was unlikely to encounter either silence, or solace.

As Wilson exited Downing Street at the rear of the premises, his official car was waiting to collect him and whisk him swiftly back to his office.

"Sorry about that. It all went on a bit," he said to his driver as he climbed into the back seat.

"The office sir?" enquired his chauffeur.

"Yes… please. Thanks."

Lifting his mobile from his jacket pocket, Wilson scanned the contact list and tapped on one of the names in front of him. He typed out a short message and pressed send. His message was written using appropriate code.

SWALLOW MIGRATION ON TRACK.
NO CHANBGE OF COURSE.

The stray "B" was deliberate and was intended as additional confirmation that the message was from him.

Seconds later came the reply. BON VOYAGE. It was the general affirmative response code used by all the key people involved in the operation.

All the way back to MI5, he was quietly working through the various scenarios now presenting themselves, mentally calculating whether he'd managed to co-ordinate sufficiently, deceive satisfactorily and plan ruthlessly enough. He reassured himself that he had, but he also knew that only time, and the events of Sunday and Monday would confirm that for sure.

After arrival, he made his way up to his office. As he turned the corner into the corridor that would lead him right to it, Welling came out of his office and hurried after his boss.

"How did the meeting go?"

"Yes, it went well. Very good. Nothing new really," Wilson replied as he walked.

"Oh, good… all on track then?"

"Certainly looks like it. Onwards," came the reply. "I need to sort a few bits and I'll catch up with you later."

"okay… Laters."

Wilson headed into his office and Welling made for the coffee unit, the latter very much in need of a caffeine dose.

* * *

For Home Secretary Wolstenholme, the afternoon had dragged terribly. Though he'd had the conversations he'd needed to have, they'd been less confident and clear cut than he'd have wished them to be.

It was creeping towards 6:50pm, he was still at his House of Commons office, and now, almost certain to run late for the engagement he had that evening. Scheduled to speak at the Annual Constituency Dinner of his fellow League and outer London MP, Diana Freeman, he had given himself until 7:00pm to get away. He'd have to return home and change into his dinner jacket and then get across to the east London seat.

He'd be lucky to arrive much before 8:15pm, probably early enough to grab at least one course. He'd certainly have to make a few notes for the speech but, if all else failed, he'd simply make the one he usually makes on such occasions. With a little luck, no-one present would have heard it.

He grabbed his coat, a couple of folders and exited his office at some pace, quickly covering the ground to his awaiting ministerial car and escort. Fortunately, one of the perks of his role afforded him the luxury of getting around, through and out of London more quickly than the average person.

"Home please, and as quickly as possible."

The small convoy managed to manoeuvre its way quickly through the few streets which separated his Westminster office from his large townhouse, depositing him door to door in less than ten minutes.

"I won't be long," he said, as he exited the vehicle. The driver looked in the mirror, watching his charge take his leave, smiling to himself at the suggestion that The Home Secretary would not be too long. That was certainly not his experience.

Wolstenholme swiftly crossed the pavement, skipped up the steps and entered the house. He knew he needed to take a shower, get changed and set off once again, and all in less than twenty minutes.

He'd better get started. But, before he did, he needed to make one quick call.

CHAPTER 23

Josh had been lying on his bed, waiting patiently for some indication that he would either see Becky again at some point that evening, or, alternatively, that he would be able to catch up with Paul and move things forward in terms of their next steps. Whilst he knew that waiting was a necessary part of the game, it was frustrating and unnerving .

It was now just after 19:00 hours and he'd not eaten, nor had there been any sign of any other activity or interaction. As the evening started to draw in, he decided to flick on his light. He got up from his bed and walked over towards the door. He was about to raise his hand towards the light switch when he stopped dead in his tracks. He was certain he heard, or had he sensed, something immediately outside the door.

Josh stood, statue-like, barely a sound emanating from his person other than the faintest of breaths, barely audible even to him, let alone anyone outside his bedroom door.

He had been convinced that there had been no-one stationed outside of his door since the first few hours following his arrival and unless things had changed, and his captors were being ever more cautious, which might be the case especially with Becky now in situ, he hadn't expected that to change.

Josh waited twenty seconds before relaxing his body a little. No key in the lock, footsteps, no knock even. Nothing.

Then, a slip of paper appeared under the door followed by the lightest of taps. This was almost comical given the situation, and were it not for the seriousness of the predicament he found himself in, it would have been precisely the kind of thing that would have normally amused him.

Stooping down to retrieve the paper, Josh pondered if this was from Paul, or, if not, from whom? Was it a set up? Should he be wary, and, if so, to what degree?

The writing was, at best, a scribble and, at worst, almost illegible. The letter "P" appeared in the bottom right-hand corner. He had to assume it was Paul and he'd also have to assume it was genuine.

The message, written out mostly in capital letters, but strangely, with some occasional lower-case letters intermingled amongst them, contained three points and an instruction to destroy it once read. At least he'd have something to eat, he thought, the slightest chink of a smile appearing across his face.

ASK TO SEE BeCKY TONIGHt

MAKe SURe SHe COMes WITH US

Be ReADY FOR SUNDAY

Josh tore up the paper into small strips and walked over to the toilet. All were crunched and dropped into the pan. The flush ensured their disposal and the one which didn't quite make it would inevitably be dealt with later.

The second of the three messages troubled Josh the most. Asking to see Becky was something he'd wished to do anyway, and as far as Sunday was concerned, he'd assumed that that was the day it would all kick off. But making sure she joins them when they go somewhere? Where? When? How would he ensure that?

He returned to his bed and lay down, his head once again resting on the now familiar pillow.

Once again, he checked his watch. Barely ten minutes had passed since he last looked. He'd been unable to settle, and he returned to the small bathroom, having another go at finally flushing away all the evidence of the note he'd received earlier. This time, success.

As he lay back down on his bed, he became conscious of

footsteps making their familiar journey towards his room. Two sets, he deduced. Not totally in sync, but almost.

Sure enough, moments later, the key turned in the lock and the door swung open into the room.

Ryan appeared and tilted his head in the direction of the door; a silent summons for Josh to make a move.

Immediately outside the room, and standing bolt upright in the corridor, was a second man, unknown to Josh, waiting for him to appear. Once Josh came into view, he immediately started to walk off, a tilt of his head encouraging Josh to follow him.

Obliging, Josh followed Ryan's unknown accomplice and made his way down the corridor and then, as usual, down the staircase and across the hallway into the room he'd become well acquainted with over the last couple of days.

As he entered, he quickly scanned the room. In addition to Ryan and his new mate, there stood CM, Paul and two other men he'd recognised from the earlier run-through outside.

"You've done well. Thank you." CM's remarks were almost as bizarre as other comments and interventions he'd heard over the last few days. Josh felt that he'd been patted on the back for a quick, emergency boiler repair rather than forcefully required, against his will, to rehearse a violent act against the state.

As per usual, Josh had decided to remain silent until he had something of import and clarity to say. After waiting for what seemed an appropriate interval, CM continued.

"There will be some work for you to do tomorrow. Not much. And then you can see Becky again. Perhaps even a coffee together or something... She's fine of course. In fact, she's just had some supper. You'll have yours shortly... back up in your room."

Josh determined that this was a moment, once again, to test his capacity to influence and control whilst he was still needed.

Fixing CM with an unblinking, wide-eyed gaze, quietly and firmly, Josh insisted, "I'll see Becky this evening or there'll be no work tomorrow. You can't treat her like a piece of dog shit and then expect me to step on her as well."

It was a point well-made and had clearly thrown CM a touch off balance. There was a moment of obvious tension, an instant nervous atmosphere, suddenly created. Josh mentally held his breath as all those present focussed on CM.

"You're quite right… I'm being unreasonable. Of course, you need to see her. She's upset… and probably frightened… very frightened." The last two words were delivered particularly slowly, deployed with venom. It was CM's turn to remain wide-eyed and unblinking as he took the opportunity to remind Josh of the parlous state his wife was in and the threat she faced. It was a reminder, well delivered, and it hit its mark.

CM's attempt to regain psychological control of the situation hadn't been missed by his team. For Paul and Josh, victory had been achieved and Josh would see Becky tonight.

Ryan, Paul, and one other of their sidekicks, were instructed to take Josh to Becky's room, give them five minutes together, and then return Josh to his bedroom.

"Search him before he enters and leaves," came the final command.

The quartet moved off and headed back upstairs. Once at the top, turning in the opposite direction to that which Josh had become accustomed to, they all headed down another hallway to Becky's room.

"Stop," called Ryan.

Josh was patted down and frisked by the unknown member of the team and, as the door was unlocked and opened, Ryan reminded Josh, "Five minutes."

Becky was stood up, presumably as a nervous reaction to her door being unlocked.

No sooner had she realised that it was Josh than she physically and emotionally crumpled before him, taking a couple of steps towards him.

The door to the room was closed and they were alone, albeit

temporarily.

They held each other, Josh issuing words of loving support and comfort as he tried as quickly as possible to get the conversation away from the emotional and on to the practical. He wanted, with all his heart, to take time, provide loving support and emotional stability, but he knew he had limited time and the practicalities had to take precedent.

He walked Becky slowly back towards the bed and they both sat down, side by side, hands held tightly.

Their conversation was whispered and punctuated by Josh with various strokes of reassurance and the frequent touch of physical support and encouragement.

What was going on? Who were these people? Why were they being dragged into this? Was it something from Josh's past? What was going to happen? All questions from Becky that Josh did his best to respond to, but which he knew wouldn't resolve her disquiet and angst.

Josh asked Becky to remain silent for a few moments and take careful note of what he was going to say. She nodded in agreement.

Becky knew her husband well. This was her time to take orders and, however possible, and in whatever way he wanted, try to carry them out. She knew that it was Josh, and Josh alone, who could get them out of this situation, and she trusted him completely.

Josh urged her to look around and explore the room and think about anything that might be useful in terms of either defending herself, or for escaping. Alternatively, hiding out somewhere if things became difficult. Although the room looked relatively bare, there would always be something. She just needed to open her mind and think differently.

Josh was also acutely conscious that, irrespective as to whether any of these things proved practical and effective, it was far better for Becky to feel she had a part to play in bringing this to an end. It was also important for her to focus on something with a purpose whilst she was effectively held hostage, rather than allowing her mind to roam in other more destructive directions.

Time had flown by and as the door was opened, Josh held Becky's head between his hands and leant over, kissing her on the lips. "I love you," he whispered. Becky nodded. "I love you too," she replied, in staccato half breaths.

Josh stood up and walked to the door, turned, and smiled at his wife. Becky smiled back as she watched her husband leave, the door being pulled tightly shut, and then locked behind him.

Immediately outside, Ryan abruptly stopped Josh and pushed him against the wall.

"Search time. Arms up," he demanded.

Josh lifted his arms outwards to shoulder height, his contempt for Ryan etched across his face.

Having concluded his unnecessarily harsh and overly firm patting and prodding, Ryan tilted his head once again and directed Josh in the direction of his room.

Once Josh had been safely deposited back inside his bedroom, all three men made their way back down the hallway before their voices disappeared along with their footsteps as they descended the flight of stairs.

CHAPTER 24

It was approaching 8:40pm as Wolstenholme's convoy arrived at the Cornerstone Hotel. Just a few minutes before, he'd dropped the local MP, Diana Freeman, a text with his approximate arrival time. She'd responded with a brief warning about the small but vocal demonstration being held outside. Having passed the information to his driver and close arm protection officers, he was told that they had already received that information and were entering via the side door of the hotel as a precaution.

Just as he alighted from the vehicle, a small number of protesters rushed around the corner of the building and started throwing eggs and tomatoes towards him. He was quickly ushered into the hotel where he was met by Diane Freeman.

"Sorry about the welcome," she said, smiling.

"Not a problem," replied Wolstenholme. "I think we are all used to this nonsense now." The Home Secretary followed his host through into the main dining room where his arrival was greeted with the customary applause that such senior figures tended to get at any League event. He smiled and waved in the direction of different tables in acknowledgement before taking his seat at the top table, briefly surveying the scene in front of him. There must have been the best part of one hundred and fifty guests, a fairly good attendance for a League event.

As the main course came and went, Wolstenholme asked the local chairman, Chris Makerfield, what time he was due to speak.

Diana immediately cut into the conversation and suggested that it should be as soon as the pudding was cleared, so that the Home Secretary could depart. "Thanks. In that case," Wolstenholme continued, "shall we move on to pudding and then we can get underway once that's cleared?"

After dessert, Makerfield rose to his feet and tapped his dessert spoon against the empty wine glass in front of him, chiming out notice of the impending introduction and subsequent speech.

After a glowing introduction, Chris Makerfield paused for effect, turned slightly towards Wolstenholme, and said firmly and confidently, "Ladies and Gentlemen, one of the finest and most effective Home Secretaries this country has ever had, and one of the League's most impressive politicians. I ask you to join me in welcoming," he paused, "Oliver Wolstenholme."

The Home Secretary rose to his feet, smiling as he acknowledged what was not only a first class and flattering introduction, but, also, felt like a very warm reception indeed.

* * *

Wolstenholme had been speaking for the best part of twenty minutes, without notes, and had assailed anything and anyone that seemed at odds with the League's hard-line positions on key issues of the day. This was Oliver Wolstenholme at his best, and the audience loved every minute of it.

Without warning and with all the unexpected suddenness that such an incident might cause, the shattering of glass interrupted the occasion as a rock flew through the air and onto a table, bringing with it the inevitable gasps and shrieks of surprise that such a violent act was intended to cause.

The diners quickly moved away from the immediate area, thankful that no-one had been hit, and the early chaos which had enveloped the scene was quickly replaced by a more calm and stoic response. Wolstenholme's protective detail had swung into action and moved with haste to enlist the support of local police officers outside the building to deal with the offender, as well as move closer to their charge to offer protection and persuade him to leave the building immediately.

"Wait!" he exclaimed. "Wait…"

"Sir, we need to leave, now!" insisted one of his detail.

"In a moment, in a moment."

With his protection officers increasingly insistent, Wolstenholme shouted above the hubbub, "Ladies and Gentlemen, ladies and gentlemen!"

As the room slowly became silent, Wolstenholme continued, "This incident is yet another example of the appalling actions perpetrated, all too frequently, by a tiny minority of law breaking, violent and anarchistic thugs. Your presence here tonight, your support for our league, your commitment to our cause, and through that, our country, is one of the reasons they will not prevail. We are made of sterner stuff, and as I take my leave, I do so in the full knowledge that–as friends and patriots–we will win through in the end. Thank you for everything you do and thank you for coming along tonight."

As Wolstenholme made his way slowly and deliberately from the room, applause erupted all around him. His smiles of reassurance as he walked past the crowd only served to underscore the respect which he had so quickly earned by those present.

As Wolstenholme eventually climbed into his car, his protection detail, together with uniformed officers surrounding his car, man-handled a few particularly aggressive demonstrators to the ground as the convoy sped off towards central London.

CHAPTER 25

The noise of the plane starting its engine, and what had initially sounded to him like it was taxiing into a take-off position, alerted Josh to the fact that preparations seemed to be getting underway. He wasn't able to see the aircraft at this stage, and no sooner had he anticipated watching it make that same banking turn over the main property that he had witnessed a short while ago, the engine noise stopped. Maybe it was just prepping for a later take-off he pondered.

Being cooped up was beginning to frustrate him. It had been almost two hours since Paul had delivered his breakfast, and he'd heard nor seen anything since. Josh had been watching through his window for any hint of movement, but none had been visible. He'd heard plenty of intermittent, inaudible speech echoing around the building, including the occasional shout, but other than the odd word, he had been completely unable to discern anything of any consequence from any of it.

Josh had been pacing about his box of a room, frequently returning to the window and carefully, deliberately, checking every square metre of ground he could see stretched out in front of him. Other than momentary glimpses of someone walking around the back of the main house, or collecting the odd container, or piece of kit still in place after the bulk of the training area had been dismantled, nothing was happening. He felt that additional tinge of anxiety as he contemplated everything that must, therefore, have been happening out of sight at the front of the main property.

Josh's thoughts turned to Becky. He was hoping that the tasks he had given her would have helped her to focus on matters other than her worries, but he wasn't entirely confident that it would have been enough to make a serious difference to her state of mind.

In the main hallway of the house, Ardoon had been watching the various comings and goings, as different pieces of kit, weaponry and supplies had been loaded onto one of the two brand new vans purchased recently for the process. One had already been fully loaded, some twenty minutes earlier, and had already set off with driver and passenger aboard. The second, awaiting the loading of a few small items, would also then be on its way.

Each of the four vehicles used to transport the supplies and equipment, as well as twenty of the men in the wider team, would deliberately travel apart from each other, to avoid the look of a convoy and the potential curiosity of a traffic police patrol.

Fitz barked out the names of ten of those assembled and instructed them to climb into the first minibus.

A few moments later, the minibus slowly moved off and, as it did so, Ardoon made his way to the front door, as if to say "goodbye" to a group of everyday house guests. He turned and walked back into the hallway, looking across to Fitz and nodding his approval. All was going well.

CM appeared from one of the meeting rooms and waved his mobile in the air. Ardoon needed to take a call. His Lordship gestured with his right hand that CM should join him in his study and both men converged on that small, more intimate of rooms, on the ground floor of the property.

Ardoon reached out towards CM and took the phone from him.

"Good morning," he said, waiting for the inevitable question from the person on the other end of the line.

"Yes... all going well... and, on time. Some of the boys and equipment have already left and the rest of it will all have left within the hour. Then, of course, it's the slightly trickier ones in the plane."

He was interrupted and listened attentively to what he was hearing.

"I know. And yes. I'm definitely leaving later."

After yet another intervention, Ardoon felt the need to provide additional reassurance.

"That conversation will happen later this morning, before we head off… he may push us, but it doesn't matter… if he wants her around for the short term, why not? We're totally clear this end and we're all running to plan. Exactly as expected. You just need to make sure you do the same."

Ardoon suddenly lifted the phone away from his ear and looked at the screen. "He's bloody gone. He can be a nauseating and irritating little wanker. Here."

CM took the phone and agreed, "He always has been."

"Right Christopher, let's aim to speak to our friendly little sleeve operator at 11:30. Get him brought to the main Drawing Room then."

"Will do," confirmed CM, turning away from Ardoon, and walking out of the room, across the hall and then, out of the main entrance to make the necessary arrangements.

Ardoon looked out at the scene. In some respects, he couldn't believe this was actually happening, but almost as astonishing as that was the fact that he found himself on the side of events that he did.

CHAPTER 26

Paul and Ryan were sitting on a plain garden bench. It felt planted in place on a small patch of beautifully mowed lawn towards one side of the main house. As CM approached, Ryan stood to his feet, slowly followed by Paul.

"Get him to the main front Drawing Room for 11:30."

Both men checked their watches, noting they had about fifteen minutes to kill before they were called upon to babysit again.

"When you've done that, you'd better go and get the wife as well… one of you. No need for both. We'll probably have to do something if past experience is anything to go by. Darren and Simon will be there, as will I, so there'll be no worries."

Both men nodded their agreement and CM turned away from them and walked back to the house.

"I presume we'll be babysitting him on the trip as well?" enquired Paul.

"Dunno," came Ryan's non-committal response, "S'pose so."

"I'll see you inside. I'm just going to have a piss."

With that Paul left Ryan and headed to the main house, disappearing into the building moments later. Ryan watched him every step of the way, a gentle smile creeping across his lips. Josh wasn't the only one who was going to be in receipt of some babysitting, he thought.

When Paul re-appeared in the main hallway some minutes later, Ryan was there waiting.

"Right then, let's get him," said Ryan, as he started making his way up the stairs, followed closely by Paul. As the younger of the two men approached the top of the staircase, he removed the gun from its shoulder holster and held it in his right hand which was hanging straight down by his side. Paul repeated the movement as he made his way along the corridor and up to Josh's bedroom door.

By this time, Josh had heard the steps heading down the corridor and had readied himself for the appearance of Ryan, Paul, or whoever else had been tasked with visiting him this time around.

The now familiar routine dutifully obliged. The door was unlocked, opened and the two men entered the room, taking the few steps necessary to do so but stopping some feet short of their captive.

"Downstairs," said Paul. With that, Josh made his way out of the room and once again followed Ryan on the almost routine journey along the corridor, down the stairs, across the entrance hall and then into the large Drawing Room.

Awaiting Josh's arrival were CM, seated, and two other men from the team that he recognised, though didn't know their names and, of course, Ryan and Paul. Hearing the door closed behind him, Josh looked around to discover that Ryan had disappeared.

"Won't keep you waiting too long I'm sure," said CM.

Josh glanced at CM before continuing to focus his gaze forwards and await further developments.

No more than four minutes after Ryan had left the room, he returned, this time accompanied by Becky, who walked over to Josh and flung her arms around him. He held her tightly for several seconds.

"You ok?" he whispered quietly and comfortingly, close to her ear.

She eased herself back from his embrace and looked into his eyes, nodding. He once again pulled her towards him and tightened his embrace, kissing her locks and holding her head cupped in his left hand.

The door to the room once again opened, and as Josh turned his head to see who had entered the room, the figure of Ardoon appeared. The door was gently closed behind him, and he made his way across the room and settled down in his usual spot in that large leather chair.

By this time, Becky and Josh had loosened their embrace, Becky standing close to her husband but no longer enveloped in his arms.

"Lovely to see you re-united for another moment," said Ardoon. "I'm sure you appreciate how important these moments are and how fragile they can become."

Pleasantries and a threat; the usual mix. Josh reflected on the fact that His Lordship was a good deal older than him but right now, he could cheerfully punch him straight in the face, if not worse.

Josh offered no response, once again waiting for a more appropriate time to engage in whatever conversation might be initiated. He knew he'd have his moment and was content to wait for it to arrive.

"Becky," continued Ardoon, "I hope that you've been well cared for: food, etc?"

Becky nodded silently; her nervousness obvious for all to see.

"Excellent. Excellent. Just the way it should be. Now, Becky, why don't you pop over here and sit down for a few minutes."

With that Ardoon gestured to the sofa. Becky looked at Josh for his agreement to this proposal, which came in the form of a nod, and then, full release of his contact with her.

"As you'll have no doubt ascertained, we are all going to do a little travelling and I wanted to be certain that we were all aware of the implications... were... ah... anything to be done which delayed or frustrated such a journey."

Ardoon was his usual quietly spoken, polite, occasionally cryptic, but all too threatening self, and Josh continued to wait for his moment.

"I wondered what you might think if you and Becky were allowed to travel together?"

Josh was both surprised and confused at the same time. He wasn't expecting to be offered the opportunity to travel with his wife and had expected to have to enter a verbal duel with his captors.

Becky had been observing Ardoon as he spoke and looked quickly over towards Josh, clearly seeking a positive response from him. Josh could see in her eyes the desire for him to agree to the proposal just made.

He determined to push back just a little, to test the purpose behind this apparently benign and almost friendly gesture.

"And?"

"Good Lord Josh, no "and" in it. A thoughtful and gentle reminder of what you have… and how important it is that what you have, remains."

The reply was, once again, charming but threatening at the same time. Josh began to realise the sense of this proposal from the perspective of his captors. First, it kept them both together and his time would be spent re-assuring and supporting his wife, both physically and mentally. Second, the chances of him doing anything to either disrupt the plans or physically intervene in any way with Becky present, thus endangering her, were remote and, third, fewer resources would be required to guard them both because of them being together, rather than apart. This was smart thinking.

Josh nodded his agreement and looked across to Becky, a smile creeping across his lips as he fixed her in his gaze. She reciprocated; the relief writ large in the expression which followed his willing consent.

"Lovely, lovely." With that, Ardoon looked at CM and gave the smallest hint of a nod. CM then gestured to the assembled team to return each of their captives to their respective rooms upstairs.

As Josh and Becky were accompanied across the entrance hall,

Fitz was barking out a set of ten more names, which saw men scurrying off towards a minibus which was readying itself for departure. Josh also caught a glimpse of a van pulling away, driver and passenger on board. With obviously fewer men about, and vehicles departing the property, it was safe to assume that things were well and truly underway.

Josh now felt that plans were focussing on Sunday and was acutely aware that he had just twenty-four hours to go before either he, or Paul, come up with something.

At the top of the stairs, Josh headed one way, and Becky the other. As he was ushered into his bedroom, he heard the door to Becky's room close and then lock. Seconds later, a repetition of just the same ritual for him.

He took the few short steps that would take him to the window. Looking out across the panorama set out before him, he was aware that most of the men involved had left the grounds by now. There was no obvious sign of any activity being undertaken at the premises and, to all intents and purposes, this might as well be just another estate in Scotland, basking in the spring sunshine with not a care in the world.

* * *

With a gap of thirty minutes between van and minibus, CM watched as the latter moved off, grateful that he would not be making such a long journey by car, or minibus.

The property seemed eerily quiet. Few men around the place, and little, if any activity to speak of. As he looked around the deserted grounds, breathing in the clear crisp air that was encouraged by a gentle breeze to rustle around the buildings and countryside surrounding him, CM considered it to have been the perfect place to make plans and train those involved and was privately delighted at how well things had gone. Few hitches and everything that needed to have been achieved, completed, and successfully so. He was content.

The pilot of the plane emerged from the main house and walked over to the aircraft. As he passed CM, he confirmed he was about to go through pre-flight checks in readiness for take-off.

"I'll get things sorted inside," CM replied. "How long?"

"Fifteen minutes should be fine," came the reply.

With that, CM turned and strolled back into the main building.

Ryan, Paul and two other men were standing together and chatting at the base of the staircase but cut short their conversation the moment CM appeared and walked purposefully towards them.

"Fifteen minutes until we are airborne," CM informed them. "You two," pointing at Ryan and Paul, "get him on the plane in ten minutes and you two," looking at the other two guys, "get Becky and get her on board now. Let's get her settled in first."

CM moved away towards the Drawing Room and Paul and Ryan watched their two colleagues making their way up the staircase, and then disappear into the corridor in the direction of Becky's room.

A few moments later, Becky appeared at the top of the stairs, followed by the two men, and commenced her descent. As she got closer to the bottom, Ryan and Paul took a few steps sideways to allow more space to open up. Once standing on the tiles on the floor of the Entrance Hall, Becky stopped and turned around, waiting for an instruction as to where she should head next.

"This way. Follow me," said one of the guys, moving past her and walking towards the open door. As she followed, the other took up position a few paces behind her.

As Becky headed out of the main entrance, she noticed the plane off to the side, and, once it became clear that that's where they were all headed, she realised she was about to board it. She started to become anxious as she couldn't see Josh and was hoping that what she had been told earlier wasn't a nasty hoax.

On entering the plane, Becky was directed to sit in the second row back on the left. After taking her seat as instructed, she fastened the seatbelt, though slightly less tightly, and therefore, more comfortably than she might normally have done had she not been pregnant. Once that was done, she looked back towards the house and kept her eyes trained on the main entrance to the building.

The two men accompanying her had taken their seats immediately behind her and hadn't spoken a word since doing so. Every so often, Becky looked at the pilot, who was continuing to do the necessary checks before take-off, and then, back towards the house. It couldn't be much longer. *Where was Josh?* she kept asking herself.

Five minutes later, Josh appeared at the front door and proceeded to walk towards the plane, closely followed by Ryan and Paul. It was a huge relief to Becky.

As he climbed into the aircraft, Paul told him he could, "Sit where you like."

It was a surprise statement but one which both he and Becky welcomed. Without delay, he made his way along the aisle and settled into the seat alongside his wife, immediately holding her hand to provide her with additional reassurance.

They both looked at each other, Josh wrapping his left hand around her already enveloped right. She repeated the exercise, and both quietly prepared themselves for the journey ahead.

Paul and Ryan had taken up seats in the row behind them but on the opposite side of the aisle.

The pilot turned, looking behind him at all six of his passengers. "We'll be off shortly."

With that, he began starting the engines and preparing for what seemed like an imminent take-off. Josh was conscious that the door to the aircraft hadn't yet been closed and assumed that at least one other passenger was likely to be joining them, possibly two, as neither CM, nor Ardoon, had yet appeared.

As the roar of the engines became more intense, out from the main house came both Ardoon and CM. *They are coming along after all*, thought Josh.

About halfway to the aircraft, CM and Ardoon stopped, had a brief exchange of words, and shook hands. CM continued towards the aircraft, Ardoon remaining in place.

Once aboard, CM took his seat immediately in front of Paul and Ryan and fastened his seatbelt. The noise of the engines became ever louder, and then, in a matter of seconds, the plane edged its way forwards and headed towards the make-shift runway that had served its purpose over the last few days.

Holding the aircraft in position at the far end of the runway, the power was increased, and the plane shivered with pent up tension before the brakes were released and the aircraft commenced its take-off, building speed metre by metre until, in no time at all, it was climbing into the sky before banking sharply in order to adopt its necessary course.

Becky and Josh looked at each other and then out of the window as the ground shrunk before them and the aircraft gained height even more quickly. Neither knew where they were headed but at least they were together.

CHAPTER 27

Eddington's morning had been as busy as usual. His constituency surgery had thrown up a dozen individual cases to be investigated before his convoy travelled on to a new army recruitment office, which he was to open that morning. More demonstrations, chanting and the odd hurled egg dogged his movements as usual.

As the Prime Ministerial convoy left the newly opened recruitment office and headed towards the venue for his constituency lunch for local activists, Eddington started to review the messages which had accumulated on his mobile.

There were two of particular importance. The first was from Lord Ardoon, the second from David Wilson.

Ardoon's message was typically forthright. Whilst both charming and often quietly spoken with others, lately, Ardoon didn't do "diplomatic" with Eddington. He was the most colourful of the party's founding members and one of its most significant donors. He always spoke his mind , forcefully, whenever he was given the opportunity to speak to his Prime Minister. As the recipient of his opinions, Eddington could either like it or lump it.

TONY - DON'T LET THE BLOODY SIDE DOWN ON MONDAY. HOLD FIRM. WEAKENING NOW WOULD BE A DISASTER. YOU HAVE MY SUPPORT IF YOU HOLD FIRM. DON'T FAIL US NOW.

Following a conversation Eddington had had with Ardoon some months ago, in which he'd confirmed his commitment to reversing the present strategy and relaxing controls and restrictions completely at some point in the near future, their subsequent discussions had become far more difficult and, at times, even tense.

This was the fourth such message that Eddington had received from Ardoon over the last three weeks.

Ardoon was a steely character, and it was clear to Eddington that he was trying to re-enforce all the earlier messages, the last one of which, urging him to, "PUT SOME BLOODY LEAD IN YOUR PENCIL."

Eddington pondered his reply but wasn't certain of the exact choice of words. He'd reply later when he'd given it some further thought.

The second message, from Wilson, was characteristically short and cryptic. Whenever Eddington communicated with Wilson, he always felt like a spy himself. Wilson tended to communicate almost entirely in code. Eddington had often thought to himself what might happen if all he wanted was a sandwich for lunch and what might actually turn up if he tried to order one.

ON TOP OF THINGS NOTB * DECISION NEEDED SUNDAY

Eddington acknowledged the text from Wilson with a simple "Noted" and looked out of the window, searching for some relief from his present trials. After the dreadful weather that had hit the southeast of the country only a few days ago, the sun was now shining and people were going about their business, making the best they could of their lives in difficult circumstances.

That Wilson felt he was on top of things north of the border, or NOTB, as he always referred to it as being, was encouraging as far as Eddington was concerned. But so much could still go wrong.

Just before 1:00pm, the Prime Ministerial convoy turned into the driveway of The Valley Park Hotel and made its way along the half mile, tree lined avenue towards the main hotel function suite. Over a hundred party members were assembled to join Eddington for lunch and hear their leader speak. Just like their Prime Minister, they too had had to run the gauntlet of the jeers, insults and occasional flying objects which had become all too familiar over the last few years.

Eddington was extremely popular within his local party, and it was unsurprising that so many had turned out to see him. He had recognised from the beginning of the Leagues existence, that a movement such as this would only grow and thrive if it had genuine grass roots support and engagement. He had always been generous with his time to ensure that his own local team was well supported and encouraged.

As his car pulled up immediately outside the main entrance doors to the function suite, his local chairman strolled in to view ready to greet him, beaming smile as usual and bags of goodwill to impart.

"Good afternoon Prime Minister," he said, "great to see you and thank you so much for making the time to do this for us."

Nick Stevens was a self-made man, hugely popular with the members and full of the kind of bonhomie that makes for an excellent voluntary leader. Always saying thank you, always having fun and always reflecting upon the little things that people did that were so important in building up loyalty and strong relationships. The local organisation was in safe hands with Nick.

"It really is my pleasure, Nick. Have we got a good crowd?"

"A good crowd? Ha! Full PM, full!" Nick's confidence and positivity was almost infectious. It was clear to see why he wasn't only successful but highly regarded too.

For Eddington, this was likely to be the last time for some days that he would be amongst such a friendly, unquestioningly loyal, and supportive audience.

As both men appeared at the open double doors through which access to the main dining area was gained, applause erupted, and everyone stood to their feet. As he made his way through the crowd, he was constantly stopped with demands for handshakes and brief congratulatory conversations. Occasional banging on the tables, along with the cheering, all added to the sense of occasion and enhanced the feeling of warmth directed towards him from those present. It seemed to take an eternity to make the distance between the entrance doors and the top table from which he'd address his supporters.

Eddington was reassured and encouraged. He was amongst his own.

CHAPTER 28

Wolstenholme had allocated himself a great deal of time throughout Saturday to step up preparations for Monday's likely showdown.

His first dozen or so calls had been to key supporters within the Parliamentary Party. Nothing intense or heavy, a "casual chat" to see how they were doing, as well as an opportunity to chat things through and find out how they were all feeling about the party. More importantly, though delicately raised, Eddington's leadership.

Most remained loyal to Eddington initially but there was an underlying concern with every one of them. Eddington, it appeared, was losing his grip on things generally and seemed to be going through "a bad patch." One major issue that cropped up often was the level of public protest which accompanied almost every Government announcement; some of which turned violent. This was an area which played directly into Wolstenholme's hands and, whilst cautious with his words, was acknowledged and generally sympathised with.

After a little more pressing, a few even suggested that it might be time for the party to start thinking about its future under a new leader. " Someone like you, Oliver." Wolstenholme, of course, remained overtly loyal, but thanked each for their support, encouraging them to voice their concerns to colleagues to "help keep things on track."

He knew that the particular individuals he had spoken to would quickly spread their influence and opinions amongst at least forty to fifty others. What none of the recipients could have known was that such a situation might be about to explode in front of them, and sooner than they had anticipated.

Glancing at his watch, he exhaled sharply through his rasping lips. Where had the time gone? He didn't want much, but he should eat something.

As he rose from his seat, his mobile rang. Glancing down at the screen to see who it was, the name "Fox" flashed up in front of him. He answered.

"Marie… afternoon."

The conversation was to be a brief one in which Marie Standing provided support and encouragement to her lover. To the ears of Oliver Wolstenholme, her ambition was almost as great for him as it was for herself.

Standing finished the call by wishing him well and urging him to make the right decision.

"Thank you… and good luck tomorrow yourself." Wolstenholme concluded the conversation and made his way towards the kitchen. Having given everyone the day off today, cheese on toast was the safest option for him to attempt.

His main concern suddenly became the whereabouts of a bottle of Worcestershire sauce.

His mobile shook and lit up, the short trilling noise indicating the delivery of a message. It was from David Wilson. This was something more important that Worcestershire Sauce.

ON TOP OF THINGS NOTB * DECISION NEEDED SUNDAY

Wolstenholme, reassured, responded with a "thumbs-up" emoji.

Now, lunch.

CHAPTER 29

The descent triggered the same feeling in Josh that he'd had on his trip northwards. Josh had taken the opportunity of their journey to be as reassuring as possible, mixing occasional references to the ground below or nature of the clouds and sky above, with nostalgic, happy memories of their earlier life and what kind of life their newborn should be provided with.

Becky had become a little more relaxed as the journey progressed, a smile passing her lips more than Josh had expected given their predicament. Such sentiment was to be short lived.

As soon as it became clear to both that the aircraft was on its landing approach, their grip tightened and looks from Becky to Josh became more frequent.

Josh gazed out of the window and recognised that they were approaching the same place where he had previously taken off from: Cambridge.

The hard touch down drew a few expletives from Ryan and one of the other men aboard. Becky let out a sharp gasp and tightened her grip around Josh's hand. With a much longer runway in front of him, the pilot braked much more gently than he'd had to do in Scotland and, soon enough, the plane came to a standstill about fifty metres from the main building. Becky looked once again towards Josh who gave her a warm smile and squeezed her hand for further reassurance.

Everyone on board gathered what little they had and began to leave their seats, heading for the exit door. Both Becky and Josh were given the go ahead to depart from the aircraft and, one after the other, they headed down the short gangway and out into the warm but breezy afternoon.

Josh held Becky's hand as they walked to the main building. As they turned the corner, he noticed a man leaning up against the wall by the entrance door. He recognised him immediately but wasn't entirely sure where he'd seen him before. It wasn't in Scotland, and it wasn't at his flat, but he definitely remembered him from somewhere.

As the entire group reached the building, Josh and Becky were preceded by CM, along with the two unnamed men, and followed in by Paul and Ryan. Immediately after them came the man who had been leaning against the wall outside. Josh remembered. He was the guy who had entered the pub when Josh had met Micky; the man Micky had spoken to at the bar. That meeting was clearly not coincidental. As for Micky, Josh thought, where was he?

CM's mobile rang. He took the call and listened for all of five seconds before it was concluded. "The cars will be here in a few moments," he confirmed.

Becky and Josh squeezed each other's hands tightly.

Looking towards Josh, CM said, "We'll all be together. There's no need for any further concerns in that regard, Josh."

Whilst it was no doubt reassuring for Becky to hear those words, Josh became ever more conscious of the impact them being together was having on a number of areas, not least his ability to act without endangering Becky. This was a clever decision by his captors and had obviously been carefully planned to precisely have the effect it was having.

Minutes later, three cars appeared outside the entrance to the building and their arrival was greeted by a "right, let's go," from CM. "Adrian, you're with Becky."

As everyone made their way outside, Becky was told to get into the first vehicle and Josh, the third. Josh nodded towards Becky and gave her a further reassuring smile. She was accompanied by the man Josh remembered from the pub, now known to be Adrian, and one other. With Josh rode Paul and Ryan, and the others all piled into the central vehicle in the small cavalcade. The three cars pulled away, staggering their set-off times. It was clear that this small convoy wasn't about to draw attention to itself by travelling together.

Becky had felt uncomfortable from the moment she'd climbed into the back of the first vehicle. Even though almost twenty minutes had passed, Adrian, the man sitting alongside her, had barely taken his eyes off her. Although she had resisted the temptation to look at him, other than when she entered the vehicle, she eventually succumbed and glanced across.

The short, young, balding man, made no movement and continued to stare at her through squinted, dark eyes, emotionless and unnerving. The sooner Becky could get out of the car, the better she'd feel about things.

Out of the corner of her eye, Becky noticed Adrian Mason look away from her and put his hand in his jacket pocket. He pulled out a long piece of string and started deliberately and purposefully tying knots in it.

As the knotting progressed, he'd occasionally look at her, lift his hands to chest height, pull the string tightly and then, as though he was calculating some form of length and measurement, carry on tying his knots. Never a smile, never a sound, never with speed and almost robotic in action and task. Every three or four knots, another look at her, and then, more measuring. From time to time, he would raise the index finger of his right hand and align it such that it rested on the length of his nose. He'd then stare at Becky for all of ten seconds before he went back to his knot tying.

Becky became increasingly uncomfortable in the presence of this man. Her journey seemed to be getting longer, not shorter, and the emotional pressure being applied by the passenger sat alongside her was becoming almost unbearable.

Occasionally, she'd notice that the driver would also observe this man's actions through the rear-view mirror, sometimes frowning or lifting his eyebrows. The fact that no one spoke through the journey made the whole experience even more disconcerting.

She looked away from Adrian Mason and out of the window at the countryside that was now speeding by, trying to distract herself from him. They'd left Cambridge and were heading south. Hopefully, it wouldn't be too much longer before she could see Josh again. But she could feel Mason's stare burning into the back of her skull.

* * *

The motorway signs continued to beckon London ever closer, but shortly before Josh convinced himself that the capital was where they were headed, the driver took a slip lane and left the motorway.

Josh looked at both Paul and Ryan, neither responding in any way. The signs indicated they were going to be heading to somewhere situated north of London, but where?

* * *

"Here." The man occupying the front seat of the vehicle carrying Becky lifted his right arm and bent it behind his head waving a large blindfold from his hand. Becky looked towards the man and saw Adrian reach up and take hold of it.

As Becky leant towards him, Adrian eased it over her head and into position, checking that it was sufficiently tight to prevent her seeing anything. It was big enough to obscure almost everything, but there were tiny gaps around some of the edges.

Suddenly she tensed and jumped, making a small gasping noise in surprise, or was it fright? She felt Adrian's hand gently rub along her thigh.

"Stop!" she shouted at him.

The touching stopped, not least as her message was re-enforced by the driver of the car. "Adrian, stop it, or your brother will hear about it." came the added instruction.

For the next thirty minutes or so, the vehicle was making far more turns than had previously been the case. Still blindfolded, Becky presumed that they were now well into the countryside, where smaller, narrower roads resulted in more turns, corners, and tight junctions.

Then, after one particularly tight turn, the road became more uneven and bumpy. For a few minutes, the car seemed to lurch and vibrate, like it was weaving its way around potholes, bumps and dips which occasionally caused it to roll a little, rocking Becky around in the back seat as each turn was taken. Then it came to a halt. The engine was switched off and doors were opened.

"Take it off," came the instruction from Adrian. His voice wasn't at all what Becky had expected. It was relatively high pitched and slightly rasping in tone. It also had a peculiar feminine quality about it which wasn't at all in keeping with this most sinister, unpleasant and calculating of individuals.

Becky removed the blindfold and handed it to Adrian. He stared at her, once again fixing her with his unnerving gaze. He let the blindfold go and allowed it to fall into the footwell of the car. Becky's door was opened by the driver who instructed her to alight from the vehicle.

"Out," he ordered. Becky climbed out of the vehicle slightly awkwardly, as she eased her frame from what was a relatively tight seating area, given her condition. Having exited the vehicle, she stretched and breathed in deeply, drawing herself up to her full height, compensating for what had been a cramped journey.

Adrian made his way around the rear of the vehicle to take up position behind her. She felt that uncomfortable presence once again. He raised his hand and indicated that she should head towards the entrance to what looked like a large house.

The main building was a double fronted property with a small lawn in front of it, two smaller cottages to the right as she faced it, and some outbuildings to the side and behind them. It felt like a tiny hamlet all of its own. There was a big, open fronted barn to the left of the main building which had at least one small van already parked up within it.

The railings that topped the surrounding wall were metal, with one small section to the left-hand side having clearly seen better days.

The cottages were semi-detached and white walled, one much in need of a coat of paint, and both were entered via a single path dissecting a small lawned garden, completely surrounded by a low, waist height, stone wall, the entrance to which had no gate.

There was a large parking area in front of the properties, enough for several vehicles. Assuming the main property had at least four or five bedrooms, this was a collection of buildings that could comfortably sleep at least twenty people.

There appeared to be some land to the rear and, with a tree and shrub lined access lane, which was at least five to six hundred metres from the road, this was an isolated spot.

As Becky approached the short path to the main house, a man appeared at the front door. He was a tall, stocky man, about fifty-five years old with a ruddy complexion, unkempt greying hair, and a red and black checked shirt with rolled up sleeves sitting atop a pair of distinctly grubby jeans.

Walking down the path towards them, he nodded towards Becky and then informed Adrian that her room was at the top of the stairs and first door on the right, handing him a key to the lock as they passed. Adrian said nothing and gave Becky a slight shove in the back. Becky turned and scowled at him.

Entering the property, it was much darker than she imagined it to be. All the doors had been closed and no lights had been switched on. The staircase in front of her was much smaller than anticipated, running up the side of the right-hand wall with a single wooden handrail to hold.

At the top of the creaky steps, she turned to the right and stopped at the door she understood to be her room. Adrian eased past her, grabbed the handle, and pushed open the door. She stepped inside the room and quickly looked around to acclimatise herself with her surroundings. A single bed, two small chairs, an old wardrobe and a window which looked to have recently had bars fitted.

Adrian put his hand in his jacket pocket and slowly pulled out the same piece of string he had been weaving and knotting in the car during their earlier journey. Becky could feel her heart pounding and was certain that it could now be so loud, and fast, that Adrian must also have been able to hear it.

She remained quiet, stared at him, and psychologically steadied herself. She was certain that Josh would urge her to be confident and strong in the face of such an undesirable individual and situation. Defiance, she contemplated, would see her through these next few moments if she were prepared to show it clearly enough.

She lifted her chin slightly and the smile across Adrian's lips broadened further. Becky noticed a gold tooth towards the back of Adrian's upper jaw. He held out his arm and allowed the string, some two feet in length, to swing a little from side to side. After a few seconds, he slowly walked across to the window and attached it to the latch. He waited for what seemed like an eternity to Becky, before turning around and walking straight past her and out of the room. He pulled the door shut behind him and locked it.

She walked over to the window, pulled the string off the latch, and threw it to the floor. After a few moments looking at it, she bent down, picked it up and re-fastened it to the window latch before sitting on the bed to gather her thoughts. She wasn't going to give Adrian the satisfaction of knowing that she was afraid of his little string tricks.

Becky looked around the room. She checked the wardrobe, moved each of the chairs and looked under the bed. Spotting a chamber pot, she became aware of the fact that there was no bathroom or toilet attached to the bedroom and, she presumed, the pot was there to serve the inevitable purpose.

From outside, the noise of another vehicle arriving drew her to the window, which gave her a view across the front of the property and off towards what looked like a small copse and wooded area some seventy-five metres away. The car, which she recognised as the second in the convoy, had arrived. The male passengers alighted from the vehicle and the driver drove the car across to the open barn and parked it inside.

She was now calculating the time at which Josh should arrive. With five to ten minutes between each vehicle, it should be any time now. She stood at the window, waiting. She wanted to see her husband arrive and nothing was going to drag her from her place until he'd appeared.

Sure enough, the third vehicle arrived just over five minutes later. The passengers exited and Josh removed his blindfold as he got out of the car. He spotted Becky in the window of the main house and smiled, winking as he did so.

She watched as he, Ryan, and Paul, strolled towards the entrance of the main house and made their way up the pathway and then, out of sight as he entered the property. She heard the footsteps up the staircase, the boards on some of the steps creaking as they all made their way up to the first floor.

As all three men walked past her door Becky heard one of the men tell Josh that she was in the room they were passing, before the door to the adjoining bedroom opened. She heard one of the men tell Josh to "get in there," and then heard the slam of the door, the turn of the key and the retracing of steps past her room and then downstairs.

* * *

Josh looked around his room. No door handle, just like his room in Scotland, a single bed, one chair and bars at the windows as per usual. He looked under the bed and discovered a chamber pot. He reached out and pulled it towards him as he stood up. Standing upright, he peered into it as if searching for something and then, with a brief chortle, popped it back under the bed from whence it came.

He walked over to the window and looked out across the vista in front of him. The perfect place to hold up, out of sight, and isolated, he thought to himself.

As he took in the positions of various vehicles, he suddenly, as if his memory had received a jolt, headed across the room to the wall which adjoined Becky's room.

He stroked the wall and patted it a few times before lowering his hand to the skirting board which ran its way around the entire room. Josh hoped that the information he'd been given about Becky's whereabouts earlier was correct.

He started tapping out "hi" in Morse Code.

· · · ·   · ·

He tried again and waited for a reply. Moments later, Becky responded.

· · · ·   · ·

One of the things Josh had taught Becky for fun many years ago when they first met, was basic Morse Code. They'd used it in all sorts of unlikely situations, and it had certainly enabled them to share a private thought or joke more than once as they tapped on a tablecloth or the arm of a chair, communicating secretly and privately with each other.

It seemed that they were even closer together now than others might assume them to be.

CHAPTER 30

After many hours of repeatedly checking over the details, and then, working through every conceivable consequence of the two different plans he was examining, David Wilson rested his pen on the last few pages still attached to the pad in front of him and sat back in his chair.

His desk was littered with pages of handwritten notes, reflecting the machinations of assorted actions and re-actions, timelines, and names, all connected with lines and arrows.

All appeared to be set for success one way or the other. His meticulous planning and careful recruitment decisions had kept things tight. It was all textbook preparation. He knew he risked his own position but only if the ambitions of the politicians involved failed to hold up; and he was confident that that was now unlikely to falter given that the stakes were so high.

He sat still, his eyes darting from paper to paper. He stopped examining everything in front of him and frowned. He tilted his head backwards, and, looking up at the ceiling for a few seconds, looked back down at the papers on his desk once again. He leant forwards slightly and selected two pieces of paper which he placed side by side.

Carefully checking the scribblings on each, he then plotted his way down the piece of paper on the right-hand side with his finger, stopping occasionally to check something against that with the paper on the left. It seemed to him that there might be something to think about. He needed to be certain.

He checked his watch. His wife had taken the children out for the morning to give him the privacy and space he needed but they were due back soon. He looked out of the window. No sign of a returning family. Wilson looked at his watch once again. He had time. He'd make the call.

Wilson held the mobile to his ear and waited for the call to be answered.

"Parksey, good morning. okay?"

Parkes was one of the best surveillance and covert operations directors in the department. He had an incredibly inquisitive mind and seemed to have an unerring ability to discover the most unlikely of plots, ideas, and suspicious situations, making all sorts of things fit into a pattern that most people never would.

Wilson had worked with Parkes before on a variety of particularly sensitive operations prior to being promoted, and his confidentiality, as well as ready acceptance to simply follow orders without question, or concern, made him the perfect man for the task in hand. He was a "Wilsonian" as David Wilson's closest lieutenants were known within MI5.

"I need something checked but I need it for my eyes only. No-one else, no-one."

"Understood," Parkes said.

"I want you to pull everything we've got on Marie Standing and Dave Welling. I mean, going right back. School, everything. I also want you to do a complete check on their movements, diaries etc and particularly out of working hours. Check it over and look for any connections or something you think might appear to be unusual. I'm not saying there is anything, by the way. I'm saying we should look. And pull the tap records on Standing's phone. My personal, and verbal-only authorisation. Understood?"

"Okay... and Welling's phone?" Parkes asked.

"We have those?"

"I can get them."

"But we can retro-check without linkage? I thought we had to get sign off for that to happen?"

"All people below certain clearances can actually be retro-checked. Including us."

"Mark," Wilson spoke slowly and deliberately, "for obvious reasons, for both of us, I think it's best that this call cannot be retro-checked. Understood?"

"Understood… this call never happened, sir."

"When you have everything, let me have any thoughts you might have. Come here to the house, however late."

"Understood."

"And one final thing," said Wilson.

"Yes sir?"

"Wipe everything for the last three months. From both our records."

"Consider it done."

Wilson disconnected the call and placed his mobile on the desk in front of him, relieved he was able to wipe calls from his record that he might have to answer too many questions about. He spotted his family coming up the road and Martin dashing up the small drive ahead of the others, no doubt eager to get started tackling his father in "Barbarian Lands."

* * *

The constituency lunch had gone well. As Eddington said his goodbyes and as his convoy pulled away, he sat back and relaxed as the tension built up from performances given throughout the day, released instantly from his body.

"What time do we think we'll get to Chequers?" he enquired of the driver.

"With traffic as it is, I'd expect it to be about an hour Prime Minister."

"Good. Thank you."

Eddington rested the back of his head against the headrest and closed his eyes. He'd grab a few moments to relax and wind down before taking another look at the papers in his red box.

* * *

"Michael," Wolstenholme said, in the warmest friendliest tone he could muster, "how are you and, more importantly, how is the little one?"

"Much better today thank you, Oliver." Michael Bonato was genuinely surprised to receive the call, but appreciated it nonetheless, "Well over the worst and we're expecting to get him out of hospital sometime in the next few days. We've actually just arrived for another visit, so you've caught me just in time."

Bonato looked down at his daughter who was tugging at his arm, insisting on making faster progress into the hospital. He tugged her back and pursed his lips demanding a little quiet from his boisterous daughter.

"I'm delighted to hear all this," said Wolstenholme, "it must be a really worrying time for you. Have you spoken to the PM about taking a day or two over Sunday and Monday to do the dad thing?"

It was most unlike Wolstenholme to be this concerned and supportive, but Bonato contemplated that he might be encountering a warmer side of Wolstenholme's character.

"I hadn't actually, as we seem to be coping okay, but it's not a bad idea. I could, I suppose."

Wolstenholme was insistent. "Promise me you'll do that Michael. It's so important that you're about with him and the rest of the family, and I can't believe that the PM won't be anything other than positive about you taking some time."

Wolstenholme waited, silently adding to the pressure for his colleague to commit to taking the time he was encouraging him to take.

"Okay. It's a good idea, and I know that it'll help. Thanks Oliver.

Good call. I'll drop the PM a message as soon as we've finished ."

"Great, and so pleased. It's definitely the right thing to do. You'll be glad you did it."

Before he entered the main entrance to the hospital Bonato selected Eddington's number from his list of contacts and tapped the screen to connect.

* * *

Wolstenholme wrapped up his afternoon of communications with a final brief text before the early supper that had been booked in with his wife.

COE not about Sun – with family - partial return Mon for cabinet only

Responding with a thumbs up symbol, Wilson acknowledged the information and then turned to his son and nudged him in the ribs.

"Dad!" Martin snapped back. "Stop it! No cheating. I'm concentrating."

Wilson smiled back and clicked the "PLAY" button. Seconds later, all hell broke loose on the foldaway as it lit up with impressive 3D vistas, both players quickly up to their necks in various challenges, mass fights and fast-moving mayhem.

CHAPTER 31

Communicating messages via Morse Code for almost two hours had been a source of huge comfort to both Josh and Becky and their latest exchange had only been interrupted by the sound of approaching footsteps and voices.

Becky quickly moved back from the wall and sat on her bed, whilst Josh stood up and walked across to the window, leaning against the frame in a relaxed fashion.

Becky's door was the first to be opened. Ryan walked in and handed her a tray on which was a plate of sandwiches, a piece of malt loaf, and a can of Coke. Having already been told by Josh that Paul was an ally during an earlier Morse Code conversation, and hearing that he'd entered Josh's room, Becky decided to try and give Josh and Paul more time to communicate.

"What's in the sandwiches. I can't eat some things," she said.

"Don't know. Haven't looked," came Ryan's disinterested response.

"I'm really sorry but can I just check and if I can't eat them, is it possible to have something else please?"

Ryan paused and nodded. Becky lifted one of the slices of bread and noted the contents.

"Cheese and tomato."

"Can you eat that?" enquired Ryan.

"I can eat the tomato," replied Becky, doing her best to gain her husband even more time.

Ryan took the few steps forward, retrieved her plate and placed it on the bed beside her. He then lifted the slice of bread on the top of each round, removed the cheese with his fingers and dropped it on the tray, closing the sandwiches up once again.

"No cheese now. Enjoy."

Ryan turned and left the room, pulling the door shut behind him and locking it immediately.

* * *

As Paul delivered Josh's food, the extra time Becky had bought them proved to be invaluable.

In whispered tones, Paul brought Josh up to date with his latest thinking. "It now looks set for Sunday," he said.

"Do we know exactly what yet?" asked Josh.

"No, still no joy there," replied Paul. "Sunday is the day everything looks to be happening. We are going to be given mobiles early on Sunday morning. Except you, of course. There are no further run throughs and there seems no reason why things should be delayed until Monday or after."

"So, tomorrow then?"

"Yes. It certainly looks that way." Paul looked back towards the door and paused for a few seconds before continuing.

"You need to be ready from now on. We'll have to take our chances as they happen. Stay close."

The sound of Becky's door being pulled shut was the cue for Paul to cease the conversation and leave Josh's room.

An identical tray of food and drink had been handed to Josh, and Paul immediately turned and headed out of the room, pulling the door to Josh's bedroom shut and locking it behind him as he went.

After checking the contents of the sandwich, Josh went back to the wall and tapped "Cheese. Your fav," in Morse Code. Back came the message: "Told him can't eat. Buy you time."

Josh smiled. He was pleased that Becky was focussed on managing the situation rather than being overwhelmed by it.

"Well done," he replied.

At the sound of a vehicle, he walked over to the window to look at what was happening outside. One of the vans, the first that had left Scotland that morning, had just arrived. It was being directed towards the open-ended barn and was neatly parked towards the rear of the building. Josh recognised the two men that emerged, both of whom walked back across to the main house, up the path and in through the entrance door.

Almost immediately, a second van arrived. Its driver appeared to be given the same instructions. The driver and passenger also entered the main property moments later.

Ten minutes later, another smaller van had appeared, and Josh realised that the entire operation, whatever it was, would be run from this property. The target had to be close. If Paul was correct, they had less than twenty-four hours before the operation began.

Josh kept an eye out for Micky, but the more Becky told him about Adrian, the more he became concerned about what might have happened to him.

Josh heard some more tapping emanating from the skirting board in the room next door and listened attentively to the letters being tapped out by Becky.

"What happen tonight."

Josh replied, "hope nothing get sleep love you."

Becky's reply was immediate, "Love you x"

The "x" had brought a smile to Josh's lips, and he reciprocated straight away. Josh allowed his mind to wander a little in the direction of the day to come, growing ever more concerned about what he might encounter, about whoever would be left at the property to guard Becky and, he feared, potentially to murder her.

The approaching steps that could be heard making their noisy way upstairs and along the hallway gave ample warning of a visit of some sort to either his or Becky's bedroom.

Josh became tense as the footsteps approached. But not for himself. Ever since he'd heard about Adrian from Becky, he'd become anxious every time her room was being approached. He had convinced himself that Adrian was likely to be the one tasked to deal with Becky at the appropriate time and was now alert to every potential movement in the direction of her bedroom.

As the key turned in the lock in the door to Josh's bedroom, he was almost relieved to see Ryan who, with a theatrical sweep of his arm, indicated that Josh should leave. Paul was waiting outside.

As all three men made their way down the narrow staircase they were met by CM and two men Josh recognised from the team based in Scotland.

"This way, Josh," said CM, indicating along the hallway beside the staircase towards the rear of the premises. As he made his way, Josh passed two rooms in which small groups of men were sitting and eating.

The final room, situated at the end of the corridor, was poorly furnished and fairly dark. Josh followed CM inside and the others followed suit. CM took a seat himself and indicated that Josh should sit on the other. The two men stood either side of CM and Paul and Ryan stood close to Josh.

"Now," said CM, "we have something for you to look at."

On cue, another man entered carrying a box which was placed on the table. Josh immediately recognised the sleeve control box.

"I want you to examine this carefully. Check it over. And please, don't fuck us about. I really don't want to have to involve Becky at this stage."

Josh unfastened the lid, opened the top and slid the front side of the box open to reveal the sleeve device.

Having already seen it some hours earlier, Josh wondered what the point of this further examination might be.

"Turn it on," said CM.

Everyone was watching Josh carefully as he activated the equipment. He was playing this strictly by the book. The extent of CM's knowledge wasn't clear and whilst he obviously couldn't operate the equipment, he may have enough of an understanding to expose any attempt by Josh to cause a problem. He'd take no chances.

Josh flicked two switches and the device lit up in front of him, the screen initially showing a green colour before slowly turning a creamy shade of white.

"Now, enter the code," continued CM.

"Enter the code?" replied Josh.

"Yes, enter the code."

Josh was slightly perplexed. "You don't enter a code at this stage. You have to detect the operational code first and then you can disarm it."

CM smiled, "Good. It's all working satisfactorily?"

"As far as I can tell, without actually testing it," responded Josh.

"Good. No need to enlist the skills of Adrian then. So much easier that way." concluded CM.

"I do have one question," interjected Josh.

CM stared back at him, saying nothing.

"Micky. What has happened to him and where is he?"

Josh became conscious that a few of the men had immediately glanced at each other, anticipating the answer.

CM remained motionless and silent for many seconds before looking at a couple of the men in the room, and then, back to Josh.

"Since you ask, Micky had an interesting little encounter with Adrian; not a man to encounter at the best of times."

Josh's immediate thought was one of sorrow. In spite of his last meeting with Micky, and his conviction that his friend had got involved in something best avoided, Josh retained a considerable amount of affection for his long-term mate and his death, though pretty much anticipated, still hurt.

"He's dead then?" Josh sought unequivocal confirmation.

"That is Adrian's way," replied CM. "Sometimes it's quick, most often... not. His talents can be uniquely distressing."

Josh hoped that Micky was one of those whose fate had been sealed quickly.

"We'll want you to check this over again tomorrow. For now, turn it off."

"Understood," replied Josh, as he carried out his instructions. "Will I need to check it operationally at some point tomorrow?"

"There's a wonderful American Civil War film in which our heroine calls out, "tomorrow is another day!" so let's see what tomorrow brings, shall we? Good evening, Josh."

As Josh left the room, Adrian was waiting outside and fixed Josh in a stare like a bird of prey zeroing in on its latest meal. Josh returned the stare, and then winked at Adrian and began whistling the theme tune to the Laurel and Hardy movies, refusing to be intimidated by him. Adrian straightened his back and stood stock-still, bolt upright and staring at Josh, clearly incandescent. Josh walked on, urged by Paul.

* * *

CM had waited for everyone to leave the room, before standing to his feet and looking into the box which was still sitting on the table in front of the chair in which Josh himself had been sat.

"This is a box of tricks that is going to change the face of this country," he quietly said to himself.

He gathered up the box in his hands and walked out of the room.

CHAPTER 32

Wilson had still not received any communication from Parkes. He was tempted to chase him but knew that Parkes would be working continuously. All that his interruption would do was further delay things.

He flicked through the messages already received to remind himself where all the key players were once again. Eddington had arrived at Chequers. Wolstenholme was also at home and was working late having spent time with his wife earlier that evening. Bonato had returned to 11 Downing Street after visiting his son in hospital and had been playing games with his daughter before getting her to bed. Strong was out to dinner in his constituency with members of his family.

"Strong has been wisely keeping his head down for twenty-four hours," Wilson thought to himself.

Wilson had also received confirmation that Standing hadn't actually arrived home yet and was believed to have gone late night shopping, her tail having lost her a couple of hours earlier and failed to re-establish contact.

Wilson's network of surveillance had been highly effective over the last month or so and he was reassured that everyone was in the right place, with the exception of Marie Standing.

He pondered on how remarkably normal and relaxed everything seemed, even though within twenty-four hours "Mixing Bowl" would be initiated and the direction of the country would change irrevocably.

He rose from the sofa and walked across to the drinks trolley, which was stationed by a large and impressive bookcase, itself crammed with paperback and hardback literary masterpieces and classics. He poured himself a small whiskey and resumed his place at one end of the sofa.

His wife popped her head around the door and informed him that she was tired and was heading to bed.

"I'll see you later. Don't be too late darling, you need to get some decent sleep."

Wilson nodded in agreement. "Sure. I'll be up a bit later."

Having closed the door behind her, Wilson was left alone to continue reviewing his thoughts and plans.

He was thinking about each of the main players and was impressed by their ability to play the game. To be a great politician, Wilson thought, you first had to be a good actor. If ever there was confirmation of such a proposition, this moment was it. Whilst almost everyone involved was preparing themselves for a tumultuous few days, they happily sat with friends and family, eating food, or playing games, as if nothing were happening at all.

As he smiled to himself at that thought, he also pondered that each of them might also make good spies and double agents. His smile suddenly turned to a frown. He gazed forward, mentally looking beyond the room and into the outer space which contained his new, anxious, and potentially worrying considerations.

"Spies too," he muttered to himself. "Spies too."

He leant forward and rested the glass of whisky on the low, solid, wooden coffee table in front of the sofa and stood to his feet. He then walked over to his desk and retrieved the papers which he'd been working on most of the morning and into the early afternoon.

He flicked through the small bundle and retrieved two particular pages. Walking back to the sofa he slowly retook his seat and laid out both sheets of paper on the coffee table in front of him, crouching over them both and slowly scanning the notes and scribbles he'd made with great care.

"Spies… double agents," he whispered to himself.

His mobile rang. It was Parkes.

"Yes?"

"I have everything and have checked it over. I'll be with you in about twenty minutes."

Wilson looked at his watch. "That'll be fine. See you later… oh, and text me when you're here. I don't want everyone woken up by the bell. I'll let you in."

Disconnecting the call, Wilson placed his mobile carefully on the coffee table alongside the papers and rested back into the cushions which both supported and enveloped his frame. Parkes' arrival could not come soon enough. He needed his suspicions confirmed or repudiated, and quickly. He knew that suspicions can all too easily lead to a state of paranoia.

* * *

Wilson had been pacing about the drawing room, anticipating Parkes' arrival, for the best part of ten minutes. As instructed, a text buzzed its way onto Wilson's mobile and he headed straight to the door to let his colleague in.

"Sorry, it's taken me a little longer than I thought it would," said Parkes in hushed tones.

"Come in. This way." Wilson headed off towards the drawing room with Parkes in close pursuit. Once inside the room, door shut, Wilson indicated that they should both take a seat. Parkes waited for his host to sit down on the sofa and then, to Wilson's surprise, promptly sat down immediately alongside him.

Parkes started to remove a lap-top from his rucksack.

"You've got something for me?" enquired Wilson.

Parkes said nothing, glancing at Wilson before eventually nodding.

"I think so."

"You think so?"

Parkes rested the laptop on his thighs. "I think so. I can't be certain of what I'm going to suggest but I do think there's a shit load of evidence that points to two people who are not playing the game you think they are."

"Show me," insisted Wilson, becoming ever more impatient about the delay he'd encountered already.

Calling up the first report, Parkes pointed to the diaries of Welling and Standing and highlighted their movements. A page existed for each of the last eight weeks.

"I went back eight weeks for the obvious reason that it was from that moment that we assumed things may well have to change. Now, look." Parkes showed Wilson the first report. "Nothing there, right? Nothing obvious at all." he confirmed.

"Nothing obvious," responded Wilson.

The second report showed texts and the third, calls. Each was again historically focussed on the previous eight weeks just like the first. After each one had been scanned and reviewed, Parkes would confirm that nothing obvious appeared to be linking either party together, other than when their roles overlapped on official business.

"Right... now look," said Parkes, bringing up a combined, fully overlapping report in respect of their diaries some in colour coded blocks.

Wilson looked at the report, taking his time to examine every component of what was being presented to him.

"I don't see anything," he said to Parkes.

"Now this one," came the reply. Once again, Parkes opened the combined and overlapping report which showed the times and dates of texts. Wilson again reviewed carefully all the data that was being presented. He shook his head, once again failing to understand what Parkes was getting at.

"Now, this one," was the further instruction. This time it was calls. Once again, Wilson examined the report but failed to spot anything unusual.

"So, nothing, right?" suggested Parkes.

"Not that I can see. This means all is okay?" asked Wilson.

"Not exactly," said Parkes. "There's something here but this is the bit that is circumstantial... but it's one heck of a circumstance, boss."

"Okay, show me." Wilson wasn't prepared to wait any longer.

"Okay, we're getting there. Now, look at this one," said Parkes, in the slow deliberate tones of a man who knew he was about to reveal a secret.

The chart he had opened on his wide screen laptop was a consolidated report including both sets of diaries along with the records, by timeline, of every text sent and call made, including duration and location.

"It still looks innocuous doesn't it," asserted Parkes.

"Parkesy, this is not pass the bloody parcel. I don't need you to unwrap any more layers for me. I just want you to show me what you think you've found." Wilson's impatience was understandable.

"On the face of it, there's nothing there to see. That's because we're looking at what's there. What if we look at what's not there? When I block everything out by colour, red for her, green for him, and then run everything again into one reporting process, we get a number of gaps. We also get the answer."

"And?" Wilson was beginning to sense that the reveal might well have been worth the wait.

"Now look."

As the full consolidated, colour coded chart for each of the last eight weeks was opened up onto the screen, there were regular lines of white space which ran across both sets of information, and, in respect of each day, they appeared in exactly the same place and lasted for almost exactly the same amount of time.

"Fuck," whispered Wilson, immediately coming to the same conclusion that Parkes had.

"There are forty-nine white bars that run across these charts," continued Parkes, "Each of which is on a different day, and each of which, is at exactly the same time give or take a minute or so. Either side of those white bars, both Standing and Welling are communicating externally with all the people you'd expect them to be communicating with."

"What were they doing? Do we know?" asked Wilson.

"That's the problem, we can't say for certain… but… look at this."

Parkes opened another report and started to explain to Wilson what he was looking at. "This is a report of all mobile calls made from within fifty metres of the location in which they were both situated when they made their last call immediately prior to, and after, these white time spaces. Of those forty-nine occasions, four numbers crop up regularly, the same two communicating with each other on sixteen occasions and the other two, thirty-three times. The first two numbers are never ever used at the same time as the second two and, after sixteen uses of the first two, we never see those two numbers again. It's only the second two."

"You're saying they were communicating with each other using these other phones, and not their own?"

"I'm speculating that that's the case. But it's a big bloody coincidence isn't it? Our problem is we can't use existing surveillance systems to retrieve most of the content, and none of these numbers had been previously entered into the systems. It's clever boss, clever."

Wilson nodded in agreement. "It is, it is. Damn."

"Until, of course, you then look at this." Parkes had held back the final reveal until the end and it truly was a superb piece of detective work and the deployment of surveillance expertise and knowledge.

Up on his screen popped the location which had been recorded each time either Standing or Welling had made a call on their usual phone numbers.

Wilson looked at the screen and then back to Parkes. This was an incredible piece of work. Both Standing and Welling were within a matter of a hundred metres of each other on every occasion that the different numbers were being used but where the white spaces existed.

"In other words," said Wilson, "either they were on those phones, or they were physically meeting one another at those times?"

"Exactly... exactly."

Wilson was intrigued. "There's no way this is a co-incidence. Fuck. We need to get a tap on those second two numbers Parkesy, and right away."

"Already done. Sorted that about a couple of hours ago once my suspicions were aroused. And you'll love this. This, for me, moves it from circumstantial to bloody certain."

"What else do you have?" pressed Wilson.

"Standing wasn't shopping earlier. She was meeting Welling. They were both within 100 metres of each other when they used their own mobiles last. Then, neither mobile was used for over an hour. I called Welling and he didn't reply. He still hasn't replied. I think she dumped the tail. I think Welling somehow found out that she was being tailed and he told her she'd been tailed for the last few days."

Wilson rose to his feet and took a few steps around the room.

"I had some suspicions earlier when I noticed that Welling and Standing had been at several meetings together over the last few months but other than looking a bit odd, it was nothing more than a hunch... what I don't understand is, what are they doing and who's fucking side is Marie Standing really on? It doesn't look like it's ours."

"It has to be the PM's. There is no other logical explanation."

"Fucking politicians. Spies and actors," muttered Wilson.

"Say again?"

"Welling and Standing. Right under my fucking nose. She's

played an absolute blinder. No wonder the PM has avoided certain issues over the last few weeks. He's bloody known that there might be trouble and even what it might be. Wolstenholme is an utter twat. I hope to God he hasn't shared too much across that bloody pillow."

"What do you want me to do now?" enquired Parkes.

Wilson breathed in deeply. "Leave Welling and Standing to me. You get clarity on the comms with Christopher and the boys ahead of tomorrow. I want to know exactly who is supposed to be communicating with who, and, what contacts Welling has sorted out inside the group. We know about Paul, but we need to be sure there are no others. We're going to have to sort out who is going to communicate with who, and when, given this fucking news. I'll think about this further and see if there's a better way to finesse it all. If there isn't, we're going to need a shitload more men to tidy this up come Monday. Thank God I've been careful with that bastard Welling."

Parkes stood up and turned to go.

"Is there anything else?"

"There will be, Parkesy. Tomorrow for sure."

Both men made their way to the front door of the house and Wilson shook the hand of his colleague vigorously. "Bloody excellent work, excellent."

"Thank you. I'll be back to you tomorrow once I've got more clarity on what you've asked for."

As Wilson closed the front door to his home, he knew he had a long night of thinking ahead of him. This was a plan that was starting to fray at the edges. However, one decision had already been taken. As soon as he got to the drawing room, he sent a text: "thirty minutes usual place. confirm" He waited less than two minutes for the response: "confirmed."

Wilson retrieved a small file from a locked drawer in his desk, quickly checked its contents and made his way out of the drawing room and towards the front door. He lifted a small jacket from one of the coat hooks by the entrance door, opened it and made his way out of the house, quietly shutting the door behind him.

Right now, time was against him and the encounter he was shortly to have was now necessary, whatever time of day or night it might be.

CHAPTER 33

It was a dull, overcast and wet Sunday morning. The Prime Minister had risen early and was already working through his papers ahead of the meeting scheduled later that morning with Marie Standing, Edward Strong and Adam Taylor.

Just after 8:00am the Prime Minister's breakfast arrived on a tray, as requested. "Ah, thank you. That looks great."

Lifting the plate from the tray and placing it on his knees, the Prime Minister began to prod at the eggs, slicing portions from the toast and using it to scoop up some of the scrambled eggs to eat. It was hard going, and he struggled to generate the appetite required to finish it off. He scraped what was left to the side and moved on to the bowl of fruit, which he also struggled with. Eddington rose from his seat and walked over to the window. Chequers was one of his favourite places and apart from the scale and historic charm of the place, the gardens were a real treat and he'd often take the opportunity, particularly whilst staying there during the summer months, to spend as much time as possible outside in the garden.

A ray of sunlight pierced the clouds overhead and shone directly through the window where he was standing. It added a further sense of wonder to the space around him and he felt the warmth rain down on his face.

As his eyes squinted in the bright sunlight, he pondered the day ahead and, for the first time, felt vulnerable to circumstances and people over which, and whom, he worried he had no control.

* * *

Josh had checked his watch several times in the last thirty minutes. He hadn't heard a sound emanating from Becky's room since he'd woken up. He decided to wait for her to make contact in case she was still getting some of the sleep he knew she needed.

Becky had also been awake for a couple of hours and was lying on her bed, deep in thought and increasingly worried about the situation she found herself in. She had decided not to wake Josh, leaving him to make the first contact. He needed his sleep, she thought, especially today.

The noisy creaking of the stairs and the voices that were accompanying the footsteps gave due warning to both Josh and Becky that they were about to have their present silence interrupted.

Sure enough, seconds later, first a key in Becky's door and, almost immediately afterwards, the same repeated action in Josh's.

"No Ryan or Paul this morning then?" Josh enquired.

"Obviously not," came the reply. Josh recognised the man from the time he'd spent in Scotland, but he was clearly not going to get any more information out of him.

"I'm working with them. Will they be here later?"

The man was already making his way out of the room and had almost pulled the door closed behind him before suddenly pausing, opening the door a little and popping his head around it to look in Josh's direction.

"No idea. Someone will pick up your tray in a while."

The man wasn't interested in any more conversation and closed the door firmly, locking it once again. No Paul and no Ryan. Where were they, but more particularly, where was Paul? Things were not going to stand a chance without him being around.

Josh stooped by the skirting board and tapped out "Hi" to Becky. Almost immediately, back came the same response and the two chatted more.

Josh was relieved that Becky seemed in reasonable spirits. He remained anxious about how she would react when things got chaotic and more threatening but was increasingly reassured that she appeared calm and focussed enough to do what he told her when it all kicked off.

Becky's security and protection had been absorbing a good deal of Josh's time, and, as he became increasingly worried that they might be separated at some point during the day, he homed in on the necessary protection which she might have to provide for herself.

He tapped out a question he believed would start getting her to think about things she could do for herself.

"Things in room to block door."

She would look again at each item of furniture in a different light.

"Bed. Wardrobe"

Becky knew Josh well enough to know that this wasn't just reassurance. She began to realise that protecting herself whilst the situation developed might prove to be essential if Josh wasn't around for any reason.

Josh sat back, leaning against the wall by his bed. He knew it wasn't ideal, but it would buy her some time.

* * *

Wilson was sitting in the same place he'd occupied the previous evening. The curtains were still drawn, and all the lights remained on. He'd returned to the house after midnight and was relieved to find his wife asleep when he eventually climbed delicately into bed, making his best endeavours not to wake her. Struggling to get anything other than intermittent sleep, he'd got up and was anxiously awaiting the first text, or call, of the day.

The door swung open, and Wilson's wife entered.

"Goodness David, it's daylight outside." She swept in and

opened the curtains, switched off the lights and confirmed breakfast would be on its way. As ever, she was organised, much in charge of domestic affairs and ran the household when it came to almost all their family arrangements.

"Thanks. I'd been working. Forgot the time."

"What time did you eventually come up?"

"I had to finish off a few things so it would have been about 1:00am. I didn't want to wake you."

"Damn good that you didn't. Back with breakfast shortly. And please remember you're out with the kids this afternoon."

He'd forgotten, of course. Whether he'd be able to fulfil today's family expectations was another matter.

Wilson rose to his feet and walked across to the window. A little dull and cloudy but there was a promise in the forecast of better weather to come later in the day.

His mobile pinged. A message. He retrieved it immediately.

"all set"

He looked at those two words for a long time. Deleting the message, he sat back down and allowed the sofa cushions to fully envelop him. The path on which he was set had no return option.

* * *

At Chequers, Eddington had been practising his address, pausing to make notes and re-write sections and sentences as he'd proceeded. There was no chance of a full run through, so he decided to wait until his colleagues had arrived and started making preparations ahead of that.

However, before they were to begin their meeting, he had one call to make.

The phone numbers used had changed so often recently that he had written down each one, every time it had changed, so as not to get confused.

"Good morning."

"Good morning, Prime Minister," replied Welling.

"I'm with Marie, Edward and Adam shortly, as you know. I'm keen to get an update on preparations for Monday. Are we ready?"

Welling confirmed that he had spoken with Marie Standing the previous evening and that she was intending to have a further call with Wolstenholme later today to finally get him to commit. At that point they'll have all they needed and could move on him. Second, the Police were prepped and ready and would be waiting for his call once everyone from the "Scottish Squad" was in place and could be surrounded and tackled. The actual locations and targets hadn't been shared with the Police yet, nor timings at this point, so no leaks could happen, but they would be all set and in position and would move immediately in receipt of his instruction on Monday. Thirdly, he was still working on Wilson and had asked a colleague earlier that morning to check his records, to see if there was anything obvious, which, so far, hadn't thrown anything up, in spite of their obvious suspicions and everything else they believed and knew.

Finally, he believed that all the mobiles would be issued to the guys in the "Scottish Squad" later that morning and, as a consequence, those working on the inside would have their instructions by the end of the day.

It was a comprehensive report and Eddington felt much more confident about the outcome. It remained concerning that parts of the puzzle had been kept from some sections of those involved but until the depth of the threat had been fully established, and how many others, at all levels, might be involved, it was felt to be a necessary and wise precaution.

It was a few minutes before 10:00am and Eddington decided to greet his guests personally at the door. He made his way out of the room and towards the entrance. They won't be long now, he thought.

* * *

Wilson hadn't expected the call he had just had from Parkes. After yesterday evening's revelations, he realised immediately that he was now directly in the line of sight and was now quite probably being targeted by other agents and officers as one of those potentially involved in the plot.

Fortunately for him, Parkes's loyalty to Wilson, as well as his political views, had successfully trumped duty and loyalty to the state machine.

With Welling having asked Parkes to check over Wilson's communication records, there was now valuable time during which a revised plan could be put into operation. Parkes would stall, Wilson would act.

"My little friend is not so clever... I'm going to nail the bastard," thought Wilson.

With twenty-four hours still to go, Wilson thought that there was ample time to construct the necessary changes to deliver success. Frustrating and disruptive though these latter interventions might be, their order, as well as the particular people involved, made for an obvious set of responses; responses which were now underway.

CHAPTER 34

Edward Strong and Adam Taylor both arrived within a few moments of each other and were greeted by Eddington just outside the front door.

Eddington had suggested that they wait outside for Marie Standing to arrive and enjoy the fresh air before they embark on their marathon session inside the building. With the weather so changeable, everyone agreed that it was a good suggestion, particularly as the latest shower had stopped and a break in the clouds had allowed the sun to temporarily shine down upon them.

"How have you got on with your speech Tony," asked Taylor.

"It's pretty much there," came the reply, "though I've not entirely finished it. We can work through the last few amends later if that's okay with you both?"

"Unlike Marie to be late," interjected Edward Strong.

"Yeah, though I did say "around" ten," came Eddington's reply. He checked his watch. It was now 10:16am.

All three men chatted for a few more minutes and then decided to go in to start the meeting. They had a lot to get through and Strong suggested that Marie could catch up when she eventually arrived. Eddington signalled that they should follow him to the large drawing room which is where they'd be based for the day.

Small talk done and dusted, coffee and tea poured, the three men started to review their approach for Monday's announcement and work through the various members of the Government who were likely to fall into line and those who were less likely to do so. All were certain, however, that the critical moment would be the cabinet meeting late on Monday morning.

About ten minutes in there was a knock at the door, which was opened almost immediately.

"Prime Minister," said the aide, "We've had a call from Marie Standing. She's stuck in a queue which is only just moving. She'll be here about 11:00am. She sends her apologies, but it was unavoidable."

"Thank you, Ben," Eddington replied.

After Ben had departed and closed the door behind him, Edward Strong made a quip about Marie being really irritated that she'd not arrived to hear the gossip. All three smiled and concurred. Adam Taylor, as he was often known to do, once again reminded his colleagues about Marie's incredible role in keeping a close eye on Wolstenholme–something they all acknowledged had been particularly critical throughout the last year.

"So, given the fact that this is going to depend on cabinet and assuming they do get behind the announcement, my statement to the House probably needs to be nailed and maybe we work back from that?" asked Eddington, clearly keen to make sure this most critical part of the process was well thought through and agreed.

"Agreed. Look, we're all pretty confident about cabinet, so let's move to the set piece," said Strong.

Though Taylor nodded in agreement, he also wanted to know whether they'd be getting an update about what Wolstenholme was doing and whether any further evidence had emerged over the last few days which would enable the appropriate authorities to act.

"We'll get to that Adam. Dave Welling is joining us after lunch. I'm hoping by then we'll have at least some clarity on what he's planning, beyond what we already know and what we suspect. Marie will also have some input for sure by then."

Working through the speech, all three men debated almost every paragraph, searching for the key words and phrases which would turn what was already a good statement, into a statesmanlike, barnstorming, and authoritative performance.

As they all began their assessment of page six, the door opened and in walked Marie Standing. "I'm so sorry gentlemen, the traffic was simply horrendous."

"You'll want a cuppa, Marie," said Eddington, "I'll get a fresh pot."

"No, no. I'll go. You carry on and I'll catch up." With that she disappeared from the room to seek out a member of the housekeeping team.

"I think she's going to be on form today," whispered Taylor, gaining affirmative nods from both of the other men present.

"Let's wait for Marie before we start again. She'll only be a few moments, and a fresh coffee would be good too," said Strong.

Seconds later, Marie returned. "All on its way," she confirmed. "Now boys, how far have we got?"

Eddington quickly recapped. Late on Monday morning, he was planning to take the cabinet through the plans to completely restore full democratic accountability to the country within three months, announce the date for a General Election and stand down much of the intelligence apparatus and surveillance structures that had blossomed over the last three to five years.

All of the security and law and order legislation that had been carried through in recent years would be repealed. Every new piece of legislation that would be introduced subsequently that related to security, and additional limitations on the activity of British citizens, would have to undergo additional scrutiny and would also carry an automatic sunset clause, limiting the length of time it could stay in place without being presented to Parliament for extension.

Additionally, all previously approved immigration controls, including the recently introduced voluntary repatriation initiative, would be replaced by a simple target number and repatriations would be halted with immediate effect. It was the most radical change of direction seen in modern times and, he knew, would inevitably split the League.

Though Eddington was anticipating that many on the hard right of his party might vehemently oppose these changes, he was also hoping that the more radical elements of The League–primarily those associated with Wolstenholme–would not resort to any campaigns of civil disobedience or illegal activity.

In spite of the intentions of his former friend and one time loyalist, Lord Ardoon, Eddington believed he could hold things together and isolate the minority of opponents in The League to a small rump. He was determined to hold as much of his party together as possible.

Eddington also confirmed that he was to see the new Leader of the Opposition a few hours before his statement, in an attempt to bring him and the official opposition on board. He doubted they'd be a problem and was increasingly confident of success given they'd been calling for such a restoration for many months.

Welling, who would be with them in a few hours' time, would update them on the terrorist attack being planned for Monday, though it had proved difficult to get sufficient irrefutable evidence about Wolstenholme's involvement at this stage. Though he was known to be completely sympathetic with the attack, and had held various conversations about it, as yet he'd been careful enough not to say or do anything which would conclusively incriminate him.

The people Lord Ardoon had assembled were on the move and had relocated to the South East. The Police were on standby to intercept them on Monday and–given existing suspicions about Wilson–Welling was now co-ordinating that directly with them. More was expected on Wilson over the coming twenty-four hours.

It was also understood that re-configured mobiles were to be issued to everyone in Ardoon's group later that morning, if it hadn't already happened. All of them had been sourced illegally but Welling had intercepted them via another undercover operative within the supplier's organisation and had arranged for two of them to be fitted with additional communications capacity so that the undercover guys could communicate directly with Welling without compromising their status. Welling had also kept this knowledge back from Wilson in case the recent growing suspicions about him were well founded.

Eddington was confident that everything was in hand to facilitate the arrest of everyone involved in the plot on Monday, and deal with the inevitable aftermath as well.

"The one risky element of this, is that, ideally, we need the plotting group to actually travel to their location and take up position in order for the police to grab them all at once. "In the act," so to speak," he concluded. "Welling will confirm how all that is supposed to work later. Must admit, it strikes me as a bit risky but I'm told it'll be far better if we catch them all in situ so there can be no doubts as to why they are there. If there is any resistance, they can all be dealt with as necessary in relatively open, isolated countryside."

"Seems everything is under control Tony," said Taylor.

"I think so… Marie, if there is anything from you,perhaps it's better to wait until Dave Welling is here?"

"Sure, makes sense," replied Standing.

"We should probably get back to the speech, Tony," suggested Strong.

"Yes," replied Eddington. "it's important we get the balance of this right," and, looking at his watch and noting that it was already 11:45, added, "Time is ticking along."

CHAPTER 35

As Josh again peered through the window from his bedroom, he watched the various small groups of assembled men chatting and rehearsing. His gaze was suddenly distracted by the arrival of a light-green coloured vehicle, which pulled up alongside the open fronted barn and parked.

Two men exited the vehicle, one heading straight across to CM, the other circling around the back of the car, opening the boot and retrieving a medium sized box. After closing the boot lid, the second man made his way to where his colleague and CM were standing and lifted the lid of the box a little, as if to show CM that, whatever he'd been expecting, had, arrived.

CM signalled to them that they should all enter the main house and, after a few seconds, all three had disappeared.

About forty minutes later, both men re-emerged, without CM, and headed over to their vehicle, stopping to exchange a few comments with one of the small teams of men closest to them, as they made their way. Once their conversation had concluded, they got into the vehicle and drove off. Josh made a mental note of their descriptions, the make and model of the car and most of the registration number; unsure about whether it contained a five, or an eight.

Barely five minutes later, CM walked out of the house and shouted to everyone to come inside for a briefing.

As everyone made their way into the building, Josh watched

Paul and Ryan appear from behind the open-ended barn and jog over to catch up with the rest of the team.

"Come on you two!" snapped Fitz, allowing them to pass him on the path to the house and following them into the property. *He never seems to be off duty*, thought Josh.

Beginning to wonder what might be happening, Josh recalled that Paul had told him that they were all scheduled to get their mobiles today and therefore assumed that the guys who had arrived with the box may well have just delivered them.

Josh could just hear the muffled, but distinct, tones of Fitz urging them all to crowd inside the room for their briefing. It was clearly fortuitous for Josh that it was both a relatively large group of people, and, also, that Fitz was to do the briefing. Both these things, he thought, would result in him being able to hear enough to get an understanding of what was going on.

It was, as he'd suspected, all about the mobiles. Each mobile was allocated to a specific person and, once operational–from the start of the mission itself, and for a maximum period of two hours at that point–each would require a personalised four-digit passcode to be inserted every twenty minutes, or the phone would lock its operator out and could not be used. Each device was only able to communicate two ways; between them and Fitz. No other contact could be made.

Additionally, all location tracking had been removed.

Fitz was advising them to key in the code as frequently as they wished both immediately ahead of the mission, as well as afterwards. "Don't get locked out," he repeated three times.

Each mobile was in an individual box with their name on it, inside of which, was the phone itself, a charger and a piece of paper, upon which was typed the four digit code unique to that particular phone. It seemed like the meeting was about to break up, until the loud, crisp tones of Fitz brought the meeting to a quieter state.

"And don't forget to charge the fucking things tonight. And again, first thing tomorrow… fully charged mobiles. Right?"

"Right!" came the unanimous response.

Josh knew that he wasn't going to get a phone, but he considered that it mattered not, as long as he could get hold of one and the code that went with it. Paul would have one that there may be an opportunity to use at some point. Josh had convinced himself that he would be able to reconfigure the mobile phone to facilitate communication with the authorities and he was determined to try as soon as the opportunity presented itself. He made his way to the wall which separated him from Becky and tapped out a few more reassuring messages of support and encouragement. He also included some information about what he'd learned regarding the mobiles, as well as Monday being the day, and reaffirmed his view that it was all useful and encouraging from their perspective.

Each response from his wife was short but positive. Josh remained concerned about her overall emotional state but continued to convince himself that she was doing better than she might, given the circumstances.

* * *

As the men dispersed, CM put his own mobile to his ear and waited for the call to be answered.

"It's me," he said.

He quietly briefed the recipient of the call, fully updating him on the state of play and the arrival and distribution of the phones.

In response to one question of obvious interest to them both, CM was particularly reassuring.

"I think we'll know pretty quickly what they'll try and get up to. And then what we'll need to do about it... But first, we'll need them both to be alone with each other, with the opportunity to chat. Maybe. Try something. Either way, his phone is tracked and bugged, so there's no chance we won't know immediately."

The call terminated shortly afterwards, and CM looked slowly around the room trying to spot anything that might have been left by anyone in the group. With nothing in sight, he exited and headed for the kitchen.

At the conclusion of the briefing, unlike most of the team, Paul had headed straight for the nearest socket and had immediately started to charge his device.

Backtracking his steps, having noticed that Paul hadn't exited the building with him, Ryan found his colleague in the utility room, sat on the only chair to the side of the washing machine.

"Bloody hell Paul, you're quick off the mark. Doesn't bloody work until tomorrow, mate."

"Yeah, I know, but you know what it's like. Everyone will wait until tomorrow and then there won't be enough charging points and then there'll be a fucking panic. I'm not taking that risk. You should do the same after me, mate. I'll charge it for you if you want?"

"Nah, I'll do it. Good call though. I'll find another socket and charge it up. I'll just top it up tomorrow morning."

Paul had determined to try and activate his mobile as soon as possible and try and make contact with his department and bosses if at all possible.

* * *

Ardoon was pleased to hear the update from CM but knew that his influence and direct control over events had now passed to those further south, not least his trusted lieutenant, Christopher.

He turned his mind to his own position and his exit plan were everything to go wrong. With so many moving parts and all too many duplicitous individuals involved, he had already determined that he needed to make his own private arrangements to disappear for a few days pending the outcome of Monday's events.

He exited via the main entrance to his home accompanied by two men, one carrying two suitcases and the other a large cardboard box. He crossed the grass area to the side of the property and headed towards the helicopter, which was standing ready for take-off.

All three men climbed aboard as the slowly rotating blades began to gather pace, until, eventually, the noise level rose considerably, the helicopter itself straining and vibrating slightly as it prepared to lift itself into the sky.

As it powered itself upwards, Ardoon looked back at his home, as well as the exercise area that had played such an important part in the training of the team and the wider preparations for the mission itself.

As the helicopter gained height and speed, it left his estate behind him and Ardoon considered that, whilst he wasn't a particularly heavy gambler, he knew that he'd rolled the dice and now he had twenty-four hours to wait and see if he'd made a wise, or foolish, bet.

CHAPTER 36

With the Prime Minister's speech all but finalised, the working lunch swiftly devoured and Welling's arrival due within the hour, the quartet of politicians moved on to discuss the more intricate patchwork of conversations and announcements that would need to be finessed by Monday.

A few minutes after 2:00pm, there was a knock at the door and Eddington was advised that Dave Welling had arrived.

"Show him straight through, please," said Eddington.

As he entered the room, all the politicians present stood and shook his hand, welcoming him to the meeting. Welling knew that this was likely to be the most important meeting of his career and he'd come well prepared and as fully briefed as it was possible to be.

After arranging for the gathering to have a fresh round of teas and coffees brought in, small talk quickly ceasing after they were delivered, Eddington invited Welling to bring everyone up to date with the situation as far as he could.

The briefing was thorough and comprehensive. Welling confirmed that the location at which the "terrorist group" was presently based was not yet known, but would be established later today. The police would be ready to act at any time from midnight tonight. The decision about whether to move earlier than Monday morning would be made if, or when, the location had been confirmed. In any event, a full briefing would be given to the police task force early on Monday morning and they would be waiting for instructions from Welling to move in and initiate the arrest of all those involved.

As had been suspected for a few weeks now, it was almost certain that the target was Eddington, and the assault was to take place a few miles from Chequers. Welling confirmed that he would advise Eddington's team when it was clear and safe to leave Chequers once everyone had been apprehended and the route was safe.

Importantly, Welling confirmed that all the mobile telephones for the terrorist group had now been delivered and there were two that had been intercepted at source and had been fitted with external communications capability. The phones had all been sourced through a French criminal group which had been infiltrated about six months ago, quite co-incidentally, to deal with another matter relating to their activities in the UK.

Fortunately, because all the mobile phones to be used by the terrorist team had been allocated unique identification codes, the two phones alloted to each of the undercover agents had been identified and reconfigured.

Welling confirmed that he had made contact with the two undercover agents. At this stage, he believed that neither of the operatives knew who the other was. This wasn't only for their own protection but also gave Welling a little more time to be certain that both were what he thought they were, and not, potentially, themselves double agents.

As the two under-cover operatives had been appointed–one by he and David Wilson, and one by Welling alone–certainty was needed that both were on side. He had signed off his texts with the initials DW, so that they would both assume it was their respective handler that was in contact with them. "It'll help at this stage for there to be a little confusion as to which DW they are dealing with," Welling confidently asserted.

Additionally, it meant that if either of them were in fact double agents, he'd soon discover that as a result of their responses and could then take appropriate action. He expected to know the reality of this situation during the evening. All eventualities had been covered.

Welling remained confident that Wilson himself would assume his messages were getting through for some hours to come, as they were being re-directed to two dummy phones, instead of those of the two undercover agents. Even if it were proven that Wilson was working directly with the terrorist group, which seemed likely, it now wouldn't matter, because he wouldn't be communicating with the agents directly in any case.

He also explained, that after the unexpected but fortuitous discovery by a neighbour of the body of an ex CPU operative who had clearly been murdered, it had been possible to cross check previous relationships and communications and they had now established the name of the former CPU operative who would be de-activating the sleeve during the attack. His wife had also disappeared and there was a suspicion that she was being held as leverage. "Paul Somerson has subsequently confirmed these suspicions."

He confirmed that it was likely that Josh was only aware of Paul Somerson being undercover at present. And, whilst there was a high degree of confidence that Josh would not decommission the sleeve in any event, even were he to be confronted with that scenario, Somerson would be there to prevent such a situation arising.

"And what are the chances of all our people and Josh's wife getting out alive?" enquired Eddington.

"It's difficult," replied Welling, "If all goes well, they should be ok."

It was not the reassuring answer Eddington was seeking but he recognised it was all he could expect, given the circumstances.

He again confirmed that there remained difficulties concerning proof of Wilson's direct involvement, as it wasn't clear, from the present information, whether or not he was actively engaged in the plot or merely a passive, but supportive, bystander. Though he certainly knew something was going on and was known to have had conversations with some of those involved, getting the concrete proof was essential and the false communication trail now established would provide such evidence.

Welling informed them that he had asked the best analyst and operative that the department had to try and establish these contacts and prove involvement. The man he had asked to start working on that, and pulling everything together, was an excellent guy by the name of Parkes, though, interestingly, he had yet to uncover anything material thus far which did suggest Wilson's involvement was not as key as was at first thought.

In the meantime, as a precaution, Wilson had been excluded from the communication loop–though he would still believe himself to be directing events, as the small number of the substitute contacts concerned had been ordered to communicate as if he were. It was only on Monday morning itself that things might get sticky, as he would be ordering Wilson to remain at home and placed under house arrest pending further investigations.

He went on to confirm that he would be reporting to Wilson later that evening to re-assure him that everything was still on track and all the arrangements for Monday were in hand. This was likely to provide further proof that all was fine from Wilson's perspective.

"And Wolstenholme?" enquired Eddington.

"He's clearly close to the operation but we've yet to get him to actually say so, or commit in a way that is obviously incriminating," responded Welling.

Marie Standing expressed the view that he was "up to his neck in it." She acknowledged that even though he clearly wanted to topple Eddington, and made no secret of that when they were together, he'd never actually proposed a violent solution nor once said to her that violence was acceptable as a means to take power.

"All that said," she insisted, "He's a devious, prize shit and, when this is over, we'll discover that his hands are all over the bloody thing."

Eddington nodded, "You may be right but until we have the cast iron evidence of his direct involvement, we can't go after him."

Welling concluded his report and asked if there were any more questions. Eddington looked around and the shaking heads confirmed that Welling had done his job, and all was both accepted and noted.

"So," recapped Eddington, "we continue with the political strategy and ensure readiness by tomorrow lunchtime. You," he nodded towards Welling, "will nail all these other areas and we await your confirmation tomorrow morning before we actually move."

"Exactly," Welling replied.

With that, Eddington rose to his feet, quickly followed by everyone else, and thanked Welling for his time, service, and support. He turned to his comrades.

"Well, we're about as ready as we can be."

* * *

Strong and Eddington had accompanied both Standing and Taylor to their cars after their meeting had finished.

"Isn't it lovely today?" said Standing looking up at the sky.

"It is," replied Eddington. "Drive safe and take care."

Marie Standing opened the car door and threw her small document case onto the front passenger seat before climbing into the vehicle, pulling the door shut behind her and immediately winding the window down to allow some fresh air to run through the car as she drove off.

"Bye boys. See you tomorrow."

Eddington and Strong waved her off before turning towards Taylor who had spoken briefly to his two close arm protection officers before climbing into the back of his Range Rover.

"I'll see you tomorrow Tony," he said, before one of his security officers closed the door and the car made its way out of the driveway, heading for home.

Strong and Eddington looked at each other for a few seconds. It was a surreal moment for them both.

"It's almost like being in a bloody film, isn't it?" said Strong.

Eddington nodded his agreement, "It is, it is."

Making their way back into the front entrance of the manor house, Eddington continued with the analogy.

"Let's hope we can manage to do all this in one take tomorrow, Edward."

CHAPTER 37

Wilson had spent most of the morning at home. It was mid-afternoon when he'd responded to a few messages from the two undercover agents and received short briefings from Police and Security chiefs. He'd been very careful not to communicate anything too detailed or specific. He was now awaiting the imminent arrival of Parkes.

Wilson had become particularly anxious after Parkes had informed him earlier that he'd received instructions from Welling to review all of Wilson's diary movements, calls and texts. Parkes had made it clear to Wilson not to communicate with Welling further until he had reviewed more information and investigated further.

Upon hearing the doorbell, he was out of his seat in double quick time, hurrying across the hall to open the front door and let his colleague in. He'd sent the family out for the entire day and both men were quite alone in the house.

"Well?" Wilson was impatient and anxious.

"So, earlier this afternoon, you've spoken with George Robbins, Clive Astle, Peter Ferris, and Leonard Sindall, each of them reporting on the final arrangements for tomorrow. Right?"

"I have, yes," replied Wilson, a frown appearing across his face.

"Astle asked you to remain available at home all day today as further reports would be coming in and everyone would need to know where you were. Right?"

"Right," Wilson replied.

"You've also received, and responded to, texts from the two agents in the field. Right?"

"Yes," replied Wilson, once again confirming what Parkes was saying to him.

"No," responded Parkes, "the messages you've received from the operatives are actually from two of Welling's men and sent from two phones which you believe to be those of our two guys within the team. They're not. They're evidence gathering boss. Your texts are being tracked, or they were. I've cleaned it all and re-directed them and now you are texting my men, Jones and Sigston, who are both playing a blinder right now. And don't worry, they are totally with us, and every reply re-confirms your actions as being okay and beyond reproach. So, text away as if you are running the operation in the way that everyone would expect to read about your actions after the event. You are totally covered."

"Jesus," exclaimed Wilson, a cold shiver running down his spine. "And?"

"All of the reports you've received, including that from Astle, are bollocks. All are now reporting to Welling except for Ferris and Sindall who are not yet involved. Robbins and Astle are also part of the Welling evidence gathering team. Astle is taking charge of the police operation personally tomorrow and Robbins is co-ordinating from HQ and directly reporting to Welling."

Wilson felt a cold tingle once again run down the entire length of his spine.

Parkes could see that his boss was clearly anxious and immediately moved to re-assure him that all was far from lost. Everything would still turn their way.

"I've been working this through, and I'm convinced we can still get this delivered."

"Bloody hell. Go on," encouraged Wilson.

"We know that Welling is the key pivot around which this whole operation now revolves. We also know that only Robbins and Astle are aware of Welling's suspicions that you're involved. The PM, Standing, Taylor and Strong are the only politicians with enough info to be a threat. The two inside agents will still believe they are communicating with you, or Welling, so that part hasn't changed. And, frankly, it doesn't matter."

With that, Parkes paused.

"And?" Wilson thought he knew what was coming but wanted to hear it.

"We take out the lot."

"All seven of them. Seven." Wilson spoke quietly and deliberately.

"Boss, The PM and Strong are dead meat anyway because they'll be taken out in the attack. We can arrange accidents for Standing and Taylor and the two cops can get taken out on the day, at some point, during the round-up."

"And Welling?"

"The same. We can do that at any time," came the reply.

"And what about the evidence they've gathered so far? Couldn't that stuff us."

"There is no evidence. I am wiping everything as we go and I've switched the traces and mobile numbers around. They think they'll be tracing your movements and messages but they won't be.. I've pulled the surveillance on you. By the time they realise, it'll make no difference and be too late."

Wilson stood up and walked around the room for a few seconds before looking back towards Parkes.

"Standing and Ardoon are already sorted," he said. "That'll happen later"

"Ardoon? Oh, okay. What, properly sorted? And Standing?"

Wilson nodded. "The others?" enquired Parkes.

"You're right. Let's deal with most of the others on the day and we'll have to take out Taylor tonight after he's left Chequers, or first thing tomorrow and Welling too. I'll deal with that."

The ruthlessness of the conversation wasn't lost on Parkes. It was why he served his boss so faithfully.

"Parkesy," continued Wilson, "you need to work your magic and clear every fucking word from any trace or surveillance operation in place. Be certain there is nothing at all left anywhere. What I need you to do then, is to set up Welling as the traitor and build a sufficient trail to lead us right to him after this is over tomorrow. The bastard may be dead, but we need him to take the fall."

"okay." Parkes nodded and stood up.

"I think I'd better make a start. We've not got much time. Do you want me to take care of anything people-wise?"

Wilson was appreciative that his colleague was prepared to get his hands bloody, but he was convinced that the talents he possessed were better deployed elsewhere.

"No, nothing. I'll take care of all that. But keep me up to date with what Welling is saying to the undercover guys. I'll need to know that when the time comes so the messages feel like they're continuing from the same person."

Parkes nodded, shook is boss's hand and both men left the room and headed towards the front door.

"We can still pull this off," asserted Parkes.

"I believe we can," came the response. "In fact, with so many casualties, even the public will want action taken. We just need to finesse this right. Off you go. And let me know how you get on."

"Will do."

With that, Parkes left the house and headed off to take all the action he could whilst there was still time to do so.

Wilson knew that both Standing, and Taylor were to leave Chequers later today and Eddington would travel into London, as planned, the following morning with Edward Strong, who he had invited to stay the night.

In the certain knowledge that his phone communications were now completely safe from interception, just like the previous evening, Wilson sent a text to the number he always contacted when he needed something "tidied up."

"Thirty minutes – usual place – confirm" read the message.

Minutes later came the confirmation he sought. Straight away, Wilson headed for the front door before pausing and deciding to leave via the back door of the property instead.

* * *

Wilson returned to his house in time to hear the clock in the hallway strike five times. He'd done what needed to be done and now had to resolve one particular matter which he knew he would have to deal with himself.

"Hello darling, how was your day? Not too bad I hope?" Wilsons's wife and children had returned.

"I need to talk to you now, if that's okay? Privately."

"Oh, of course. What's the matter?" she replied.

"Come through to the drawing room."

Both made their way to the drawing room, Wilson closing the door after they had both entered.

"Something has blown up, something really important, and I need to deal with it. There's going to be a lot of coming and going tonight and tomorrow and I need you to take the kids and go and stay with your mum and dad for the next couple of days."

After a few seconds silence, he added; "Please."

She knew that this was unusual but also that he wouldn't have asked if it weren't necessary. Throughout his entire career, Wilson's wife had been a model of support and encouragement and had always accepted that the nature of his job meant that he would, at times, have to be away, cancel things, leave abruptly or even fail to turn up at something. She hadn't only married him but accepted that she had also married his job.

"Okay. Understood. I'll get packed and then we'll leave as soon as I've checked it's all okay with mum and dad."

Wilson took the two paces forward that separated him from his wife and kissed her. "Thank you."

"Are you okay? Is everything going to be alright?" she enquired.

Wilson smiled, "Of course. Don't worry. I just need the house and the space for forty-eight hours."

She smiled in response and left the room to make the necessary preparations.

Once his wife had left, Wilson's smile immediately left his lips. He knew that his home was unlikely ever to have witnessed the activities he was planning later that evening.

CHAPTER 38

Josh and Becky had been cooped up all morning, but had been unexpectedly allowed out of their rooms and taken outside the house for a brief, accompanied, but most welcome, walk.

As they strolled across the small parking area in front of the building and made their way towards the small copse, hand in hand, it was clear to Josh that Becky was under considerable emotional strain.

"This will all be over soon. It's going to be alright."

Becky let go of Josh's hand and wrapped her arm around his waist seeking closer contact and comfort. Josh reciprocated and folded his arm around her shoulder, kissing her on the cheek as he did so.

As they reached the side of the copse, Ryan interrupted the moment. "Around, not in," he said. The two men accompanying Ryan said nothing.

With that, Josh and Becky made a detour and took the small path alongside the trees around the side of the barn.

Josh moved his other hand across Becky's stomach and gently caressed it.

"How's this going?" he asked. "All okay I hope."

Becky looked up at him, tears welling up in her eyes.

Josh moved his arm from around her shoulders and caressed her head, pulling it towards his shoulder as he tilted his own head towards hers.

"Please, don't worry. It'll be okay."

Becky looked up at him once again and shook her head before resting it back onto Josh's shoulder.

"Have you thought through and prepared everything we've chatted about?" he whispered.

Josh had determined to change the subject and get Becky to focus on protecting herself along with more practical matters.

Becky nodded her head, "Yes, I think so."

Josh gave her a reassuring hug, squeezing her tightly once again.

"Right, that's it. Back to the house." Ryan's latest intervention was not welcome and their all too brief time together had been drawn to a close.

Within a few minutes, they were back in their respective bedrooms, locked away with only their Morse Code messages for company.

* * *

An hour or so later, Paul unlocked Josh's door and delivered an afternoon drink.

As he stood inside the room, he swung the door closed and raised his right index finger to his lips to hush any potential response Josh might have decided to deliver.

"I've made contact and I'm awaiting more information and instructions as to what the fuck we need to do," Paul whispered. "We're not on our own anymore though."

Josh was enthused and wanted to press Paul for more information.

"What's happening? Are we going to get support tomorrow?"

Paul again raised a finger to his lips. "More info later. Be ready. Got to go."

"Paul!" Josh was less than pleased at the short conversation and demanded a better response.

"Got to go," responded Paul once again, "but there's another agent other than me. Need to find out who it is."

"What, inside? Here?" Josh pressed for more information again.

Paul nodded and headed out of the room, pulled the door shut behind him and locked it.

Josh was both frustrated and relieved to hear the information. Another undercover agent could be crucial in helping them, but how was contact going to be made and what plan was going to be drawn up?

Josh sat on his bed and relived each moment of the training he'd gone through, straining his mind for clues as to who the second agent might be. As he considered each option, he became more confused and less certain. *It could even be Ryan*, he thought to himself, allowing a gentle smile to cross his lips.

Josh walked over to the bedroom window and looked out across the scene set out in front of him.

It was a beautiful evening, with just a few clouds making their slow and stately way across the skyline. His incarceration for most of the day had made him both impatient and frustrated.

CHAPTER 39

Gaining entry to Standings London flat had been easier than Green had feared it might be. With a shared main entrance door to the building itself, he had bided his time before making his attempt. It didn't take too long.

Fortunately for him, he was assisted by a charming elderly lady, who had helpfully opened the door for him as he struggled with a small step ladder, a few pots of paint and a wooden handheld container with some brushes and a paint roller in it. His white overalls and a cap completed his disguise.

"Thank you, love," he said, "I've tried that bell for the last ten minutes but it's just not working. It's not easy when you have to carry all this lot. Hope you didn't have to come down too many stairs?"

"Oh no. I'm only just along the way there. We do get problems here from time to time with those intercom things," she replied. "It can be most annoying. Which flat are you looking for?"

"Number 17."

"Ah yes, you'll need to go to the first floor. It's about half a dozen along. The lift is just there. Working on a Sunday? You must be a glutton for punishment, young man."

"Ha, yes. Gotta work when it's there. Thank you. And thank you for your help."

The elderly lady made her way down the short flight of stairs on to the pavement leaving him alone inside the main entrance hallway.

Green was one of those men most of his colleagues would prefer not to talk about and someone who politicians would deny existed. He carried out the kind of tasks that his handlers always dreaded going wrong for fear of their activities becoming more public.

He was the perfect man for the job. Average height, average build, average looking, nothing particularly distinguishing. He had a completely neutral accent and an ability to take on the appearance of any occupation with complete ease. The one fundamental difference between him and "Mr Average," was that he was immensely fit and strong and was well trained in the art of killing and murder. He was ruthless, clinical, and emotionless and had never once failed to deliver the results expected of him. It was why Wilson had such a high regard for him and why Wilson had always kept him for his exclusive use. In fact, after seven years exclusively reporting to Wilson, it was unlikely that anyone else in a senior position would recall his existence, let alone know what he looked like.

Green looked up on the board and quickly scanned it for Flat 26. As he'd expected, it was on the second floor and after he'd completed the short journey by lift, he made his way down the hallway towards Standing's flat.

As he walked, he was further encouraged, realising it was right at the end of the corridor. The opportunity to prepare everything, once inside, without any likelihood of interruption, was perfect.

Having put on a pair of gloves, he checked out the door. Two locks and no alarm. He looked up and down the hallway and then, around the immediate area and noticed that, just like downstairs, apart from one camera outside the main entrance, there was no CCTV or other form of security camera in place. A perfect place for him to carry out his duties.

Immediately, he set about picking both locks, occasionally checking along the corridor to make sure no-one was observing what he was doing. No-one appeared and in less than a minute, he was in.

He pushed the door shut behind him, but before doing so, looked at the type and strength of the two locks. He was keen to ensure that he could force both from the door frame with his own strength to give the appearance of forced entry. He would gently loosen a couple of the screws holding the lock in place during the next hour or so.

He placed his paint pots, ladder, and container along the hallway and looked around the flat, taking careful note of any of the areas which might have yielded valuables or items of interest to a thief. Once done, he retraced his steps and then proceeded to ransack the place, removing a small number of the more valuable items of interest, dropping them into the wooden box of brushes.

Every so often, he'd stop and wait for ten to fifteen minutes so as not to cause too much noise over a prolonged period. This needed to be a particularly quiet ransacking. He had at least a couple of hours and decided to use the time available to make a comprehensive job of it.

The inside of the flat was now a complete mess, its contents strewn across the floor in each room, and much of it smashed in the process. Green sat down on one of the chairs in the lounge area and scanned the mess, looking for the most suitable item with which he could deliver the *coup de grâce*.

As he did so, he noticed the upright, solid, wooden knife block in the kitchen. It was the perfect size to allow him to use both hands and, as a result, would deliver any final blow with greater effect and force. He lifted the block from its place and tipped it upside down, allowing all the knives to fall to the floor. He then left it on the kitchen unit for later use.

He returned to the lounge and once again sat down. Checking his watch, he knew he had at least another hour to wait. Green leant backwards, resting his head on the back of the chair, stretched both legs out in front of him and closed his eyes.

* * *

Having parked her car in the reserved space at the back of the building, Marie Standing grabbed her possessions and papers from the passenger seat and vacated the vehicle,heading off towards her flat.

It had been a long day and she was looking forward to putting her feet up and having a long soak in the bath later that evening. She knew that Monday was going to be a tense and difficult day and wanted to take full advantage of the time she had that evening. In addition to the one call Standing had already made, she had worked out the order in which she'd be speaking to other close cabinet members over the next few hours and had decided that she would start that process immediately after she'd had something to eat.

As she slid the key into the lock and pushed open the door, it was a matter of seconds before she began to see the wreckage in front of her.

"Oh no…" her heart sank. She fought back the tears and tried to stiffen her resolve as she pondered what might have been stolen, and, particularly, what things of sentimental value might no longer be a part of her life.

Closing the door to the flat behind her, she made her way into the lounge and stopped abruptly, scanning a room of open drawers, smashed items, and up-tipped, damaged furniture.

She knew that she needed to report it to the Met as soon as possible and reached into her pocket to retrieve her mobile phone. As she turned and took a step backwards to head towards her bedroom, she felt a heavy and painful impact to her neck and shoulder that sent her tumbling sideways and straight into the door frame of the lounge. As she hit the frame, it knocked the wind out of her, and she crumpled on the floor gasping for air.

She looked up towards the blurred figure towering above her and raised her arm to protect herself as she saw an object bearing down. The wooden knife block crashed down onto her arm and then, once again, her neck.

Wincing and moaning in pain, she was again struck with great force, knocking her out cold and leaving a gash several inches long to the side of her head. Now unconscious, for the fifth and final time the wooden knife block was hammered into Standing's skull. The damage had been done.

Green dropped the knife block and, with one hand, closed her mouth and held it tightly shut, with the other he pinched her nostrils together. He calmly counted out the number of seconds he believed he needed to ensure death and then checked her pulse.

His job done, Green moved into the kitchen and quickly removed his white, blood splattered overall, rolled it up and neatly packed it away in the wooden brush box. He then removed his shoes and tucked them down the side of the box.

The replacement, identical white, but still paint splattered overall, neatly folded and packed into a clear plastic bag, had been removed from the box earlier and placed on the kitchen table for use once the deed had been completed. Having completed his change of shoes and clothing, he slipped on a new pair of gloves.

Gathering up the ladder, paint tins and box, Green exited the property and pulled the door shut behind him. Placing the items he was carrying on the ground, he scanned the hallway stretching out ahead of him and listened for any noises which might denote the arrival of someone, either by lift, or stairs. He could hear nothing. It was quiet.

He held the door handle to balance himself and then threw his body at the door as hard, and with as much force, as he could. The loosening of the screws had done the trick and the locks gave away and the door was smashed open by a foot or so, tearing the wooden frame a little as it did so. The crack of the splintering wood was loud, but over almost instantly. Green looked down the hallway and, again, nothing was seen or heard in response to this latest noise.

Easing the damaged door closed as best he could, he gathered up his items and proceeded to leave the building. He encountered no-one and returned to his vehicle, packed the items away in the boot and calmly and quietly drove away from the scene.

* * *

Welling had started texting Wilson as soon as he'd left Chequers. He was keen to try and eke out further evidence of Wilson's involvement but also knew that their scheduled meeting later that evening needed to take place as agreed or any suspicions aroused might put the whole plan at risk. Welling would report everything to Wilson as he would normally do, but based upon Wilson's expectations, rather than what was being prepared behind the scenes.

For Wilson, it was important that Welling didn't suspect that he already knew everything and that the meeting, as planned, should proceed, but for different reasons. For Wilson, it was imperative to get Welling to meet anywhere but at his home.

The texts between the two were chess-like in their approach. Both men were thinking several moves ahead and always carefully considering the consequences of each message.

Wilson spotted his opportunity after Welling had suggested keeping close family members of key people involved separated and protected during the run up to Monday. He immediately fired back a message to Welling that he hoped would tempt his junior colleague into an affirmative response.

"Agreed. No families in any of this risky stuff. Please suggest somewhere for meeting tonight away from my house and I'll meet you there - family all here tonight - don't want them involved at this stage."

Welling became uncomfortable about this deviation from what was scheduled, but also recognised that what he'd normally do was to facilitate such a request. If he didn't, it might raise suspicions.

He reassured himself that he would also be at a location of his own choosing and not Wilson's.

"Sure – I'll get back to you with new location. Still 7:45?"

Wilson was pleased that this change had been agreed.

"7:45 it is. I'll wait to hear from you re location."

As he sat deliberating on the location he would propose, Welling checked his watch. It was 6:38pm. He had enough time to communicate with the undercover agents, and assuming they could both reply sufficiently promptly, he would also be able to get to Wilson in time for 7:45pm, assuming it was somewhere close.

* * *

Wilson had been waiting, anxiously for details of the new location at which he'd meet Welling and it was now becoming increasingly urgent. Once again, he checked his watch, 7:08pm. And again, 7:11pm. And again, 7:13pm.

The message alert evoked relief but the location was potentially problematic.

"Dots place – 7:45"

Dot's Place was the code name for one of the safe houses in central London used by the security services, and, whilst it would be safe for both men to meet there for obvious reasons, it had comprehensive, twenty-four-hour surveillance coverage in place, directly linked to the central surveillance unit. Anything that happened there would be both recorded and filmed. Given the circumstances, Welling was certain to have ensured that everything said and done would be monitored.

"Okay – see you there" Wilson's reply was quickly followed by another text, this time to Green.

"usual place – 9:15pm"

It wasn't at all the message that Green expected to receive but he acknowledged it and would do as he was asked.

Wilson had decided to walk the relatively short distance

to "Dot's place" and immediately set off on the twenty-minute journey. He'd determined to use the time to think his way through the tactics he'd use and comments he'd make. In some respects, this might be the perfect moment to take advantage of the surveillance in place.

He did his best thinking on his feet and the stroll would give him all the time he needed to develop an appropriate conversational strategy. Everything he would say would be designed to prove his loyalty and support for the Prime Minister and the Government.

* * *

Eddington's mobile had sounded off a few times over supper, with messages from Welling, all of which the Prime Minister had relayed to Strong.

"He's a bright boy that Welling," said Eddington. "If he gets Wilson to say anything compromising, we've got him."

"Wilson is the brightest we've got. He might be a little snake but as we both know Tony, that's his greatest strength. I'll lay a twenty that Welling comes away with nothing more than a few possibly incriminating sentences, if that," replied Strong.

"Hm, well, you may be right but at least he's trying to nail him."

There was a knock at the door and the conversation ended abruptly.

"Yes, Jamie?" said Eddington.

"It's The Cabinet Secretary, Prime Minister. He says it's urgent."

"Okay, put him through." Eddington rose to his feet and walked over to the table and waited for the phone to ring.

"Hello?"

Eddington listened to the message he was being given, occasionally looking towards Strong and then away into space again, each time his expression becoming more serious as the seconds ticked by.

"Thank you. Will you give me a further update first thing in the morning please."

Eddington slowly replaced the receiver and looked across to his colleague, ashen faced.

"What's happened?" enquired Strong.

"It's Ardoon. He's been killed in an accident. His helicopter crashed this afternoon. Everyone on board, killed."

"Good God," responded Strong. "That's dreadful. Are they certain it's him?"

"They are," replied Eddington. "It's tragic. What a dreadful end."

Neither man spoke for a while, taking in the news and contemplating the loss.

"We may have had our doubts about him of late, but this is a huge loss, and he was amazingly good to me over many years," said Eddington.

Strong paused for a few seconds before asking the inevitable question, given Eddington's reference to the circumstances prevailing.

"Christ. Foul play suspected? It's not impossible."

"They don't think so, but it's too early to say... I know we had real concerns about him, for bloody obvious reasons, but it's still a shock. I'm probably only here because of him, Edward."

"I understand your sentiments, Tony, but you'll forgive me if I don't entirely share them. You'd better draft a statement I suppose. But be bloody careful what you say."

Strong's advice was entirely appropriate given what might be happening tomorrow and both men agreed to work on something necessarily diplomatic, so that it could be released later that evening.

* * *

Approaching the street which was home to "Dot's place," Wilson briefly recapped his tactics, as well as the general approach he'd take towards Welling during the conversation which would certainly follow. He felt that his head was clear and that he was prepared, and ready.

As he climbed the four steps towards the front door, he deliberately looked up at the camera positioned some four feet above the door itself and briefly smiled. He was to look relaxed and calm, fully aware that we was being monitored. It was a meeting between two colleagues, after all.

Shortly after he rang the doorbell, he heard some footsteps making their way towards him and, shortly afterwards, the door was opened by Welling. Wilson was invited inside.

CHAPTER 40

Having conducted two briefings with the team, one in the afternoon and the other running into the early evening, Fitz had managed to conveniently extricate himself from the rest of the group and return to his bedroom. He'd taken a quick shower in one of the two downstairs bathrooms and headed to his room to change, before once again joining his colleagues for supper a little later.

The texts had come thick and fast and most of the answers he'd sought were forthcoming. His expectations that Paul was the other undercover agent were confirmed and he'd been instructed to make contact with him and agree the necessary lines of communication to facilitate, and maximise, the success of whatever action they would be instructed to take the following day.

The latter point was the only piece of information Fitz found slightly confusing. It wasn't clear to him why Wilson would be changing his orders this late in the operation. However, Fitz reflected on the fact that Wilson would certainly have his reasons, and he, unlike Wilson, wasn't in possession of all the facts.

As he made his way downstairs, Fitz decided to create the need for some time with Paul under the pretext of reviewing some of the more detailed aspects of the plan involving Josh. Quite how he'd do that at this stage wasn't entirely clear. He'd take his moment when it came.

Paul's messages had been broadly similar to those Welling had exchanged with Fitz, though Paul was advised that the other undercover agent would make themselves known personally to him within hours.

* * *

Paul decided to make his way into the main dining area. He would make himself as available as he could over the next hour or two to make a potential contact easier. When he arrived, he poured himself a drink and joined a couple of the other guys who had obviously decided to do the same thing.

A few minutes later, four others appeared, shortly followed by Fitz, who shouted across the room at Paul.

"Somerson, bring that drink over here. You're still a few seconds adrift at the end and I want to go over it with you a few more times."

The others all looked at Paul and smiled, a couple of them making a few wise cracks at his expense. He grabbed his drink and made his way across the room and joined Fitz at a table in the corner.

In whispered tones Fitz opened up the conversation.

"Just shut up and listen. You've had a few texts. So have I."

Paul was completely astonished and, at first, speechless. Could Fitz really be the other agent? The last person he expected to be a double agent was the man in charge of planning and executing the operation.

Initially, despite his desire to jump in and fully engage, such was his surprise that he held back and waited until he could be absolutely certain Fitz was who he claimed to be.

Helpfully, there was a good deal of banter amongst all the other men and the noise levels were loud enough to obscure most of the conversation Paul and Fitz were having. In ones and twos, every so often, others in the group would appear and join colleagues, leaving Paul and Fitz to their conversation.

Both men recapped the messages each had received and agreed that they needed to keep in touch closely if they were to make sure that they delivered what would be asked of them tomorrow.

Fitz, still a little confused about his final message, asked Paul what he'd been told about the plans for tomorrow.

"Just that I'll get instructions tomorrow morning, early," he replied.

"Me too," said Fitz, who then decided to push Paul a little further to establish his original orders.

"You got your original orders from Wilson, yeah?"

"I didn't get any, particularly. I was just told they needed someone undercover to keep an eye and be ready to act either when contacted, or on my own initiative if necessary. I had no idea there was anyone else undercover. Don't know why they didn't tell me that."

Fitz pressed on.

"Who's they? Wilson?"

"Yeah, and his sidekick, Welling. They both spoke to me and said they wanted me for this job. I guess I'm expected to take my orders from you. I certainly haven't had any. . I guess it's up to you now." replied Paul.

Fitz was re-assured by Paul's almost immediate acceptance of his seniority. Clearly, Paul was there to do as he was told. Though he didn't know exactly what Welling's role was in all this, if he'd been with Wilson at the time of Paul's secondment as an undercover agent, he figured that it should be okay.

"Okay, makes sense. I'm planning to station myself with your unit tomorrow to make sure everything gets done. We'll need to make sure Josh does what we need him to at the appropriate moment. And, obviously, we'll need to deal with everyone who's left."

Paul, still a little cautious, found Fitz's description of Josh's involvement a little strange but took it at face value, assuming he meant that they would both need to make sure that Josh would not deactivate the sleeve when the time came. However, he did think it a little odd that Fitz's words could be interpreted in two ways.

"Sure, understood. What about Ryan?"

"What about Ryan?" replied Fitz.

"He's trigger happy and excitable. He might fuck things up when everything kicks off, especially if he reacts too quickly to Josh."

"He'll be fine," responded Fitz. "You'll be there, I'm there, and as well as Ryan, I'm bringing in Des. So, that's four of us managing the Josh scenario. It'll all be fine. It's afterwards that we'll get the most trouble, but we'll sort a lot of that before the cops arrive… the element of surprise will help massively. After it's done, we've got to take a shit load of people out in short order."

Some of this was new to Paul, as well as being a little confusing and contradictory from his perspective, but Fitz clearly had a plan and seemed completely aware of his responsibilities and objectives. Paul would do the best he could when the time came.

"We best stop this and mix with the other guys," said Fitz. "We'll check in later."

Paul nodded and both men left their table and joined others elsewhere in the room.

CHAPTER 41

Wilson and Welling both knew that the conversation between them needed to be as sensitive and carefully conducted as each of them could manage.

Knowing that Welling did not know that his real intentions were known to Wilson, he was determined to get statements from Welling that would look completely compromising after the events of Monday, and took the initiative.

"So, I'm anxious that there are no gaps in planning for tomorrow if everything we fear might happen, kicks off. Are we certain that there is sufficient flexibility re response times for the Police and support units? You need to be all over this. I hope you are."

Welling had fully expected to give his boss an update on planning and preparation but this first question was clearly loaded, and his response carefully crafted as a result.

"There's a little anxiety over the exact timings of course, that's inevitable, but everything is set up so that moves are only made once we know everyone is in place and you give the signal to move."

Wilson rewound the response and pondered his next move.

"That sounds a little complacent to me. I think we need to have far greater certainty and a lot more flexibility baked into this. I know it's late in the day, but I think we need to have at least a little contingency. I think you should also be involved in triggering the response teams. It'll be much better, and probably safer, if something unexpected happens, if we both have the authority to act."

Though Welling was taken aback at this suggestion he remained poker-faced. It made no sense if Wilson was as deeply involved as suspected.

"Wouldn't you rather have the final say so on this?" Welling enquired.

"Of course, but I can't see anything other than good coming out of a backup in case things go wrong."

"Go wrong?" pressed Welling. "Like what exactly?"

Wilson shared his anxieties about the effectiveness of the operation in a number of small, detailed areas, particularly those in which Welling was involved. Once again, Wilson revisited the main issue as he saw it.

"The crucial importance of getting the timing of the Police operation right cannot be underestimated and we should be totally convinced we've got that right. We should make sure we both agree that moment. You need to have authority to authorise action to be taken. Not just me."

Welling paused before answering. This was not how he expected the conversation to go.

"So, what are you suggesting. You want us both to approve the response?"

Wilson leaned in towards his colleague. "Yes. Are you saying you don't agree, or you don't want it?"

"No," replied Welling.

"Well, what are you saying?" Wilson was insistent on getting a positive response. "Do you want to have the joint authority or don't you?"

Welling gave the only answer he could.

"Yes."

"Yes what?" pressed Wilson. "Be clear and stop mucking around. Do you want this responsibility or not? I need to hear you say it. It's too important for your bloody equivocation."

"I want the authority to authorise the response. A contingency makes sense."

"Good," said Wilson. "It makes sense to have a contingency like this and you're certainly the best placed to hold that."

Welling moved quickly to summarise the situation.

"Yes, agreed. It makes sense."

As the cat-and-mouse of a conversation began to draw to a close, Wilson expressed his doubts about the level of protection that the Prime Minister was receiving and, for the first time, floated his concerns that there might be a small cohort of people within the security service itself that was co-operating with the terrorist cell.

"I know this'll sound extraordinary, especially at this late hour, but I've been concerned about this for some weeks now and I think we need to run another round of checks on everyone to make sure there's nothing we've missed. Can you get that done immediately?"

"Sure, I'll get Parkes to do it. He's incredibly good at that kind of thing and he'll spot it if it's there. Who, specifically, do you have in mind?"

Welling waited for the response.

"That's the point, I don't have anyone in mind but it's just a hunch. I just want it checked."

Welling nodded. "Okay."

For forty-five minutes, both men had verbally boxed their way through fifteen rounds, only to emerge with what looked, to Welling, like a draw at the end of it all.

After asking Welling to call him at any time later that evening once the checks had been completed, Wilson made his excuses and left the building.

Once alone, Dave Welling pondered whether he'd managed to get any further forward with his attempts to further incriminate Wilson. He had not. Wilson's brazen confidence and extraordinary performance had left his colleague quietly impressed by the breathtaking scale of his deceit.

Welling left the building about five minutes after Wilson and headed home to his flat in Kennington. With only hours left before a day of huge import, he wanted to get home as quickly as possible. He determined not to speak to Parkes but would communicate that all was well with the checks to Wilson late that same evening.

Feeling pleased with himself for what he considered to be a total victory during the verbal sparring, Wilson briskly made his way to the location at which he was meeting Green. He turned the corner onto the canal path and walked the forty metres or so to the place of rendezvous.

It was almost dark, and it wasn't immediately clear whether Green had yet arrived. Approaching the large overhang of trees and then, shortly after that, the bridge, the perfect location for a secret meeting gave up its other participant from the shadows. Green had arrived.

"Standing?" Wilson's one word question drew the response he'd been seeking.

"Done," replied Green. "Unlikely she'll be found until tomorrow morning at the earliest."

Wilson calmly acknowledged the information and moved on immediately to the more important task Green was to undertake.

"Delay Taylor. He's second place to Welling. You need to deal with them both tomorrow morning. But Welling first… and early tomorrow, not tonight. I want him to continue planning tonight and he must be allowed to finish all that, and send his messages etc. But, it's critical that you recover all his phones, laptops and stuff. The laptops will be useful for later, but it's the phones particularly. We're now following every message he sends." Green continued nodding throughout as Wilson outlined the latest instructions. "Parkesy will be with you tomorrow and will let you know as soon as you need to get in there. He'll meet you outside Welling's block. Once you've had his instructions, move immediately. We can't afford any delay at that point. Literally every second will count. Welling must remain alive. You're to keep him quiet, and alive, until you get told otherwise. Timing is critical here. Parkesy will take the mobiles and leave you. You'll have to sort Taylor in between all that. I appreciate that'll be tricky."

"What if he's on the move or in a public place and not in his flat?"

Wilson was clear, "It's unlikely, as he'll be at home first thing. That's where you need to get him. If it's different, improvise."

"And does it matter how or when he's found?"

"It's beyond all that. We'll just have to take the risk. Just kill him once you get the call from Parkesy."

"Those mobiles will certainly be password protected. Do you need me to get the passwords from Welling?" enquired Green.

"Leave that all with me… I've already sorted that. Just get the job done. After it's all over, Parkesy will get the phones back to you in Welling's flat. He'll then send a message from there and then you'll need to kill Welling immediately, at that point. Timing will be all important. Don't forget that."

"How many mobiles does he have?" asked Green.

"I'm assuming there are two, possibly three, but I want all of them. Parkesy will certainly know by tomorrow."

"Boss, I definitely need extra help to get both of these done within a few hours of each other," said Green, clearly concerned about the extra work he'd been asked to do at such short notice.

"Do what you need to do, but no loose ends. If you must use outside help, close the door on it immediately afterwards. No potential leaks and no loose ends. None. Be outside Welling's from 05:30am."

Green nodded, "Okay… That it?"

Wilson nodded, turned, and walked away, retracing the steps he'd taken only five minutes earlier.

Green watched Wilson disappear before leaving himself, pondering who he might enlist to assist him.

* * *

By the time Welling had opened the door to his flat, it had turned

10:00pm and he filled the kettle, grabbed a mug, and added two spoons of sugar and one of instant coffee. Followed by a dash of milk, and then, hot water, stirring the contents as he made his way to the lounge, he sat himself down on the sofa.

The next series of texts was going to be the most difficult he would have to send. He knew he had to take the risk however, because without Paul knowing that there was some doubt about Fitz, the entire plan could come crashing down if he wasn't prepared.

"Alone?"

A few minutes later, a second text arrived, "OK"

"Agreed plan with Fitz?"

"Not yet - giving me orders in morning."

"Be alert. Fitz may be double"

"Double?"

"Yes – not clear – be alert!"

"He will not help me stop this?"

"Possible he's there to deliver it – not stop it – you must be careful and alert in case"

"Do we know for sure?"

"We don't – but possible"

"Is it all on for sure?"

"Yes," confirmed Welling. "instructions to you tomorrow – whatever - carry them out"

"Understood – need to go"

"OK – will confirm all tomorrow"

Paul flushed the toilet and left the cubicle, acknowledging one of the other men who had entered the bathroom to use the facilities. He washed his hands and bade his colleague goodnight.

All the way back to his room he was contemplating the consequences of Fitz being a double agent and working with the group as opposed to against them. This wasn't going to be remotely straight forward, and he would somehow have to rely even more on Josh than he'd expected.

Paul pondered further the slightly unusual responses Fitz had given to him earlier and, given this latest information, his fears that Fitz may not be everything he'd hoped for, were a distinct possibility. His situation, and that of Josh, had just deteriorated further.

CHAPTER 42

No-one had waited for the sun to prompt their early rise from bed on Monday morning. Few had had anything that might be remotely considered a good nights' sleep, and for the key players, Sunday had rolled into Monday with barely a pause in between.

Paul and Fitz had woken early and were awaiting their instructions. Just after 6:30am they each received their first message of the day.

"will send instructions before 9 – co-ordinating timings - DW"

Welling had already had his first conference call with the on-site police leadership team and had agreed that they would begin deployment as soon as the terrorist group had taken up position but not move in until the final order was given. Once that threat had been neutralised, the PM's convoy would be given clearance to depart Chequers. Immediately after that, Wolstenholme and Wilson would be placed under arrest and all the other suspected conspirators would be rounded up within hours. Welling would co-ordinate all timings and movements between the different component parts to ensure everything was effectively managed.

With everything now set, Welling called Eddington and confirmed that the operation was "a go" and that Eddington's team would get confirmation from him once it was safe to depart.

Eddington was relieved that things were moving along so well and was re-assured that Welling was clearly on top of things.

Just after 06:50am Parkes closed his laptop and gave a short instruction to Green that he'd been waiting for, "go, right now."

Green, Parkes, and their three colleagues, immediately exited their vehicle and made their way into the building and up the stairs to Welling's third floor flat.

After a quick check left and right, Parkes knocked on the door, each of his colleagues standing to one side of the doorway to avoid being seen.

Welling was surprised to have a caller this early but given the present situation, anything was possible. He was about to open the door when he suddenly become suspicious and, immediately, cautious. He eased aside the covering of the door spyhole and gazed through it.

Though surprised to see Parkes standing there, he could only have arrived on his doorstep because of something urgent .

Parkes knocked once again. Welling opened the door, and, immediately upon doing so, Green and his three colleagues charged into the flat, forcing Welling backwards, causing him to fall over onto the hallway floor as he went. Two of the men jumped on top of him and held him in place whilst the third man closed the door.

Green, gun in hand, knelt down by Welling and pushed the end of the silencer into his face.

"Not… a… sound," said Green.

The men rolled Welling over on to his front and bound his hands behind his back, before pulling him up and placing a strip of tape over his mouth. They dragged him into the lounge area and threw him onto the sofa.

Parkes immediately walked into the lounge and picked up two mobiles from the coffee table and checked them against his laptop. As the seconds ticked by, Green impatiently kept prompting Parkes to confirm whether or not he had what he needed.

"Well?"

"Wait," responded Parkes, "nearly there."

A few moments later came the confirmation Green had been

seeking.

"Got 'em."

With that, Parkes left the room at pace, and exited the flat.

Green once again pressed the silencer into Welling's head. "Not. A. Sound." With that, Green stood upright and looked at the three men entrusted to keep a close eye on their captive.

"I'm away," Green informed his team. "Watch him closely… no marks." As Green made his way to the exit, he turned to one of the three men, "You, with me."

Green was moving at pace. He knew he had less than a couple of hours to initiate the plan to deal with Taylor and then get back to Welling's flat in time.

* * *

Parkes arrived at Wilson's home some twenty minutes later and, once inside, immediately set about connecting to and accessing both mobiles. He brought up all the messages delivered thus far on his laptop so that he and Wilson could follow the history before starting to use them for their own purposes.

It was clear that one was being used to communicate with both the police and Eddington, and the other, Fitz and Paul.

"Ready to use them?" enquired Wilson.

"Nearly. Just checking something else." A few moments later came the confirmation Wilson was seeking. "Okay, ready."

Wilson began sending his first message. It was to Fitz.

"Its go. deliver as originally instructed – deal with others straight after – exit location - DW"

The acknowledgement from Fitz came almost immediately. Once received, Wilson began his message to Paul.

"Instructions are to proceed with plan – Josh to co-operate – police operation in place to be initiated once shooting starts – PM will NOT be in car – take out vehicle as planned - arrests needed whilst in progress - DW."

It wasn't exactly the message Paul had expected but he was relieved that the good guys seemed, at last, to be on top. There was clearly an elaborate plan to allow the attackers to be rounded up, as well as those involved elsewhere. This would also allow time for him, Fitz–assuming he was onside–and Josh, to deal with Ryan, and whoever else was with them. He would then get back to their location immediately to try and rescue Becky.

Wilson received Paul's acknowledgement, a thumbs up emoji, and turned to Parkes, nodding his satisfaction at the responses received.

Paul was keen to ensure that Josh knew this information as quickly as possible and he made his way downstairs to the kitchen to get Josh's breakfast.

The ground floor of the building was a hive of activity and almost everyone was either having a quick breakfast, making preparations, or chatting in their operational groups, going over and over their respective roles.

Paul grabbed a piece of fruit and a glass of orange juice and quickly made his way towards Josh's room. He was pleased that there was, as yet, no sign of Ryan. Upon entering the bedroom, he quickly handed over Josh's breakfast and informed him of the plan. Josh was initially anxious about carrying out his part, not least because of the safety of the driver of the targeted vehicle but was persuaded by Paul that all of that would have inevitably been taken care of because "they know this is coming." He advised Josh that Fitz had just told him that smoke grenades would be substituted and, in any event, if worst came to worst, he planned on missing with the second grenade, whatever happened.

Minutes later, Paul left Josh alone, who immediately began a further Morse Code exchange with Becky. All would be fine, a plan was in place, but as soon as they had all left she was to commence the plan they'd hatched between themselves the previous day. To secure herself in her room and deny access to anyone in the property until he, or Paul, returned.

Becky responded with confirmation that she understood her instructions, urged him to take great care and concluded with several X's. His final message of "I love you" was reciprocated.

Wilson sent his first message of the day using Welling's phone at 07:55am to the police chief in charge of the operation and confirmed that all was go for around 10:15am. He confirmed that he was co-ordinating with the PM, and his team, and that he would send a message as soon as the Police were to commence the operation and begin making their arrests.

An immediate acknowledgement of his message was received. Wilson knew that the critical messages would all have to be delivered by voice, and in person, but he'd deal with that issue closer to the time.

The return of Green and his colleague to Welling's flat by 09:40am confirmed that the plan to murder Taylor had been carried out but the precise details were unknown and, by the time they were likely to become known, Green anticipated that it would be too late to impact anything in any event.

Welling was still on the sofa, both men guarding him wearing their gloves, as instructed.

"How much longer?" one of them enquired.

"Not long now," responded Green. "Soon."

Eddington received his first call from a cabinet member just after 07:30am and the second before 08:00am. Both calls were prompted by Taylor's conversations the previous evening and Eddington was pleased with the response so far.

Strong had joined Eddington for a leisurely breakfast in his study and was delighted to hear that good progress was being made.

"Two down and two to go from Adam's lot," Eddington confirmed to Strong. "I've only heard from Davies via Marie, but we'll get more, I'm sure. She called him on her way home last evening so she must be doing the rest this morning."

"Well, we're building the coalition we need. Slowly but surely.

Mine will all be in touch between 08:30 and 09:30 and I don't think you'll have a problem. I really do think that we're ready for this now."

Strong was increasingly confident about the results of their collective efforts and was looking forward to Eddington cementing the support during the follow-up calls that would be made to him.

"I've heard from Dave Welling and it's all set up for later. We'll get the go ahead when the police have completed their operation. I must admit, I'll be glad when this bit is all over," Eddington said.

"Agreed. It's all a bit nerve-racking."

Eddington's landline telephone rang once again. It was the Technology and Enterprise Secretary.

"It's Christine, I'll catch you later," Eddington informed Strong.

Edward Strong gave his boss the thumbs up and left him to it.

* * *

As Josh looked out of his window, preparations were clearly moving at pace. All the vehicles to transport the team to the target location were parked outside the property in a line and he could hear Fitz barking orders to separate groups of men.

As his anxiety rose, he once again looked at his watch. It was just after 08:45am and with just thirty minutes to go before the time he'd understood from Paul that they were to start moving into position, he was anticipating a knock at the door at any moment.

Watching four men climb into the first vehicle and drive away, Josh became acutely aware of the momentous moment he was witnessing, and it had all of a sudden become particularly real.

Josh's door was unlocked, and he was asked to leave his room, joining both Paul and Ryan on the short journey downstairs and out towards the car that was waiting for them.

As Josh climbed into the back seat, he took a few deep breaths to try and calm his nerves. He was no stranger to dangerous missions but this one was at an altogether different level. His focus was to get his part over with as quickly as possible, and then, somehow, to get away and head back to the property to get Becky to safety.

Moments later, Paul and Ryan climbed into the back seat either side of him, Fitz took the front passenger seat, and another man took on the role of driver. All the other vehicles had left and only Adrian Mason appeared to be remaining. He was obviously the man charged with despatching Becky once the job had been done, thought Josh.

As the vehicle drove away, Adrian Mason checked his mobile phone for the time. It was 09:10am and, with at least an hour to wait, he decided to take a walk around the grounds of the property. As he strode out across the parking area, Becky watched him head over to the barn, look around and then head off towards the small, wooded area some hundred metres away.

She quickly moved across to the bedroom door and concentrated intently, listening for any noise that might indicate someone else was in the property. After a few minutes, she'd convinced herself that she was alone, save for Adrian, and decided to put in place the barricade she'd promised Josh she'd do immediately upon his departure.

Bit by bit, she eased the wardrobe across the bedroom floor, eventually managing to manoeuvre it into position to one side of the door. In spite of her condition, she toppled it over onto its side with one heave, blocking the door, preventing it from being opened inwards. She then dragged the bed into position, again, bit by bit, until it was wedged between the wardrobe and the wall opposite, effectively anchoring the wardrobe into position.

A little breathless, she then tipped the mattress up against the wardrobe to create an additional protective barrier between her and any gunfire which might ensue once entry into the room was discovered to be impossible. Whilst Josh had told her that it would effectively deal with any bullets from a handgun, she certainly hoped that that would be the case.

* * *

Wilson moved on to the next phase of his plan. He sent a message to Welling's phone, checking on whether Welling had established confirmation of potential double agents operating within the team and urging Welling to contact him as soon as possible. Wilson would also place three calls to Welling, two to three minutes apart leaving voice-mail messages along the same lines.

Being alive at the time of these messages and calls, Welling would appear to have deliberately ignored warnings and suspicions from Wilson of impending disaster. The plan to establish Welling as the double agent was well underway and being neatly pieced together.

Additionally, whatever would now happen, Wilson's own cover had now been established and had been re-enforced by these messages and calls, all of which, provided him with an effective alibi. Confident that everything was now in place, and using Welling's phone once again, Wilson's last message, before initiating the whole plan, was to the police officer in charge. It simply said;

"hold. slight delay. all terrorists not yet in place. will call when go"

CHAPTER 43

Though the connection could have been better, in spite of the slightly muffled tones, the message received was clearly understood by the head of Eddington's security detail; the way ahead had been cleared and it was a "go" for Eddington's convoy of vehicles to leave Chequers.

Eddington and Strong were told that all was ready and that they would need to be leaving in about five minutes if they were to get to Downing Street comfortably on time for cabinet.

At that moment, Eddington's phone also received a message from Welling's phone confirming "all good to go."

"It looks like a successful operation," said Eddington.

"Excellent," responded Strong. "We can catch up with the rest of the cabinet on the way."

Both men made their way to Eddington's vehicle and, as soon as they were aboard, the three-car convoy moved off and began its journey towards central London.

* * *

Wilson waited in silence. He and Parkes were both taking great care to assess the appropriate timing of their next moves.

"It's going to be about now," said Parkes.

Wilson looked across to him and lifted the index finger of his right hand as if to silence his colleague. He was still calculating travel time.

"Not yet... not yet. We need to be sure. Ten minutes to leave the building and five minutes to get there. We need the cops to be seconds, barely a few minutes late."

Moments later, Wilson flicked through the names and numbers listed on one of Welling's phones and dialled the police chief in charge.

"It's me. Go! Go!" Immediately, he hung up, giving no time at all for there to be any attention paid to his voice.

Wilson handed both mobiles to Parkes.

"Get these back to Welling's place, totally clean and print free, other than Welling's of course. Tell Green to deal with him but make sure we get all the credible evidence we need to establish his deceit."

Parkes took the phones, made his way out of the building, and hurried back to Welling's flat. He and Green would deal with Welling and give themselves the perfect alibi at the same time. Failing to stop Welling at the last moment, but killing him in the process was a neat and entirely credible cover story.

Wilson could now do nothing but wait. The die was cast.

* * *

The team had been in position for about ten minutes, each section of the group quietly waiting where they should be, out of site and anticipating the moment to carry out what they had been trained to do, to the highest level.

Josh was kneeling on the ground checking over the sleeve operating unit and Paul, who had rested the RPG against the hedge next to him, was also kneeling a few feet away. Ryan and Fitz were standing on the other side of the gateway, and the fifth of their number was ready to load the RPG at the appropriate moment.

Josh had noticed that only Fitz was in possession of a semi-automatic machine gun. The others were all only carrying handguns. Someone must have changed the orders at the last minute relating to who could carry what firearms. With only two men to worry about, and the fire power that Paul and Fitz had between them, they should be able to deal with the situation easily once the mission had been thwarted.

Suddenly, all four of Josh's colleagues looked at their mobiles at the same time. Vibrating into life, it was the confirmation they'd been waiting for and they all crouched down against the hedge in preparation.

The tension was palpable as the moment approached. Josh could feel his heart thumping away in his chest. His thoughts were not only of the immediate violence to come, but also, of his wife who, he'd hoped by now, had barricaded herself into her room. He knew that somehow, he had to arm himself and get back to that property as quickly as he could.

As the seconds ticked away, each one seemed like ten. Then, suddenly, and without any warning at all, a huge explosion shattered the calm and silence of what was, hitherto, a beautiful sunny day.

As the pall of smoke rose into the air, the revving of car engines and the screeching of tyres on tarmac, was all the confirmation needed that the mission was underway and that the first strike had now been made. Paul was becoming increasingly anxious.

Was this really how it was supposed to be?

Within seconds, two cars sped past the gateway behind which Josh's group was hidden, as they sought to make good their escape. It didn't take long before the next phase of the operation delivered its expected explosion, this time accompanied by some light gunfire.

The four men hiding behind the hedge with Josh checked their phones as their final message alerted them to their task.

"Ready!" shouted Fitz, as more gunfire punctuated the air. Sirens in the distance and more gunfire, which sounded all too close for comfort, added to the general cacophony of noise enveloping the entire locale.

Paul rested his hand on Josh's shoulder. "Ready?" Josh nodded in response and started preparing the sleeve control unit. He was ready.

Fitz stood to his feet, raising his machine gun to waist height and Ryan drew his weapon in readiness. Paul had loaded the first grenade and his colleague was ready with the second.

Moments later, the trap was sprung. The approaching car slammed on its brakes as it sought to manoeuvre itself between the gate posts seeking a route to safety. The front driver's side of the vehicle clipped the hedge and prevented its progress through the gap, the blackened rear windows preventing Josh, Paul, or Fitz, confirming whether there was anyone sitting in the rear.

Once clear and accelerating through the gap, the slight stall in the vehicles progress had given Josh a few extra seconds and, as the sleeve unit let out its single but continuous tone, Josh shouted "Done!" to Paul who immediately unleased the RPG at the vehicles rear. The noise was deafening, and the point of impact sent the vehicle hurtling into the air and onto its side some forty metres from the gateway. As the second was loaded, Paul immediately knew that this was not a smoke grenade.

Paul unleashed the second RPG which failed to hit its target, exploding a few feet away from the vehicle.

Fitz, clearly annoyed at the miss, immediately shouted, "Shit!" and ran towards the vehicle peppering it with bullets as he closed in. Ryan took a few steps forward, initially intending to follow his colleague towards the upended vehicle, but then stopped and turned to face Josh and Paul.

Ryan's hesitation, and those critical consequential seconds, were all Paul needed. He'd already drawn his gun and fired two shots at Ryan, who immediately crumpled in a heap.

As Josh instinctively, and at speed, raced towards Ryan to retrieve his gun and arm himself, he heard several additional shots behind him. Josh turned and watched as Paul fell to his knees, his left arm dropping to his side, blood streaming from his upper body. The fifth man in their team also stumbled backwards and collapsed against the hedge.

Josh was about to head towards his stricken colleague to provide whatever help he could, when Paul was struck by several bullets which forced him over and onto his back. Looking back in the direction they had come from, he saw Fitz swivel towards him, clearly intent upon serving him with the same fate.

The unexpected silence, quickly followed by Fitz's urgent attempts to draw his handgun, meant crucial seconds gained by Josh. He grabbed Ryans gun and stood up from his position behind Ryan's body, pointed the gun at Fitz and walked forward towards him, firing as he went. One, two, three hits and Fitz was down before he had any chance to respond.

Josh looked back towards Paul and, for a few seconds, fully absorbed the sadness Paul's death had caused him. Paul had saved his life and he knew he'd failed to do the same for him.

The distant sirens were altogether louder and the gunfire more prolific. A helicopter had now appeared overhead, and he could hear the voices of armed police offices calling on various members of the group to surrender as intermittent gun fire peppered the atmosphere.

Josh set off at pace across the field towards the small wood a few hundred metres ahead of him. As he passed the smouldering car, he checked on the driver. Dead. Fitz had clearly finished him off.

As he stood to his feet, Josh glanced through the upturned vehicle and looked towards the back seats. A chill was immediately sent racing up and down his spine. Two men lay dead in the rear of the car, one he recognised as Eddington.

Somehow, things had gone horribly wrong. His only objective now was to get to Becky.

As he reached the wooded area, he heard a few bullets whiz past him and the shouts of "Stop, armed police!" confirmed that he was now being chased down himself. He ducked down and pressed on. The helicopter was now directly above him, but he knew he was unlikely to be easily seen or targeted because of the canopy of green that shielded him from view.

Whilst he was confident of the general direction of travel, he was aware that he'd need to refine his route shortly if he were to get back to the hideout quickly. As he emerged from the small, wooded area, he immediately recognised the little horse trough he'd spotted by the side of the T-junction during their trip to get into position earlier and headed off at pace. It was the quickest quarter mile or so that he'd ever run. By this time, the helicopter had established his whereabouts and was hovering directly above him. Loudspeaker instructions from overhead were urging him to stop and surrender himself. The sirens grew louder as his pursuers tracked him down. He would not give up. He knew he had to keep going at all costs and was determined to lead the police to the building where his wife was imprisoned.

As he turned into the track which would lead him to the main property and its complex of outbuildings, he thought he could hear gun shots coming from the house. His pace quickened and he was praying he wasn't too late. As he ran into the open area immediately in front of the main house, he saw a man climbing his way to the top of a ladder propped up against the window of Becky's room. As Josh closed on the building, he saw the man smashing some of the panes of glass and firing a few shots indiscriminately into the room. It was Adrian Mason. Clearly, he'd not managed to gain entry to the room from the inside of the house and had sought to carry out his instructions from the outside.

The noise of the helicopter overhead had covered Josh's arrival and Adrian Mason had neither seen, nor heard him, arrive.

Josh stopped and took aim. Steadying his arm he loosed two shots, each hitting its target, and Adrian fell from the ladder almost instantly and crashed to the ground.

Josh immediately ran up the path towards the main entrance door, only to feel a sudden, agonising pain, as he fell to the ground.

He knew he'd been shot. He tried, in vain, to get up. He felt weak. His sight failed him, and everything got darker around him as he drifted into unconsciousness.

CHAPTER 44

Three days later, the House of Commons commenced its first evening session for twelve years and a packed House was brought to order by the Speaker.

"Order, order," came the familiar words but there was nothing remotely familiar about the circumstances surrounding this statement. "The Prime Minister."

As Wolstenholme stood to his feet, supported to his right by The Chancellor and new Deputy Prime Minister, Michael Bonato, there was no noise, no support, or opposition, not even a murmur. A silent and sober House of Commons greeted the new Prime Minister at this saddest and most devastating of times.

"Mr Speaker," Wolstenholme paused and looked slowly around the House. "Mr Speaker, in one of the most distressing and desperately sad weeks ever witnessed by our country, I rise to my feet, shaken to my core as a consequence of the outrages that have been committed."

Warming to his task, and now receiving more overt support from MPs across the chamber, Wolstenholme continued in the same vein.

"This entire episode has been nothing less than an assault on our values, an assault on our democracy and, yes, an assault on the essence of what it means to be citizens of the United Kingdom. The cold-blooded murder of our Prime Minister, and other senior members of the Government, by a ruthless, destructive and thuggish group of terrorists and criminals, has picked away at the fabric of our nation and woven a blood-soaked intervention forever into the rich tapestry of our national life and history."

Slow, steady, and statesmanlike, it was the opening to a speech that gave voice to the sentiment the whole House of Commons, as well as the country, was experiencing.

As each piece of information about the events of the fateful day emerged, it was explained and reflected upon in some detail. The deaths, the assassinations and all the horrors that Wolstenholme was outlining at the Despatch Box, added to the sense of despair and sorrow. Tributes were paid to fallen politicians and public servants who had "Quite literally given their lives in the service of their country."

Wolstenholme pressed on. "The infiltration of our security services by those hostile to the state, the deceit of key senior officers within it, the worst example of which was Dave Welling–now dead– is clear. The duplicitous actions of some senior politicians, coupled with the dangerous, ill-judged interventions by some members of different houses of this parliament, have all compounded, still further, the extent to which institutions have been compromised and the safety of our people put at risk."

Wolstenholme touched on the bravery of many, including undercover officers who had lost their lives and an ex special forces operative now fighting in hospital for his, whose wife , fortunately still alive, had been kidnapped to provide the terrorists with the worst kind of leverage imaginable.

The police officers who had been involved in a ferocious gunfight around the countryside of Buckinghamshire, four of whom had lost their lives and a further nine of whom had been seriously injured. Whilst all twenty-three of those involved in the attack had lost their lives, the hunt continued for those providing back up and support. There were believed to be many such individuals.

The country's new Prime Minister then moved on to what would have been controversial ground but now seemed almost tame in comparison to what had just taken place.

"As a consequence, and until such time as we can be certain that there are no further plots, no more dangerous terrorists at large, no more murders to be committed and no more disloyal and treacherous public servants amongst the ranks of our departments of state, be they politicians or civil servants, members of the security services or military personnel, the full force of the law will continue to apply."

"Elections will have to be postponed, relaxations in respect to individual control orders and civil gathering restrictions will be re-introduced and tightened further, and no reviews will take place with regard to any presently operating Act of Parliament, including the recently introduced Abolition of Jury Trials Act. Though there may have been many in this House who might have been opposed to such a proposal, the enormity of this weeks' events has forced such an approach upon the Government."

Wolstenholme moved towards his conclusion.

"Mr Speaker. Members of this House of Commons. There have been few moments in the entire history of this place when we have witnessed an attack so vile and despicable that it has struck at the heart and soul of our country. Our institutions compromised, our politicians butchered, our people now anxious and our freedoms, yet again, set aside as a consequence. Challenging moments throughout history have been met in this House with resilience, fortitude, and an unerring determination to see right done and evil conquered. This will be another such moment. This Government and this House will not fail in its duty."

Wolstenholme retook his seat alongside a tearful looking Bonato to his right, and, to his left, a number of empty spaces on the Front Bench where those murdered politicians would have sat, a folded union flag resting on the green benches in their places.

As the House of Commons erupted in support of a truly bravura performance, Wolstenholme looked up at the balcony and picked out one smiling face. Wilson hadn't only enjoyed the performance but was quietly celebrating a job well done.

END

Printed in Great Britain
by Amazon